LONDON BOROUGH OF BRENT LIBRARY SERVICE

Ealing Road Library, Wembley HAO 4BR
Tel : 902 9218

Open 9 a.m. – 8 p.m. (Weds. 1 p.m., Sats. 5 p.m.)

Please return this by the latest date below or overdue charges may be made. Books and recordings can usually be renewed unless in demand. Please quote item number and date due when renewing by post or by 'phone.

1. DEC. 1979	10 OCT. 1980		
	11. NOV. 1980		
22. DEC. 197	29. DEC 1980		
-5. JAN. 1980	20 FEB 1981		
25. FEB. 1980	-9. APR. 1981		
-8. APR. 1980			
16. APR. 1980	10. AUG 1981		
12. JUL. 1980			
-6. SEP. 1980			

D1346115

L & Co.   P 7.

303   949   200

New Arrivals,
Old Encounters

BRIAN ALDISS

New Arrivals, Old Encounters

Twelve Stories

JONATHAN CAPE
THIRTY BEDFORD SQUARE LONDON

'New Arrivals, Old Encounters' © 1977 (originally published under the title 'Horsemen'); 'The Small Stones of Tu Fu' © 1978; 'Three Ways' © 1978; 'Amen and Out' © 1966; 'A Spot of Konfrontation' © 1973; 'The Soft Predicament' © 1969; 'Non-Isotropic' © 1978; 'One Blink of the Moon' © 1979; 'Space for Reflection' © 1976; 'Song of the Silencer' © 1979; 'Indifference' © 1979; 'The Impossible Puppet Show' © 1974.

Jonathan Cape Ltd, 30 Bedford Square, London WC1

British Library Cataloguing in Publication Data
Aldiss, Brian Wilson
New arrivals, old encounters.
I. Title
823'.91FS   PR6051.L3

ISBN 0–224–01681–4

ACKNOWLEDGMENTS

'The Small Stones of Tu Fu' appeared in *Isaac Asimov's Science Fiction Magazine*; 'Three Ways' and 'The Soft Predicament' appeared in *The Magazine of Fantasy and Science Fiction*; 'Amen and Out' appeared in *New Worlds*; 'A Spot of Konfrontation' appeared in *Penthouse*; 'Non-Isotropic' appeared in *Galileo*; 'Space for Reflection' appeared in *New Writings in Science Fiction*; 'Indifference' appeared in Lee Harding's *Rooms of Paradise*; 'The Impossible Puppet Show' appeared in *Factions*, edited by Giles Gordon. To all concerned, thanks and acknowledgements.

Printed in Great Britain by The Anchor Press Ltd
and bound by Wm Brendon & Son Ltd
both of Tiptree, Essex

For Harold Boyer
who taught me all I know
and much I still don't know

Contents

New Arrivals, Old Encounters

It was a quiet planet. The quiet had reigned for century piled on century. Until the Earth ship came.

Beings externally resembling humans lived on the quiet planet. Their hamlets, villages, towns, slowly covered the habitable parts of the globe. As they spread – slowly, slowly – they drove out the species of animal which had occupied the land. But the animals were not ferocious, and in many cases lived in the hedgerows and copses close by humanoid habitation. They did not prey on the humanoids, or the humanoids on them.

The quiet planet's sun was old long before the first amoebae stirred in its oceans. Although it occupied a fifth of the sky at noon, the sun's red warmth was thin. Evolution was a slow affair. The pain of life, its joys, were muted. Even the struggle for existence was curiously muted.

Over half of the planet was land. The oceans were small and shallow. Much of the land was not habitable and the humanoids spread out only slowly from the equator. They encountered deserts where the sand never stirred. Storms were rare. Periods of calm prevailed for hundreds of years. Great silences lay over the land. Until the Earth ship came.

Muffled against heat, the people moved through barren regions before settling in clement valleys. Their villages were modest. They were great cultivators. It was their pleasure to

9

tend the land, to groom it, to serve as its acolytes. The god they worshipped lay in the soil, not in the sky.

They bred domestic animals, obtaining from them eggs, milk, cheese, in great variety. Their rapport with the animal kingdom was so close that they hesitated to slaughter anything for fear of the pain it brought them.

The humanoids procreated rarely. Group marriages took place between four or more people and they lasted throughout life. The children remained many years in childhood, but often became independent when young; then they would strap a few necessities on their backs and move into the hills, to live among the wild things. With adolescence, some inner call would bring them back to the nearest town. In a short time they would settle down to congenial work, marry, and enjoy a life of domesticity without regret. After death they were buried in cemeteries under the open sky, with a carved stone to preserve their names. This was the way of existence on the quiet planet for many millennia. Until the Earth ship came.

The humanoids were in some respects a simple folk. When they slept, they did not dream. When they suffered, they rarely wept. Their pleasures were faint. Yet the sloth of their evolution, its iron peacefulness, had given them integration. They were whole.

Within that wholeness they enjoyed much complexity. From the outside, their lives might have appeared dull. Their interior life was so rich that they required no foolish distractions.

In a village called North Oasis, because it was in the high latitudes, on the fringes of a vast, stony desert, lived a marriage group of five men and women who served as leaders of the community. Their name was Brattangaa. Many generations earlier, the Brattangaas had begun to build a Common. Now the present generation of Brattangaas completed it.

New Arrivals, Old Encounters

The village lay in a valley, sheltered by hills. The Common stood on the edge of the village.

After the work of the day was done, the people of North Oasis came to the Common. They had no particular reason for meeting face to face. But they derived a mild pleasure from each other's physical company. They sat together on benches round peat fires, touching each other. They drank their sweet-sour parsnip wine. Nerdligs moved among them, slow and woolly. The evenings were unbroken in companionship. Until the Earth ship came.

The senior male Brattangaa stood at the window of the tower of the Common. Evening was fading into dusk, dusk into night, in the slow dying of the day. He looked out at the landscape, which at this hour appeared almost lighter than the sky. As was the case with his people, Brattangaa's interest was much less in the sky and the heavens than in the things of earth.

He could see the stone roof of his own marriage home-stead from the tower. Inside he could sense the mind-bodies of his domestic stock, easily distinguishing the shapes of one from the next. He could sense the roots in the ground, growing towards a slow fruition.

His attention moved to the cemetery. There, under the ground, he could still catch a faint scent of his parents, grandparents, and even great-grandparents. Their presences, ever fading, were like faint lights caught in a great fog.

It was all of fifty miles to the next little town, also cling-ing to a brook at the fringe of the stony desert. It had no tower like this. Brattangaa could sense the lives of the people of that town; he knew them well, exchanged peaceable greet-ings with them, learned the news of the day. He could sense those whose mind-warmth was most akin to his own, his friends, as well as those whose mind-warmth was so different as to make them especial friends. Some welcomed him in – most did – others put him away with a friendly image, a wreath, a stained wooden door, an empty pewter plate, because they were too occupied with other things.

Brattangaa also sensed the people he knew by eyesight, the people of North Oasis, including his companions in the room below. He was not absent from them, or they from him. A jostling and enriching harmony prevailed. Until the Earth ship came.

As he sensed contentedly over the land, up the hillside, he saw with sudden terror a great flame standing in the sky. Such was his alarm that all in the room of the Common below also sensed it and turned their full attention towards what Brattangaa saw. In North Oasis, people did the same. More faintly, many people in the distant town did the same. Under the earth, even the dead generations protested.

All watched as the flame burned in the darkening sky. Ferocious light and flame beat upon the hillsides. And then the Earth ship came.

In the ship were five women and four men. They were of many colours and many nations. They talked in one language but they dreamed in nine.

Great excitement seized them on landing, as they set about their pre-exploration tasks.

'Kind of a drab-looking place, I'd say. Still, signs of habitation right enough.'

'Can't wait to get out of this damned can. How many months we been cooped up in here?'

'Break out the carbines. Don't talk so goddam much.'

'Chance to get in some big game hunting, maybe. Just imagine a great big bloody steak, fresh off the bone!'

'Atmosphere great. We can land ten thousand colonists right here within a twelvemonth.'

'We're made, you realise that, made! Grab a few of the higher life forms, take them back to Earth. Imagine the sensation.'

'Could be some nasty things out there.'

'We can handle anything that goes. From now on in, we're in charge, baby.'

'And remember we come in peace.'

They went through an hour of rigorous sterile-drill, moving from chamber to chamber, bathed in changing wavelengths and liquids designed to prevent them from contaminating the atmosphere of the planet they had discovered.

At last the great ground-level hatch slid open, grating slightly as it went. The nine stood there in their foil coveralls, weapons slung easily on their shoulders. Then they stepped out, walked on the hillside.

In their heads, in their minds, thoughts raced. A tremendous voltage of various thought-levels, some rising from depths beyond the conscious, beyond control, images hammered on the anvil of a ferocious evolutionary past. They looked down on North Oasis.

To Brattangaa in the tower, and to those who sensed him in the room below, in the little town, and in the distant town, nine strange flesh-like shapes formed on the hill. From that moment of contact, poison spread. Emanations, streamers, dark clouds, poured out of their minds. The emanations assumed definite configuration.

All the myths of Earth – the whole husbandry of the imagination – burst upon the startled people of the quiet planet. From clashing cultures, warring climates, ancient enmities, the images came, as the nine space travellers moved forward unknowing. With them came a terrible music – such music as had never been heard before upon the quiet planet, music that slashed at the eardrums like heavy claws.

Accompanying the music came wind. It blew upon their mind-senses like a storm. It whirled upon their mental landscapes, it hammered upon the doors of their consciousness. It blew down chimneys and roofs. It was irresistible.

And on the pinions of the storm, on the surge of the music, above the brows of the clouds, rode the legends of

Earth, all those terrible things in near-human form which haunt the human mind.

Pale Nazarene and sweating Buddha, elephants, cats, monkeys, serpents, gods, goddesses, grotesques with many heads, beasts, dragons, things of fire, streamed forth from the hill. Demons, devils, angels, ghouls. Never had such things been loose before upon the brow of this placid world. They formed a plague to which there was no local immunity.

Immediately their bad news spread across the face of the globe. Neighbour communed with neighbour, town with town, province with province, until every being on the quiet planet, humanoid or animal, stood and stared, transfixed by the terrible monster unleashed upon their defenceless minds.

Last to emerge from the psyches of the nine figures on the hill were four creatures more terrible than any other. Even the frenzied music, even the storm, died as they arrived, as they rose in the saddles of their steeds. Darkness fell upon the face of the planet. Beneath the soil, the lights of the dead flickered out.

Forth streamed the four horsemen. Eyes staring, foreheads ablaze, muscles straining, they goaded on their great steeds. With flaring manes, the four horses leapt eagerly forward, rejoicing to be free.

The planet was theirs. As the nine space voyagers began slowly to descend the hillside, they saw nothing of what the humanoids saw — the flowing manes, the flashing hooves, the brandished weapons.

Pestilence, Famine, War, these were their names, with Death close behind riding an old grey nag. Death's long beard fluttered in the wind as he galloped into the valley. Over his shoulder he swung his long scythe. The broken minds fell before him.

Breathing ash, he stooped to gather up the bodies lying in his path, stooped, laughing over the dying and the dead.

There was a plentiful harvest for him on the quiet planet, when the Earth ship came.

The Small Stones of Tu Fu

On the 20th day of the Fifth Month of Year V or Ta-li (which would be May in A.D. 770, according to the old Christian calendar), I was taking a voyage down the Yangtse River with the aged poet Tu Fu.

Tu Fu was withered even then. Yet his words, and the spaces between his words, will never wither. As a person, Tu Fu was the most civilised and amusing man I ever met, which explains my long stay in that epoch. Ever since then I have wondered whether the art of being amusing, with its implied detachment from self, is not one of the most under-valued requisites of human civilisation. In many epochs, being amusing is equated with triviality. The human race rarely understood what was important; but Tu Fu understood.

Although the sage was ill, and little more than a bag of bones, he desired to visit White King again before he died.

'Though I fear that the mere apparition of my skinny self at a place named White King,' he said, 'may be sufficient for that phantasm, the White Knight, to make his last move on me.'

It is true that white is the Chinese colour of mourning, but I wondered if a pun could prod the spirits into action; were they so sensitive to words?

'What can a spirit digest but words?' Tu Fu replied. 'I don't entertain the idea that spirits can eat or drink – though one hears of them whining at keyholes. They are forced to lead a tediously spiritual life.' He chuckled.

This was even pronounced with spirit, for poor Tu Fu

had recently been forced to give up drinking. When I mentioned that sort of spirit, he said, 'Yes, I linger on life's balcony, ill and alone, and must not drink for fear I fall off.'

Here again I sensed that his remark was detached and not self-pitying, as some might construe it; his compassion was with all who aged and who faced death before they were ready – although, as Tu Fu himself remarked, 'If we were not forced to go until we were ready, the world would be mountain-deep with the ill-prepared.' I could but laugh at his turn of phrase.

When the Yangtse boat drew in to the jetty at White King, I helped the old man ashore. This was what we had come to see: the great white stones which progressed out of the swirling river and climbed its shores, the last of the contingent standing grandly in the soil of a tilled field.

I marvelled at the energy Tu Fu displayed. Most of the other passengers flocked round a refreshment vendor who set up his pitch upon the shingle, or else climbed a belvedere to view the landscape at ease. The aged poet insisted on walking among the monoliths.

'When I first visited this district as a young scholar, many years ago,' said Tu Fu, as we stood looking up at the great bulk towering over us, 'I was naturally curious as to the origin of these stones. I sought out the clerk in the district office and enquired of him. He said, "The god called the Great Archer shot the stones out of the sky. That is one explanation. They were set there by a great king to commemorate the fact that the waters of the Yangtse flow east. That is another explanation. They are purely accidental. That is a third explanation." So I asked him which of these explanations he personally subscribed to, and he replied, "Why, young fellow, I wisely subscribe to all three, and shall continue to do so until more plausible explanations are offered." Can you imagine a situation in which caution and credulity, *coupled with extreme scepticism*, were more nicely combined?' We both laughed.

'I'm sure your clerk went far.'

'No doubt. He had moved to the adjacent room even before I left his office. For a long time I used to wonder about his statement that a great king had commemorated the fact that the Yangtse waters flowed east; I could only banish the idiocy from my mind by writing a poem about it.'

I laughed. Remembrance dawned. I quoted it to him:

'I need no knot in my robe
To remember the Lady Li's kisses;
Small kings commemorate rivers
And are themselves forgotten.'

'There is real pleasure in poetry,' responded Tu Fu, 'when spoken so beautifully and remembered so appositely. But you had to be prompted.'

'I was prompt to deliver, sir.'

We walked about the monoliths, watching the waters swirl and curdle and fawn round the bases of a giant stone as they made their way through the gorges of the Yangtse down to the ocean. Tu Fu said that he believed the monoliths to be a memorial set there by Chu-Ko Liang, demonstrating a famous tactical disposition by which he had won many battles during the wars of the Three Kingdoms.

'Are your reflections profound at moments like this?' Tu Fu asked, after a pause, and I cogitated on how rare it was to find a man, whether young or old, who was genuinely interested in the thoughts of others.

'What with the solidity of the stone and the ceaseless mobility of the water, I feel they should be profound. Instead, my mind is obstinately blank.'

'Come, come,' he said chidingly, 'the river is moving too fast for you to expect any reflection. Now if it were still water ... '

'It is still water even when it is moving fast, sir.'

'There I must give you best, or give you up. But, pray, look at the gravels here and tell me what you observe. I am interested to know if we see the same things.'

Something in his manner told me that more was expected of me than jokes. I looked along the shore, where stones of all kinds were distributed, from sands and grits to stones the size of a man's head, according to the disposition of current and tide.

'I confess I see nothing striking. The scene is a familiar one, although I have never been here before. You might come upon a little beach like this on any tidal river, or along the coasts by the Yellow Sea.'

Looking at him in puzzlement, I saw he was staring out across the flood, although he had confessed he saw little in the distance nowadays. Because I sensed the knowledge stirring in him, my role of innocent had to be played more determinedly than ever.

'Many thousands of people come to this spot every year,' he said. 'They come to marvel at Chu-Ko Liang's giant stones, which are popularly known as "The Eight Formations", by the way. Of course, what is big is indeed marvellous, and the act of marvelling is very satisfying to the emotions, provided one is not called upon to do it every day of the year. But I marvel now, as I did when I first found myself on this spot, at a different thing. I marvel at the stones on the shore.'

A light breeze was blowing, and for a moment I held in my nostrils the whiff of something appetising, a crab-and-ginger soup perhaps, warming at the food vendor's fire farther down the beach, where our boat was moored. Greed awoke a faint impatience in me, so that I thought, Before humans are old, they should pamper their poor dear bodies, for the substance wastes away before the spirit, and I was vexed to imagine that I had guessed what Tu Fu was going to say before he spoke. I was sorry to think that he might confess to being impressed by mere numbers. But his next remark surprised me.

'We marvel at the giant stones because they are unaccountable. We should rather marvel at the little ones because they are accountable. Let us walk over them.' I fell in with him and we paced over them: first a troublesome bank of grits, which grew larger on the seaward side of the bank. Then a patch of almost bare sand. Then, abruptly, shoals of pebbles, the individual members of which grew larger until we were confronted with a pile of lumpy stones which Tu Fu did not attempt to negotiate. We went round it, to find ourselves on more sand, followed by well-rounded stones all the size of a man's clenched fist. And they in turn gave way to more grits. Our discomfort in walking – which Tu Fu overcame in part by resting a hand on my arm – was increased by the fact that these divisions of stones were made not only laterally along the beach but vertically up the beach, the demarcations in the latter division being frequently marked by lines of seaweed or of minute white shells of dead crustaceans.

'Enough, if not more than enough,' said Tu Fu. 'Now do you see what is unusual about the beach?'

'I confess I find it a tiresomely *usual* beach,' I replied, masking my thoughts.

'You observe how all the stones are heaped according to their size.'

'That too is usual, sir. You will ask me to marvel next that students in classrooms appear to be graded according to size.'

'Ha!' He stood and peered up at me, grinning and stroking his long white beard. 'But we agree that students are graded according to the wishes of the teacher. Now, according to whose wishes are all these millions upon millions of pebbles graded?'

'Wishes don't enter into it. The action of the water is sufficient, the action of the water, working ceaselessly and at random. The playing, one may say, of the inorganic organ.'

Tu Fu coughed and wiped the spittle from his thin lips.

'Although you claim to be born in the remote future, which I confess seems to me unnatural, you are familiar with the workings of this natural world. So, like most people, you see nothing marvellous in the stones hereabouts. Supposing you were born – ' he paused and looked about him and upwards, as far as the infirmity of his years would allow – 'supposing you were born upon the moon, which some sages claim is a dead world, bereft of life, women, and wine ... If you then flew to this world and, in girdling it, observed everywhere stones arranged in sizes, as these are here. Wherever you travelled, by the coasts of any sea, you saw that the stones of the world had been arranged in sizes. What then would you think?'

I hesitated – Tu Fu was too near for comfort.

'I believe my thoughts would turn to crab-and-ginger soup, sir.'

'No, they would not, not if you came from the moon, which is singularly devoid of crab-and-ginger soup, if reports speak true. You would be forced to the conclusion, the inevitable conclusion, that the stones of this world were being graded, like your scholars, by a superior intelligence.' He turned the collar of his padded coat up against the breeze, which was freshening. 'You would come to believe that that Intelligence was obsessive, that its mind was terrible indeed, filled only with the idea – not of language, which is human – but of number, which is inhuman. You would understand of that Intelligence that it was under an interdict to wander the world, measuring and weighing every one of a myriad single stones, sorting them all into heaps according to dimension. Meaningless heaps, heaps without even particular decorative merit. The farther you travelled, the more heaps you saw – the myriad heaps, each containing myriads of stones, the more alarmed you would become. And what would you conclude in the end?'

Laughing with some anger, I said, 'That it was better to stay at home.'

'Possibly. You would also conclude that it was *no use* staying at home. Because the Intelligence that haunted the earth was interested only in stones; that you would perceive. From which it would follow that the Intelligence would be hostile to anything else and, in particular, would be hostile to anything which disturbed its handiwork.'

'Such as humankind?'

'Precisely.' He pointed up the strand, where our fellow voyagers were sitting on the shingle, or kicking it about, while their children were pushing stones into piles or flinging them into the Yangtse. 'The Intelligence – diligent, obsessive, methodical to a degree – would come in no time to be especially weary of humankind, which was busy turning what is ordered into what is random.'

Thinking that he was beginning to become alarmed by his own fancy, I said, 'It is a good subject for a poem, perhaps, but nothing more. Let us return to the boat. I see the sailors are going aboard.'

We walked along the beach, taking care not to disturb the stones. Tu Fu coughed as he walked.

'So you believe that what I say about the Intelligence that haunts the earth is nothing more than a fit subject for a poem?' he said. He stooped slowly to pick up a stone, fitting his other hand to the small of his back in order to regain an upright posture. We both stood and looked at it as it lay in Tu Fu's withered palm. No man had a name for its precise shape, or even for the fugitive tints of cream and white and black which marked it out as different from all its neighbours. Tu Fu stared down at it and improvised an epigram.

> 'The stone in my hand hides
> A secret natural history:
> Climates and times unknown,
> A river unseen.'

I held my hand out. 'You don't know it, but you have released that stone from the bondage of space and time. May I keep it?'

As he passed it over, and we stepped towards the refreshment vendor, Tu Fu said, more lightly, 'We take foul medicines to improve our health; so we must entertain foul thoughts on occasion, to strengthen wisdom. Can you nourish no belief in my Intelligence – you, who claim to be born in some remote future – which loves stones but hates humankind? Do I claim too much to ask you to suppose for a moment that I might be correct in my supposition ... '

Evidently his thoughts wandered slightly, for he then said, after a pause, 'Is it within the power of one man to divine the secret nature of the world, or is even the whisper of that wish a supreme egotism, punishable by a visitation from the White Knight?'

'Permit me to get you a bowl of soup, sir.'

The vendor provided us with two mats to lay over the shingle. We unrolled them and sat to drink our crab-and-ginger soup. As he supped, with the drooling noises of an old man, the sage gazed far away down the restless river, where square sails moved distantly towards the sea, yellow on the yellow skyline. His previously cheerful, even playful mood had slipped from him; I could perceive that, at his advanced age, even the yellow distance might be a reminder to him – perhaps as much reassuring as painful – that he soon must himself journey to a great distance. I recited his epigram to myself. 'Climates and times unknown, A river unseen.'

Children played round us. Their parents, moving slowly up the gangplank on to the vessel, called to them. 'Did you like the giant stones, venerable master?' one of the boys asked Tu Fu, cheekily.

'I liked them better than the battles they commemorate,' replied Tu Fu. Stretching out a papery hand, he patted the boy's shoulder. The boy gave a shy smile before running after his father. I had remarked before the way in which the aged long to touch the young.

We also climbed the gangplank. It was a manifest effort for Tu Fu.

Dark clouds were moving from the interior, dappling the landscape with moving shadow. I took Tu Fu below, to rest in a little cabin we had hired for the journey. He sat on the bare bench, in stoical fashion, breathing flutteringly, while I thought of the battle to which he referred, which I had paused to witness some centuries earlier. A small affair.

Just above our heads, the bare feet of the crew pattered on the deck. There was a prolonged creaking as the gangplank was hoisted, followed by the rattle of the sail unfolding. The wind caught the boat, every plank of which responded to that exhalation, and we started to glide forward with the Yangtse's great stone-shaping course towards the sea. A harmony of motion caused the whole ship to come alive, every separate part of it rubbing against every other, as in the internal workings of a human when it runs.

I turned to Tu Fu. His eyes went blank, his jaw fell open. One hand moved to clutch his beard and then fell away. He toppled forward – I managed to catch him before he struck the floor. In my arms he seemed to weigh nothing. A muttered word broke from him, then a heavy shuddering sigh.

The White Knight had come, Tu Fu's spirit was gone. I laid him upon the bench, looking down at his revered form with compassion. Then I climbed up on deck.

There the crowd of travellers was standing at the starboard side, watching the tawny coast roll by, and crying out with some excitement. But they fell silent, facing me attentively when I called to them.

'Friends,' I shouted, 'the great and beloved poet Tu Fu is dead.'

A first sprinkle of rain fell from the west, and clouds hid the sun.

Swimming strongly on my way back to what the sage called the remote future, my form began to flow and change according to time pressure. Sometimes my essence was like steam, sometimes like a mountain. Always I clung to the stone I had taken from Tu Fu's hand.

Back. Finally I was back. Back was an enormous expanse, yet but a corner among the dimensions. All humankind had long departed. All life had disappeared. Only the great organ of the inorganic still played. There I could sit on my world-embracing beach, eternally arranging and grading pebble after pebble. From fine grits to great boulders, they could all be sorted as I desired. In that occupation I fulfilled the pleasures of infinity, for it was inexhaustible.

But the small stone of Tu Fu I kept apart. Of all beings ever to exist upon the bounteous face of this world, Tu Fu had been nearest to me – I say 'had been', but he forever *is*, and I return to visit him when I will. For it was he who came nearest to understanding my existence by pure divination.

Even his comprehension failed. He needed to take his perceptions a stage further and see how those same natural forces which create stones also create human beings. The Intelligence that haunts the earth is not hostile to human beings. Far from it – I regard them with the same affection as I do the smallest pebble.

Why, take this little pebble at my side! I never saw a pebble like that before. The tint of this facet, here – isn't that unique?

I have a special bank on which to store it, somewhere over the other side of the world. Only the little stone of Tu Fu shall not be stored away; small kings commemorate rivers, and this stone shall commemorate the immortal river of Tu Fu's thought.

Three Ways

When a big fish dies and is beached in the shallows, belly upwards, the minnows dart about it. Tremulously brave, appearing and disappearing, they approach the enormous carcass. They eat. More and more arrive upon the scene. The water teems with little greedy fish.

The *Bathycosmos* was all but home. It lay in the shallow of space, in a cislunar orbit about Earth where its gravitational pull could not disturb terrestrial tides. Little police flitters, media craft, supply torpedoes, cruise ships, military patrols, approached the gigantic research vessel as close as they dared. They drifted across the great cliff of hull, glittered in sunlight, disappeared into shadow, were gone. The *Bathycosmos* remained.

Despite its bulk, it was itself a fugitive thing.

Deck XLII, Section A. The photographers and spectrum-analysts had been roused from cryogenic sleep. They had undergone the rituals of exercise and dance, and had taken their first semi-liquid meal. Digestion began again, after many Earth years. They were feeling more like human beings, less like revenants.

Williamz, Premchard and Dale even managed to laugh again. The noises came out rusty and hollow and brave.

Williamz: 'All right for you, Acharya, you're a lazy swab – you enjoy lying in bed.'

Premchard: 'Suppose you were right for a change, I still

25

prefer a nice warm bed, not an ice box. Even fast asleep, I still missed my nap at midday.'

Dale: 'Directly we get down to ground, I'm heading for the nearest warm bed. With a woman in it – one at least, to ward off frostbite.'

They jumped about, chuckling at the sensible movements of their limbs.

Lucas Williamz was a small ageless man with a dapper dark beard which had faded slightly under the weight of icy light years. In repose his face held melancholy, but he cultivated cheerfulness as an art. He put an arm about his friend A. V. Premchard and said, tenderly, 'You'll soon be back in the squalor of your native village, Acharya. Better you than me.'

Acharya Vinoba Premchard was a lightly built Hindu with a proud hook nose. He took life almost as seriously as he took photography. 'And you, Lucas – back to the asepsis of your flat in Bonn. Better you than me. Will you make another intergalactic journey, do you think?'

Jimmy Dale was a big man with heavy shoulders. He had been born in San Diego and had spent his childhood on the ocean. There was something solitary about him; he answered Premchard seriously, 'I'd go out again if Doug Skolokov wanted me to. He's a good leader. You, Lucas?'

'Not flaming likely,' Williamz said. 'Once to the end of creation and back is enough. You, Acharya?'

'We will see, we will see. In any case, why do not the ferries take us down to Earth?'

'You heard the announcement. A strike among the computer operators at Port Authority. Some things never change, let the centuries do their damndest ... '

But some things did change. They were summoned for a rehabilitation briefing. As the two hundred men and women of Deck XLII, Section A, settled down, the big screen lit and a plain-faced woman, speaking from Earth, addressed them without preamble.

Three Ways

'Welcome home, travellers of the *Bathycosmos*. You will find your home planet in many ways the same as when you left it, for planets are slow to change. All the same, we think it helpful to advise you of certain aspects of life which are different from when you left. You and your ship are under the jurisdiction of Corporatia. We appreciate that you may have problems in adjusting to us and our social institutions, and intend to do all we can to assist you through the transitional period. When you reach ground, you will be dispersed according to your appropriate demographic area.'

A slight movement which could be interpreted as unease rippled through the audience. Premchard raised an eyebrow interrogatively at Williamz. The woman on the screen continued to look pleasant but firm. She regarded them all.

'First, you will be glad to know that the Great Ice Age is abating. The average temperature in the Northern Hemisphere is two degrees warmer than when you left. The North American continent and much of Asia are now clear of glaciers up to a latitude of approximately forty degrees and Western Europe to fifty-two degrees. Cargo ships can again sail round the tip of South America, or through the English Channel. Many of the large centres of civilisation have plans to reoccupy surface sites, while the Third World – which of course has been less severely affected by the centuries of cold – reports considerable immigration to non-equatorial zones.'

Her words had come voice-over. On the screen, images gave flesh to her sentences. Satellite shots showed the greyish white mantle receding from Peking and the ruins of New York. Gigantic slabs of ice launched themselves off the Irish coast. In underground caverns, walls of metal glowed and came thunderously together. In a haze of golden dusty sunset, whites and blacks jostled in Central Africa for a north-bound train.

'Climatic disturbances have inevitably been followed by civil disturbances. These have been quelled, often with considerable loss of life. Severe curtailments of individual liberty

27

have been necessary in the public interest. You will be issued with regulations on your return to your several countries, and we advise you to familiarise yourself with them as soon as possible. As you will discover, it has been necessary to introduce capital punishment for a number of offences. Restrictions will be lifted as soon as the emergency is over.

'Owing to the severe climatic conditions which have dominated Earth ever since the *Bathycosmos* left, national frontiers have markedly changed. We have suffered two large-scale nuclear wars in the interim. The Advanced countries have been the chief victims.'

The audience was now standing; individuals cried out in anguish as they viewed the screen. Rioting, violent clashes between civilians and fleet armoured vehicles, fire-cannon shooting down vast underground streets, tanks shovelling aside bodies, rocketships plunging like daggers into the lunar crust, heads flying from bodies under the sweep of a machine with horizontal blades, lines of missiles darkening a china-blue sky – these images and more conveyed a magnitude of terror the woman's voice tidily concealed.

Nuclear explosions billowed outwards, rising on savage thunder, duplicating and reduplicating their thunder, climbing to the clouds, setting the clouds boiling, turning cities to charred feathers. Metal men marched, storming down tunnels to subterranean cities. Corpses lay rigid for one last military inspection. A man with a clipboard shouted wordlessly. People with prosthetic limbs attempted some kind of reconstruction. Men stood in queues or lay in hospital beds, faces armoured in pale smiles for the camera.

'You may find your own country has disappeared or has been entirely reorganised. In the common interest, there are now only five demographic areas or countries. These are Corporatia, Socdemaria, Communia, Neutralia, and Third World, the divisions being for the most party ideological. This may sound confusing but, as soon as you land on Earth, officials from the Demographical Centre will meet you and try to allocate you to your native area, if it still exists, and to the descendants of your family, if that exists. Never fear, we shall see that you readjust. Meanwhile, welcome back to Earth! Welcome to Corporatia!'

In forty-eight hours the strike was over. The rumour aboard the *Bathycosmos* was that the strikers had been shot before a firing squad.

As they travelled down to the landing site in a ferry, jostled on all sides by other members of the research vessel, Premchard said, 'Now we feel glad we signed on. We certainly had the best of the bargain – ten years' orderly scientific life for us, 120 years of disorderly recession for Earth ... '

'That's relativity in a nutshell,' said Jimmy Dale.

'I'm sure your great-great-grandson will be pleased to see you, Lucas, even if your Western ideas of progress have taken a hard knock.'

Williamz laughed. 'You Hindus, with all your flaming black gods, years and generations mean nothing to you.'

They bounced in their upright cradles as the ground rushed to meet them.

'Tell me, Williamz, you racist bastard, why are you so down on Hinduism, just because it's so reactionary?'

'I'd slosh you one, Acharya, if I could get out of this harness. If you must know, though I'm of Australian stock, my maternal grandmother was a Bengali. So I take a sort of family interest in your Indian idiocies.'

'Not India any longer – Third World. Not Australia either – a sub-department of Neutralia. So stuff that up your billabong, chum!'

They were down. Low grey buildings raced by. A glimpse of distant ice. The mouth of a great hangar into which they rolled. Darkness. Then lights, loudspeakers, grey-clad officials proceeding towards the craft.

A. V. Premchard found himself afflicted by an extreme form of agoraphobia when he left the shelter of the ferry. The outside world rendered him absolutely catatonic; he had forgotten how everything moved outdoors, how uncertain perspective was. He had forgotten such problems as irregularities underfoot, winds that blustered, temperatures that changed. The blue of the sky terrified him – never had he seen such a senseless colour.

Even inside, matters were little better. He had forgotten that rooms had windows, that people shouted and came and went meaninglessly, that corridors had ugly angles. He had forgotten how to negotiate stairs. Even doors were not as they had been on the *Bathycosmos*; on Earth they tended to slither away as you reached to grasp them.

People shouted. Methods of address had changed.

He tried to curl up in an armchair. Armchairs had changed.

He spent two days being examined or interrogated and filling in forms. To add to his disorientation, he could not make out where exactly on the globe he was. He was in Corporatia City, but that told him little. He knew he was in Corporatia because the flag, a melancholy affair of white and grey with a red fist rampant, flew everywhere. He was not sure where Corporatia was. It looked like Greenland but could have been Los Angeles or Milan. He met only women, women clad in grey shapeless uniform.

On his third day – the authorities had installed him in a singularly noisy hotel, The Syringe, ten floors underground – he found that it was no fun being a Hindu in Corporatia. Corporatia was at war with the Third World. Well, not actually at war. But there were hostilities. A frontier was under dispute. His beloved India was still somewhere in existence, but now called Hindustania; there was a fashion in Corporatia to refer to the Third World as Anarchania. As far as Premchard could ascertain, chaos was the order of the day there; terrorism and destruction were rife. Corporatia was eager to take over Anarchania, to protect it from the evils of Communia.

'For you, Premchard, bestest advisement is become of

Corporatia citizenship, third grade with skin allowance, forget terrestriality at odds.'

The language was difficult to understand.

Premchard stuck to his metaphorical guns, occasionally waving his star contract in a minor official's face, or in the eye of a computer. It was explained to him that his contract was 120 years old and made with dead officialdom in a dead land. He explained that the insurance covered all such eventualities, secure in the knowledge that several hundred fellow crewmen of the *Bathycosmos* were explaining precisely the same point in other sordid little offices.

On the evening of the third day, they conceded that it was possible for him to draw a certain sum of money due to him after his long service – not the fortune he expected because, owing to successive devaluations and continued inflation, the *groatime* had fallen to an all-time low.

He took what they paid him, staring with some nausea at the face of the woman on the plastic *groatime* note. Presidess Wjeilljer.

The authorities also conceded that it was possible, despite everything, to travel to Anarchania, were he fool enough to wish to go. Once he was there he would no longer be a government responsibility. He signed a form to that effect, checked out of The Syringe – yes, with regret in face of the new challenges, and caught something called a hedgecar, powered by human wastes.

'Oh Kancharapara!' said A. V. Premchard to himself. He tried to avoid imagining what terrible forms of progress might have overtaken his native village of Kancharapara, lost somewhere in the wilds of – what was that again? – oh, yes, Anarchania ...

Lucas Williamz discovered that he was afflicted by a virulent form of agoraphobia immediately he left the ferry. He tripped and fell on the naked ground, and could hardly bring himself to get up. He had fogotten the awful randomness of outside, the beastly irregularities underfoot, the temperatures that changed, the winds that blew. He had forgotten the horror of trees, the nastiness of bushes, the weird geometries of buildings designed for exposure to atmosphere. He had forgotten noise and violent motion and the stark idiocy of a blue sky overhead.

He ran trembling into the shelter of the nearest building. Little reassurance was to be found there. The rooms had doors that slithered away when you attempted to reach them and windows that revealed the unstable atmosphere – *clouds!* – beyond. He no longer knew how to negotiate stairs; he hated the ugly angles of corridors, the stench of public rooms, the grotesque people who walked clumsily, shouted, and made meaningless journeys to and fro. He had forgotten the crowds.

He was terrified of strangers. They talked in a funny way. They looked at him in a funny way. He hated the official portraits of Presidess Wjeilljer.

He tried to curl up in an armchair, but armchairs had changed.

The authorities installed Williamz in a ghastly hotel called The Antidote where, to his alarm, he was given a room two storeys above ground level. He could not sleep. He drank, but alcohol did not agree with him. He spent two days being examined and interrogated. He filled in many forms.

To add to his depression, he was unable to discover where he was. He knew he was in Corporatia City, the capital of Corporatia; the Corporatia flag, a dreary white and grey affair sporting a clenched fist, flew everywhere – more proof of the unstable atmosphere. Unfortunately he was not sure where Corporatia was. It looked like Iceland, but it could well have been Berlin or Toronto.

His applications to be returned to his home in Melbourne, Australia, were answered on the third day. Williamz was informed that Melbourne was a city in Neutralia, and that Corporatia was in a state of hostility with Neutralia. He would be returned on a prison posting. He had half an hour to pack.

He was ready in twenty-one minutes.

He said to the official who collected him, 'Things seem pretty bad here, don't they?'

'You're a criticism-issuer? You should have achieved deadness last century, so belt it,' she said. She began methodically to confiscate valuable items in his luggage.

Jimmy Dale also was struck by galloping agoraphobia. An armoured car took him to a hotel called The Arena and left him there. He climbed on his bed and lay thinking about the great drunken celebration he had planned with his mates on the *Bathycosmos*. He spent all the next morning filling in forms and the afternoon back on the bed watching holo-vision. There were only two channels. Both showed a good deal of Presidess Wjeilljer.

He brightened up when a news show came on at six o'clock and there was Commander Doug Skolokov, captain of the *Bathycosmos*, being interviewed by an intellectual-looking young lady dressed in a kind of sack.

'Tell me, do you have a pleasure be back on Earth, Commander?'

'It's obviously going to take a little time to adjust – there have been big changes – but yes, sure we're glad to be home. Ten years is a long time.'

'Yep, 120 years long. Family is of you dispersed, making death-time over generation, haven't you just hit the obsolete situation on a redundancy interface with the Great Now?'

The Commander smiled determinedly at his interrogator.

'We are not redundant. The world always needs brave men. We return from a successful mission as planned, bringing a tremendous store of vital knowledge to the world. We have spoken with the quasars. Knowledge can never be irre-levant. You appreciate that.'

'Appreciation depreciation. Culture-of-you knowledge is

gone by for us. Now's Great Now in Corporatia with past culture knowledge banned, obsolete, death-time stuff, I must express. Satisfaction of Citizeness Law, statutory.'

'Do I understand you to say –'

'Yep, speechway of you also hits the redundancy interface, Commander, thanks, many problems for brave boys of you from defunct epoch. Nighty!'

Cut. A Govment Bond Marvels the Mond.

Presidess Bonds with her stress.

Dale switched off and lay in an anguished torpor.

Through him ran the fear of extinction. He wanted a woman. It occurred to him that he had seen only women since leaving the ferry. All the officials had been women, the reception staff at The Arena were women – but all uniformed and so plain and drab that they hardly counted as women. Not the sort of women Dale needed.

He staggered out, fighting back agoraphobia. The streets were deserted. It was almost dark. Automobiles drove on whichever side of the road they felt like, moving slowly, hooting as they went. Dale kept to the sidewalk, hugging the buildings, feeling like a fugitive.

After quarter-of-an-hour's walking, he found a bar. One hunched figure clutched a glass in the semi-darkness; otherwise the dump was deserted.

Dale ordered a beer. 'Can I get a woman round here, barman?'

'What category freak you, Les?'

He looked again. The barman was a woman. 'Sorry, I wasn't thinking.'

'You not from Corporatia? What category freak woman?'

'No, no, I'm not a woman, I'm a man. Look, my identity card – Jimmy Dale. What's happened to all the men?'

The barwoman laughed. 'Who needs men? Satisfaction beats the faction.'

The figure at the other end of the bar lumbered over. It was a gigantic woman with drooping jaws and fangs, looking rather like a bulldog.

34

'You some death-time fag libbed from that antique star-boat, baby?'

'Yeah, yeah, where are all the men, that's all I asked?' He stood up for safety, confronting her jowls.

'Masck war-makers, we carcerate the father-lovin' lot, Les!' As the bulldog-like woman spoke, she reached out a gigantic mit. Dale struck her hand down. With a deftness at total variance with her cumbersome bulk, the woman kicked him just under the kneecap.

Dale knew how to handle himself. Instinct made him duck in pain, but he seized the opportunity to butt her in the great expanse of her stomach and jab two fingers hard into the region of her kidneys.

She let out a sound like a fast-boiling kettle and he ran limping from the bar. A nation of degraded women – was it possible! He shuddered with an emotion between shame and horror.

Best to limp for home. Before he could get back to The Arena, the police picked him up. A tough woman with a small moustache pinned him to the wall and looked at his identity card.

'You nascent San Diego, Bert?'

'You can read.'

'I scan, you divvy, Masck. Antique two-sex union?'

'Jesus Christ.'

'In the car. Some Guck non-additional ovdeh re detail of you.'

'I've done nothing, officer, what've I done?'

She looked threatening and her mates moved nearer. 'In the car, Bert. No voking. You nascent San Diego, where's now part Communia. We hoot you down the station for an enemy spy.'

They started beating him up as soon as they had him in the back seat.

Allahcutta was an enormous city straddling the Ganges. Its streets were choked with people, its buildings overflowed with them. From every open window, faces gaped or washing hung. People squatted or slept on steps, on the roofs of bus shelters, on slow-moving vehicles. The gravy-coloured river was covered with boats and rafts and rubbish. Heat and stink rose from the city with a resonance matched only by its febrile noise.

A. V. Premchard found himself confronting a reasonably helpful rehabilitation officer whose English he could understand. The interview was conducted in the corner of a high-ceilinged room which had once been the linen-room of a hotel.

'My wish is simply to return to my village and remain there while I consult the records and discover what has been happening since I left Earth.' He controlled his breathing to retain his calm.

'Yes, yes, very creditable, Mr Premchard, but naturally past history is not so very popular – not, not actually illegal, you understand – but we must look always to the future. In that way we protect the citizen.'

'Corporatia was so very horrid.' He was too polite to mention that he found his own country – well, this country – also very horrid. Even the room they were in stifled him. Other supplicants sat before other desks, behind which clerks fidgeted amid their flimsy fortifications of paper and hardware. One supplicant had brought in two hens in a basket; perhaps the birds were to be offered as a bribe. 'Has the world been overcome by ideology? I wish to enquire about such things.'

'You see, Mr Premchard, it's a process, a due process. You must cultivate an understanding, you see.' The man spread his hands in a dispirited gesture.

Premchard was too listless to ask what process. Mistaking his listlessness for doubt, the officer said, 'I might as well ask you what is the purpose of the universe. It's a silly question.' He shook his head, sorrowing at its silliness.

'No, not at all. That is a vital question. Once we cease to be interested in the answer to such questions, our spiritual life is dead.' He actually found himself banging his fist on the desk. The desk trembled and people looked round at him. 'Let me add that I have been into the universe – yes, the great universe itself.' Premchard was overcome by how far the universe seemed from this stuffy little room. 'I could give you a glimpse of that magnificence by telling you that the purpose of the universe is growth, expansion. Growth is its purpose, as spiritual growth is the purpose of the human spirit. Can you understand that?'

The official sat looking at him without answering, or even appearing to search in his mind for an answer. An official at the next desk got up and went to one of the enormously tall cupboards which filled the wall-space. Premchard saw, as the man withdrew a form-pad, that the cupboard was filled mainly with the relics of yesterday, a happier era: old plumes, turbans, drums, bugles, sashes, sheets, petticoats, white satin sandals, blankets impeccably folded, old flaccid white dress waistcoats, cummerbunds wrinkling like yards of tripe, speckled mosquito nets, all pressed together in a kind of flock compost.

'Now as for the matter of Kancharapara,' said the official at length, ignoring Premchard's last remark. 'Your village is only five hundred kilometres' distance, so perhaps you can walk to it. Transportation has an immense scarcity. On the other hand, perhaps you could attempt in the city to place a mortgage on a donkey or similar quadruped. Then you would be there more promptly. Good day.'

It was a kind of train. Sometimes it attached a snow plough to itself. Sometimes it left the rails and put on caterpillar tracks.

Only rarely did it stop at a station. It stopped in the sidings or else in open country. It shunned centres of population because it was a prison train and because it stank; the two qualities were complementary.

Williamz lay in one of the trucks with twenty other villainous-looking men. They were clad in rags and filth and they stole every possession he had. He hated and feared them, lying by himself in one corner as the axle rattled hard beneath his shoulder. It was dark in the truck, dark and cold except when – twice a day most days – the grill opened and the guards who travelled with the train flung in the rations.

As the days went by, Williamz adjusted to the company. He came to realise, as have others in the long history of persecution, that the finest and most independent minds are to be found in totalitarian prisons. He listened to their talk. He ceased to despair; he joined in the conversations. He learned.

And they were eager to learn from him. To them Williamz was a freak, an aboriginal great-grandfather or great-great-grandfather who had outlived his age; but he was a miraculous freak, and they listened more eagerly to his tales of a forgotten Earth than to his story of exploration on the *Bathycosmos*. They called him the Miracle.

There was time enough on the train. Time for all history. At one point they were shunted on to a ship. Whiffs of a great ocean came to them. They endured a month at sea. Then they travelled overland. According to the best-informed prisoners, they had sailed from what had been the U.S.A. to what had been Europe, and from what had been a Spanish port they travelled the immense journey overland to what had been Williamz's native land of Australia. Men died in the truck, villains and heroes, two a week on average.

Yet they exulted. They were leaving Corporatia. After the last nuclear war, the women of Corporatia had risen in revolution and killed most of the remaining men. Women had never ruled a modern state; they learned Realpolitik the hard way. For some centuries, men would be better off outside the hated frontiers of Corporatia.

'Still, women are part of mankind,' Williamz said, recalling a woman he had loved more than a century ago.

'Ideology,' growled one of his new friends. 'It's a virus. The world is dying of it.'

With a nail they tried to draw Miracle Williamz a map

of the new world. Enormous ice movements had hammered out new shapes from the yielding continents. To counter-balance gigantic depressions elsewhere, a plate had risen from the ocean east of Australia revealing a new land – Zealandia – almost the area of Australia. It stretched from the New Zealand islands in the south almost to the Ellice Islands in the north. In these pristine lands, the old drama of exploration and settlement was being re-enacted. New legends were being born from the territories.

To this new world many of the prisoners dreamed of escaping.

They thought it could never happen, but the time came when the train stopped for longer than usual. The rations stopped too. The Corporatia guards, women all, were going home. The frontier had been reached.

Neutralia took control of the train. First came light, then soup, then bread, then hot water. The train pulled into a small township. The sick were removed from the trucks and carted off to die or recover, according to temperament. Showers, rudimentary clothes, were provided. Everyone wept or embraced. The journey continued.

The day dawned when they arrived at New Sydney. Then the endless form-filling and interviews began again. The most frugal accommodation seemed luxury. They wept, laughed, scratched.

One afternoon, Miracle Williamz was at last free to take himself off to a hostel and draw some pay, provided he reported to the Aliens Bureau every morning at nine. He thumbed a lift to the bay and hired a horse.

He mounted the horse and rode to the beach. Sand stretched before him, sand and water and sky. The months of incarceration in the prison train had cured his agora-phobia; all he wanted was space – the spaces of Earth. He set stirrup into flank. The horse began to move.

Along the great strip of the beach they galloped. Far across the water he could see land, a bar on the horizon which represented the great new territories of Zealandia, a raw small continent the size of old Australia. They had told him: white settlers were already there, hewing out fresh homesteads, driving in sheep and camels and cattle. He rode the faster. The waves crashed on the shore.

He yelled as he rode. He pulled his clothes off, stuffing them under the saddle, rejoicing in the fresh chill. Yelling, he spurred the mare into the waves. When she would go no farther, he flung himself from her back into the water.

Ocean burst over his head. Miracle Williamz rose, gasping. It was bloody cold. He struck out, frightened, elated. At last the synthetic tang of the ship and the stink of the prison train were voided from his nostrils.

Only when he was exhausted did he swim ashore to where the mare stood tossing her mane upon the barren sand.

Commander Doug Skolokov said to his three female interrogators, 'You have threatened me with torture and death. You must do what you will with me. My only concern is not for myself but for the men who are in my command and for the knowledge I have brought back with me.'

'We have explained,' said the chief interrogator, a woman called Brady, 'that your knowledge is obsolete or, at best, irrelevant. As for your men, they will be employed as we see fit. We are not savages.'

Brady had learnt to speak an archaic version of English Skolokov could readily understand. The trick made him think her civilised, so he tried another appeal to her conscience.

'Then behave like civilised beings. In the West, science and the individual have been respected for many centuries – that respect has made the West great. I demand a full accounting for all the men on the *Bathycosmos*!'

'You cannot demand. So much you and the others must learn before you have a place in our society. "Times have changed." Did they have that saying in your bygone day? To guard the things you profess to admire, we have to be vigilant. Men had gone mad. They would not give up war. Wasn't war the other thing that made the West great? We want no part of it. In Corporatia we live on the verge of disaster, threatened by climate and enemies – and those enemies are men. We are prepared to give you free passage to any enemy male country you name, as an expression of our leniency.'

'This is my country. Or it was.'

Brady got up and lit a thin white stick which she stuck in her mouth. 'It was and it isn't any longer. But you will never accept that, will you?'

He hung his head, sick with weariness. They always woke him and brought him here at an ill hour. As far as he could tell, he was incarcerated far below the surface of the world. And they were burying him under a hostile ideology.

'You have to be vigilant, you say. The science we brought back from the universe might help you to be strong and safe.'

Brady coughed and fanned smoke from her mouth. 'Oh yes, we know that view of science. Science is never neutral, always an ultimate instrument of death in the hands of men. Skolokov, we are going to have to teach you and your men – those who still remain in Corporatia – to think like women. Guard, take him away!'

By the side of the track, white flowers grew in the grass. Bees bumbled from blossom to blossom, burying their shoulders in dusty stamens. A patrolling hornet swooped in occasionally, seized a bee about its powdered middle, and headed away without pause for its nest.

The track led slowly uphill, mile after mile. The jungle grew nearer the track. The trees stood stiff and lifeless, awaiting the monsoon. A. V. Premchard moved at a measured pace, letting the sweat run from his brow and face on to his shirt. A pack containing his worldly possessions cut into his shoulders.

He heard a train ahead and, a quarter of an hour later, crossed a single pair of rails. The rails shone and hummed in the heat. He gained the top of the sharp rise which lay beyond the railway and rested himself against an aged banyan. Ahead of him, on lower ground, stood Kancharapara. From reed-beds rushes grew tall and brittle, their tattered flags reaching almost to the eaves of the outlying bashas. To one side of the reed-beds boys shouted as they bathed their water buffaloes in the village pond. Everything seemed as he remembered it.

An old man approached Premchard. His head was shaven and he walked with a stick. Premchard greeted him politely.

'This is Kancharapara? I can scarcely believe it. I was born in this very place, and have been away too long.'

'Life is hard in Kancharapara, as elsewhere. I see by your face that you have some deep trouble, young sir.'

'No, you're mistaken, old fellow. Not really trouble. Knowledge. Knowledge sets you apart.'

Silence fell between them and the tree shaded them. At length the old man said, 'In Kancharapara nobody is alone. The gods are close to Kancharapara. Although the gods are sometimes harsh to us, they keep us together as a family. I will walk with you to see Mr Shantaram, the chief landowner, for I know it inwardly that you will find peace here.'

Peace! thought Premchard to himself. This Hindu obsession with peace! How he admired it, and in truth peace he wanted himself, yet the idea was based on a mistaken cosmology. With 330 million gods, Hinduism had no room for facts, and the fact was that all the human dramas of Earth took place within a context of the violent explosion of the universe. Suppose he told this old man that all organic life was simply a side-effect of that primal explosion which set the universe in being, that there was only the explosion, and that anyone who went in quest of peace or stability in the midst of an explosion was mad?

He blinked his eyes and listened to the bees and the cries of the boys in the pool, and could scarcely credit his thoughts. He had a pang of longing for Dale and Williamz;

they would understand. If he were to live here in this village, he must remain mute about his knowledge.

So all he said to the old man, mildly, was, 'I am pleased to learn that I shall find peace here, but how do you happen to know that?'

The old man nodded his head, starting down the worn path to the village before replying.

'Because I am an old man and know all who were born here. You I have never seen before. Therefore, if you are forced to claim that you were born here, the place holds something for you that you need. If you need it, so you will receive.'

Premchard looked up at the hazy sky as he followed down into the village. Everyone on Earth was blind and didn't know it. Yet, in their darkness, some had developed second sight.

The bed was disordered, its bottom sheet rumpled and stained. It stood in a neat suburban bungalow. It was owned by a man called Moresby, at present on relief work in the Dividers. Williamz had been in and on the bed with Mirindah Moresby almost non-stop for forty-eight hours. He looked back at the bed as he left the room, then passed out of the house and out of Mirindah's life, walking downtown like a man refreshed.

At the Zealandia Office, he spoke to a small, grey, bespectacled female clerk who made him welcome and said, 'You have only to fill in this form, Mr Williamz, and you get a pass to visit the new territory of Zealandia for five years. The Neutralian government will book you a passage over on a government ship and pay that passage, and give you a grant of 150 greens besides. Neutralia has been badly hit over the last century by one natural disaster after another, and resources are low. Now that things are looking up, we claim Zealandia as a colony, and we want it developed as fast as possible.'

'Things are looking up, are they?'

'Inbloodydubitably,' said the small, grey, bespectacled lady.

Sighing, Williamz looked at the form and started to fill it in. Every now and again, he consulted the clerk. It took him an hour and twenty minutes to answer the questions. The clerk accepted the form and posted it through a slot.

After another ten minutes had passed, a big man in a khaki shirt appeared and took Williamz into a side office.

'Your application for a passage to the New Territories is turned down. I wonder you bothered applying.'

'What you mean? What's wrong?' Williamz asked, straightening up and looking belligerent.

'You know what I mean.' Belligerence returned.

'I don't or I wouldn't ask.'

The big man put a big finger on Section 4a of the form Williamz had filled in. 'Maternal grandmother. Nationality. You put Bengali. Right or wrong?'

'Right, of course. Why should I lie? The old lady's been dead for the best part of a century and a half ... You're not objecting to my age, are you?'

The big man grew red about the chops. 'Are you so thick you need it spelling out, Chuck? You've got coloured blood only a couple of generations back, so you aren't eligible for a passage. There's a Whites Only policy in Zealandia, as if you didn't know. Scarper, pronto.'

When he left the building, Williamz headed straight for some of the friends he had made on the prison train. They listened in sympathy, though not without chuckling.

'Did you think that kind of prejudice would die out just because you've been away for a few years, Miracle? Prejudice is basic – which is why those of us who suffered at the hands of Corporatia stick together. Welcome to the club. Of course we'll get you across to Zealandia. You'll make your fortune there in five years, if you don't get killed first.'

Williamz looked at his knuckles. 'All the time I was away, I just wanted to get home. Now I'm here, and it isn't the same.'

'You've got to keep moving on,' they said.

They offered him a drink. 'What's this new place like?' he asked.

'What you might expect. Raw, unformed, just risen fresh out of the sea, pretty near three million square miles – say about the size of Australia or the old U.S.A. The rawest wilderness man ever confronted. Two things in particular you need to take with you if you intend staying.'

'What are they?'

'Why, a rifle and a woman, what else?'

The airship *Trader Dawn* flew steadily on a north-east bearing, heading for the settlement of Capricorn. It passed over the magnificent Three Kings waterfall, lost in its own spray, through which tumbled the remains of deep ocean still trapped in the centre of the new continent. It passed over that misplaced ocean itself, laconically christened Three Kings Water. It passed over what had been the deep-drowned bed of the Pacific and was now raw earth. It arrived above Capricorn Broads.

Sundown was at hand. Constant volcanic activity in Zealandia brought sunsets of peculiar brilliance, unmatched anywhere in the world. Crimson and carmine and orange and heliotrope flashed among the piling cloud along the western rim of the world as the airship circled. The craft disturbed thousands of flamingos feeding in shallow water. They rose, taking to pink wing, thundering overhead as the ship sank almost noiselessly on the airfield beside the lakes.

Three men climbed down from the airship. Two of them were dressed in the rough fashion of Zealandia traders, in silvered plastic tunics and pants, decorated with patches, tassels and plumes. The third man was tall, slightly stooped, and greying at the temples; he wore a kind of shabby uniform, with a gun strapped to his shining leather belt.

'Where's Williamz?' he asked the others. 'Which way?'

One of the traders caught a light satchel thrown down from the airship and said, 'He'll be in the village. Anyone will tell us. We have to satisfy these guards first.'

He indicated two guards approaching. One guard stood back and covered them with a laser; the other came forward and said, 'Who are you and what you want? Have you a permit to sit that thing down in our territory?'

'Where did they dig you up from?' asked the trader. 'My name's McFee and this is my oppo, Flanagan, and we look in on Miracle every four months or so. What are you all wound up about? War on or something?'

The guard chewed things over before replying, and said in a reasonable tone, 'You guessed it. There is a war on, and it ain't a joke either. This is Miracle Land and that's Herbert's Land over the water. They're enemies of ours and we're enemies of theirs. If you ain't from Herbert, I'll take you to Miracle, Mr McFee.'

Capricorn was a drab settlement, its houses and offices built from prefabricated sections made in the new continent's manufacturing area in the south-east, which had once comprised the islands of New Zealand. On Capricorn's low roofs, solar panels gleamed in the last of the sunlight. The only things to relieve its insignificance were plantations of young eucalyptus and palm trees behind the town, and the dark snouts of a volcanic chain behind the trees.

As they walked down what passed for a street, they saw a few ground-effect vehicles moving slowly. The population was predominantly male. Some men rode horses and a group of four drove before them a herd of goats no bigger than cats.

The guard dropped McFee's party at a low building which called itself a hotel, promising to fetch Miracle if he was available.

'Let's go in and get a drink then,' said McFee to his two companions.

'This seems a pretty rough place,' the tall man in uniform remarked as they made their way into the bar.

'Many a worser place out this way,' said Flanagan, and ordered three beers.

'Yes, but calling a feud across a lake a war ... '

'That's politics. Increases a man's dignity.'

The glasses were bucket-sized. Flanagan and McFee flung down two apiece before the man in uniform had finished his. They were about to order more when a messenger arrived to announce that Miracle would see them.

Miracle Williamz sat in a chair in a plain room over the bank. He rose to greet them as they entered.

He had spent ten years in the new lands. His space pallor was gone, baked into a brick red by the sun swinging above Capricorn, the latitude of the township. His hair was thinning on top and, like his uniformed visitor's, greyed about the temples. He had become thickset, and his beard straggled. He no longer smiled as readily as he had done, and his look was strictly evaluative as he fixed it on his visitors.

McFee came forward, shook Williamz's hand and slapped his satchel down on the desk.

'There's your mail from the mainland, Mr Miracle, and the *Trader Dawn* is out on your strip, loaded with the things you ordered.'

'Have you brought the seed, McFee?' Miracle's voice rasped.

'Every gramme of it. Every gramme you ordered. I fetched it from the Brisbane Horticultural Unit myself.'

Miracle nodded curtly, dismissing that subject as if satisfied, while he set his scrutiny on the uniformed man.

'And who might you be? You're no trader. You're not government, are you? I'm the only government here. This is my town, Capricorn.'

'So I gather, Williamz, and the territory all round for a considerable distance.'

'I'm called Miracle now. Not Williamz. I'm a Zealandian. I asked you who you were.'

The uniformed man smiled. 'After more than a decade,

why should you recognise me? I was your skipper on the *Bathycosmos*, Williamz. My name is Doug Skolokov. These gentlemen gave me a passage from Old Sydney.'

Miracle walked in front of the uniformed man, scowling, finally grinning and setting his fists on his hips.

'Commander Skolokov. So it is! I'd even managed to forget the *Bathycosmos*, never mind you. Welcome to my domain.' He did not offer his hand, and still regarded the other closely as if expecting a hostile move.

'I'm pleased to have found you,' said Skolokov. 'You seem to have fared better in the intervening years than I have. Can I take you somewhere and buy you a drink to celebrate?'

There was one window in the room, through which the sky now showed the blue of night. Williamz walked over to the window and turned about.

'McFee, Flanagan, be my guests for the night. Settle yourselves comfortably in the hotel and get yourselves drunk. Bill me. Right now, I want a private talk with Commander Skolokov.'

Having spoken, he stood unmoving. McFee and Flanagan looked at each other and left, clearly displeased with this summary treatment. The door closed behind them and Miracle and Skolokov confronted each other.

'So it's still *Commander* Skolokov, after all these years ... '

'I told you my name was Doug Skolokov. I said nothing about the Commander bit.'

'Hmm.' Miracle rubbed his nose and crossed to a cupboard. 'I've a lady waiting for me, Commander, and little enough time to spare for you, but maybe we'll take a drink before we part.'

Glasses and a bottle appeared. They sat down facing each other.

'Just a few years ago, this spot was three thousand metres under water. We're sitting on top of a million years of oceanic bottom sludge. When we have shovelled out the salts, it's going to grow the most fantastic crops of new foodstuffs the world has seen since Eden. Isn't that something greater than all space, than all those light years we travelled?'

Skolokov shook his head, smiling. 'Not for me it isn't. A whole part of me never came back from out there. A whole part of me is still communicating with the quasars.'

Williamz hunched his shoulders, drank, said nothing. A silence opened. Skolokov broke it, speaking rather hastily.

'Well, things have worked out well for you on Earth, I can see that. I ended up in a Corporatia prison. The women aren't so hostile now. They've settled down as the years have gone by, as I always knew they would. I admire them. I've come to terms with them. They're taking a new interest in technology, now that Communia is getting back into space, and we're planning – '

Miracle made a sharp horizontal cutting movement with his hand across the desk. 'Save the news, Commander. I've forgotten all that. Couldn't care a cuss. Let the big nations slug it out. They're done for, if they but knew it. The future's right here, here where I stand. New nations are being born. Energy ... Raw energy, right here ... I plan that we'll unite with Herbert's Land – it's Herbert's daughter I'm just going to see, fine tough girl – and we'll fight the Fiji nation on our northern frontier. This is where life expands, not in space. I was in space, remember – in a flying prison.'

Skolokov blinked, but said calmly, 'New nations, old stale thoughts. How will your feud with Herbert look to history? It's in space that new philosophies, new systems of thought are born. The government of Corporatia is building a new ship, *Bathycosmos II*, going farther and faster than our old ship, and I'm to command it.'

Emptying his glass, Miracle said, 'Good luck.' He looked angry, unused to men who contradicted him.

More silence.

Sighing, Skolotov emptied his glass and stood up. 'I'll be going.'

Miracle jumped up, red in the face. 'Is that what you came

here for, what you wasted your time for? A free drink? Couldn't you have saved us both the trouble?'

Skolokov looked him in the eyes.

'I came to ask you a question, but you've already answered it.'

'Okay, then you ask it now.'

'I've demanded and got permission from my government to take a certain quota of experienced men into deep space. We'll be away nearly three hundred terrestrial years this time. I wanted you along as chief photographer. It was your fine visual record as much as anything that convinced the women of Corporatia, including the Presidess, of the necessity for another voyage.'

Miracle smote his forehead. 'Holy goats, you're mad, Commander. Leave all this that I've built, that I've fought for?'

'I said, you have already answered my question.'

When he was alone again, Miracle paced about the room, muttering to himself. After a while he stood in the middle of the floor, staring blankly ahead. He looked at his hands, which shook. 'Three hundred years ... ' he said aloud.

The satchel caught his eye. Automatically he went forward and opened it, spilling envelopes on the table. He sorted them through. One bore an Anarchania franking.

He sat heavily at the table and slit open the foil with his thumb. Pulling a single sheet of paper out, he began to read.

Dear Lucas,

After four years' pause, I try again to see if a letter will reach you, my old friend. Perhaps by now you have forgotten your Indian pal Acharya, but I still recollect you vividly and wish for your company.

Life in the world is very terrible and so I think it will always be until men cultivate the eternal side of their nature. I am living in my native village of Kancharapara as if I had never been away, yet the years of space claim something of my being.

Three Ways

My great-great-grandson, Sunil, and his family look after me. I want very little. I need only the porch of their house, where I sit all day, meditating or speaking with the villagers when they need advice. In this way I can digest the experience of a lifetime that has been lived as few other men have lived. I offer my wisdom to others. You see, I would not be silent.

The Commander Skolokov came to visit me. He tracked me down through the bureaucracy. I would not go away with him to space again. For any experience, once is enough satisfaction.

But to see you again would be a great satisfaction. In my most profound meditation, I am aware that you are still alive. I know that you have much. Here we have nothing, but we need nothing. People work hard, but the village does not depend on the outside world, not even for electricity. Only kerosene we need, and that we buy with surplus grain when the harvest is good. The drinking water is pure.

Come here and you will be looked after. We will turn old age into an autumn of wisdom. Too many things get in the way of life, but here on my porch life is pure.

> Your friend,
> Premchard Acharya Vinoba

Miracle made to tear up the letter. Then he tucked it back in its envelope. He tucked the envelope back into his pocket. He stood up. He laughed briefly, patting the pocket.

Then he went downstairs to meet Herbert's daughter.

She was a fine strapping lass who would know how to raise sons for a new nation.

Amen and Out

The day had begun mightily, showering sunshine over the city, when Jaybert Darkling rose from his bed. He tucked his feet into slippers and went over to the shrine by the window.

As he approached, the curtains that normally concealed the shrine slid back, the altar began to glow. Darkling bowed his head once and said, 'Almighty Gods, I come before you at the start of another day dedicated to your purposes. Grant that I may in every way fulfil myself by acting according to your law and walking in your ways. Amen.'

From the altar came an answering voice, thin, high, remote.

'Grant that you may indeed. But try to remember how you offered the same prayer yesterday, and then spent your day pleasing yourself.'

'I will do differently today, Almighty Gods. I will spend the day working at the project, which is surely dedicated to your ends.'

'Excellent, son, especially as that is what the governors employ you for. And while you work, reflect in your inner heart on your hypocrisy, which is great.'

'Your will be done.'

The light died, the curtains drew together.

Darkling stood there for a moment, licking his lips. There was no doubt in his mind that the Gods had him taped; he was a hypocrite.

He shuffled across to the window and peered out. Although, as a human, he played a not unimportant role in the city, it was primarily a city of machines. It stretched to the horizon, and most of it moved. The machines willed it that way. Most of the giant building structures had never been entered by man, and they moved because it was convenient that they moved.

The walls of the project gleamed brightly. Inside, Darkling's immortals were imprisoned. Thank Gods that building did not move!

Hypocrite, eh? Well, he had faced the terror and glory of the idea since he was a lad. The Gods had seen to that.

Undressing, he walked towards the shower, and looked at his watch as he went. In seventy minutes he could be at the project; today he surely would try to be a better man and live a better life. There was no doubt it paid.

He cursed himself for his double thoughts, but they were the only kind he knew.

Zee Stone was also late in getting up. He did not approach the shrine in his small room. Instead, as he staggered across to the bathroom, he called, 'I suppose I'm due for my usual bawling out!'

The voice of the Gods came from the unlit shrine, deep, paternal, but on the chilly side. 'You wenched and fornicated yesterday night: in consequence you will be late on the project today. You do not need us to tell you you were in sin.'

'You know everything – you know why it was. I'm trying to write a story. I want to be a writer. But whenever I begin, even if I have it all planned out, it turns into a different story. You're doing it, aren't you?'

'All that happens within you, you try to blame on things outside. That way you will never prosper.'

'To hell with that!' He turned the shower on. He was young, independent. He was going to make good at the project and with his writing – and with that brunette with yellow eyes. All the same, there was a lot in what the Gods said; inside, outside, he hardly knew the difference. His hated boss, Darkling; maybe much of Darkling's nastiness existed only in Stone's imagination.

His thoughts drifted. As he splashed under the warm water, his mind returned to his current story. The Gods had more control over him than he had over his characters.

Dean Cusak got up early enough. What delayed him was the quarrel with his wife. The morning was fresh and sweet; the quarrel was foul and stale.

'We're never going to make that little farm,' Edith Cusak grumbled as she dressed. 'You were going to save and we were going to go to the country. How many years ago was that? I notice you've still got your mouldy ill-paid job as doorman at the project!'

'It's a very responsible job,' Dean squeaked.

'How come it's so ill-paid then?'

'Promotion just didn't come my way.' He got his voice a tone lower and went into the bathroom to brush his teeth. He hated Edith's discontent because he still cared for her; her complaints were justified. He had held out the vision of a little farm when they got married. But he'd always – admit it, he'd always been so subservient that the powers-that-be at the project found it easy to ignore his existence.

She followed him into the bathroom and took up the argument precisely at the point to which his thoughts had delivered it.

'What are you, for the Gods' sake? Are you going to be a yes-man all your life? Stand up for yourself! Don't be a mere order-taker! Throw your weight about down there, then maybe they'll notice you.'

'That's your philosophy, I know,' he muttered.

When she had gone into the kitchen to dial breakfast, Cusak hurried back into the bedroom and knelt before the bedside shrine. As the light came on behind the altar, he clasped his hands and said, 'Almighty Gods, help me. I'm a terrible worm, she's right, a terrible worm! You know me, you know what I am. Help me – it's not that I haven't struggled, you know I've struggled, but things are going from bad to worse. I've always served you, tried to do your will, Gods, don't let me down!'

A fatherly voice filled the air, saying, 'Reforms are sometimes best performed piecemeal, Cusack. You must build your own self-confidence bit by bit.'

'Yes, Gods, thanks, I will, I will, I'll do exactly as you say – but ... how?'

'Resolve to use your own judgment at least once today, Cusak.'

He begged humbly for further instructions, but the Gods cut off; they were notoriously untalkative. At last the doorman rose to his feet, struggled into his brown uniform jacket, brushed his hair, and slouched towards the kitchen.

'Even the Gods call me by my surname,' he mumbled.

Unlike Dean Cusak, who had a wife to keep him in check, unlike Jaybert Darkling and Zee Stone, whose lives were secure, who showered most mornings, who enjoyed the fruits and blondes of later twenty-second century civilisation, Otto Jack Pommy was an itinerant. He possessed practically nothing but the shrine on his back.

It had been a bad night for Otto, wandering the automated city, and only when dawn had broken did he find a comfortable deserted house in which to doss. He roused to find the sun shining through a dirty pane on to the stained mattress on which he lay, and remained for a long time angrily entranced – he was an acid head and had taken his last ration of LSD only a week ago – by the conjunction of stains, stripes, and fly specks there, which seemed to epitomise so much of the universe.

At length, Otto rolled over and snapped open his portable shrine. The light failed to glow behind the altar.

'What's matter? You lot feeling dim too? Expecting me to pray when you can't even light up like you used to? Gods! I spit on 'em!'

'Son, you know you sold your good shrine for this poor

56

cheap one that has never worked properly. But as we come to you through an imperfect instrument, so you are the imperfect instrument for the performance of our will.'

'Hell, I know, I sinned! Look, you know me, Gods, not the best of men but not the worst either. Leave me alone, can't you? Did I ever exploit anyone? Remember what it used to say in the pre-Gods book: "Blessed are the meek, for they shall inherit the Earth"? How about that, then?'

The Gods made a noise not unlike a human snort. 'Meek! Otto Pommy, you are the most conceited old man that ever inflicted prayer upon us! Try and behave a little less arrogantly today.'

'Okay, okay, but all I want is to go and see Father at the project. Amen.'

'And buy a new battery for this altar. Have you no reverence?'

'Amen, I said; amen and out.'

The Immortality Investigation Project occupied a few acres on the centre of the city. This contrast with the space stations, which were always situated outside the cities, was one on which Jaybert Darkling had dilated at length to some of the governors on the project.

'It's symbolic, isn't it?' he had said pleasantly. 'Man forges outward, ever outward – at least, our machines do – but the important things lie inward. As one of the sages of the twentieth century put it, we need to explore inner space. It's a sign of that need that although our precious space stations lie on the outskirts of town, we find room for this great, this metaphysical project, right at the centre of things.'

Right or not, he said it often enough to silence most of the governors.

Before getting down to his paper work on this fine morning, Darkling went briskly on a tour of inspection. Robots and machines had care over most things here, but the housing and guarding of the Immortals was his responsibility. As he walked through into the first Wethouse, he saw with some disapproval that young Zee Stone was on duty and flirting with a slight blonde secretary.

'Stone!'

'Sir!'

They walked together into the ante-chamber of the Wethouse, pulling on boots and oilskins.

In the Wethouse itself basked the Immortals. The project housed thousands of them. This first hall contained perhaps twenty, most of them unmoving.

The temperature was maintained at a rigid seventy-two degrees Fahrenheit. From the high ceiling, showers spouted. Round the walls, taps gushed, their waters running across the tiles into a pool that occupied half the floor space. In the centre of the pool fountains played. Cool jets of air, hurtling in at ceiling level, made tiny localised clouds and random cloudbursts that played hydropic variations in the chamber.

Statuesquely, the Immortals stood or lay in the water torrents. Many slumped half-submerged on the sloping edges of the pool, their eyes unblinkingly looking at some distant scene. The waters, beaten to a broth by the downpour, lapped round their limbs.

Yet they themselves conveyed an impression of drought. Not a man or woman here was less than 180 years old. They resembled planed wood planks with the grain standing out strongly, so covered were their skins with the strange whorls and markings that represented hallmarks of immortality. From the time when they first took the series of eight ROA5 injections, they had been plunged into the extreme throes of old age; their skin had wrinkled and dried, their hair thinned, their marrows shrivelled. They developed the appearance and postures of mummies.

That phase had passed. Gradually, they penetrated the senility barrier. Their skin flattened again, smoothed curiously, became as patterned and strange as oak planking.

These were external signs only. Inside, the changes were infinitely greater.

'What are you thinking about this morning, Palmer?'

Darkling asked of one reclining figure that lay wallowing at the pool's edge. He squatted in his oilskins, putting his face down to Palmer's, with its great brown and black whorls as if time had set a thumbprint over it.

It took a short time for Palmer to begin to answer, rather as if the message had to travel to Mars and back before reaching his brain.

'I am pursuing a line of thought that preoccupied me some sixty or so years ago. Not so much a line as a nexus of thought.'

Since he then fell silent, Darkling had to prompt. 'And the thought is ... ?'
a shade. Some of us here discussed the idea of a language of
'I couldn't say in words. It is less a thought than ... than colour. If we had a language of colour, I could tell you precisely about what I was thinking.'

'The idea of a colour language was aired and dismissed long before I took over here,' Darkling said firmly. 'The consensus of opinion was – and you Immortals agreed – that colours were far more limiting than words: fewer in number, for that matter.'

Palmer thrust his face into a jet of water and let it play gently on his nose. Between gasps he said, 'Many more colours exist than you know of. It is simply a matter of registering them. And my idea is of a supplementary rather than a substitute language. If this other business the group was talking about, a way in which an eye could project as well as absorb light, comes to anything, the colour language may have a future.'

'Well, let me know if you think of anything.'

'Okay, director. Coinages will be forthcoming.'

As they padded away through the rain, Stone said, 'Does that sound like a fruitful idea to you?'

Darkling said, 'There I must keep my own counsel, my boy. To the untrained mind, even their fuzziest ideas can be dangerous – like slow depth-charges, you know. It takes an expert to evaluate their real worth.' He remembered what the Gods had said that very morning and added, with an effort, 'Still, off the cuff, I'd say it sounded like an unfruitful idea.'

The two men walked among the wallowing bodies, exchanging a word here and there. One or two of the Immortals had something fresh to offer, which Darkling noted on a waterproof slate for one of the trained interrogators to follow up later. Most of the ideas they gleaned here were not practicable in terms of man's society; just a few had revolutionised it.

The immortality project was a failure in its origins: this protraction of life proved too eccentric for anyone to volunteer to become an Immy. Nevertheless, by preserving these strange old failures, the project was skimming off a useful by-product: ideas, and rearrangements of old ideas. The Immies now represented a great capital investment – as the governors were aware.

At last the morning round was finished and Darkling and Stone made their way to less humid quarters, where they removed their boots and oilskins.

'Don't seem to be earning their keep much these days, do they?' Stone commented. 'We ought to ginger them up a bit, cut off their water supply or something.'

'What an immoral idea! Useless, too, because it was tried many, many years ago. No, we have to face it, Stone, they are different from us, very different.'

He towelled his face vigorously, and continued, 'The Immortals have been cut off from man's root drives. For obvious reasons, the only drives we can inherit are those that manifest themselves before reproduction. It was argued in times past, quite dogmatically, that there were no other drives. Well, we see differently now. We see that once through the senility barrier, man is no longer a doing creature but a thinking creature. Vice versa, we see that we on the green side of the senility barrier are doing rather than thinking creatures – another idea that would have upset our ancestors. Our thinking is just embryo thinking. These

Immortals are our brains. Frankly, in this star-going age, we can't afford to be without them.'

Stone had switched off several sentences ago. Hearing his boss's voice die, he said, in a vague tone of agreement, 'Yeh, well, we ought to ginger them up or something.'

He was thinking his story. What he needed was new characters – young ones, who wouldn't have to think at all.

'We cannot ginger them up!' In Darkling's voice was a sudden rasp that shook Stone to full attention. His superior swung towards him, his little moustache twitching, as if with a malevolent life of its own.

'Your trouble is, Stone, you don't listen to what's being said. The Immortals are merely given care here, you know – this isn't a prison, it's a refuge from the complex world outside.'

He had never liked Darkling; that went for his moustache too. Putting on a calm and insulting drawl, he said, 'Oh come now, sir, let's not pretend they aren't prisoners. That's a bit hypocritical, isn't it?'

Perhaps it was the word 'hypocritical'. Darkling's face went very red. 'You watch your step, Stone! Don't think I don't know of your activities with Miss Roberts when you should be on duty. If one of the Immortals wished to leave us – which never has happened and never could happen, because they live here in ideal conditions – they would be free to go. And I'd back their decision against the governors.'

They looked at each other in helpless antagonism.

'I still think it would be a miracle if one got away,' Stone said.

As he left the room, Darkling reached for his pocket shrine. There was something about Zee Stone that put him in need of spiritual comfort.

When Otto Jack Pommy arrived at the project, he was in a fine ecstatic mood of resignation. Resignation filled him, and he executed every gesture with pugnacious resignation.

While he completed the questionnaires it was vital he fill

in before speaking to an Immy, while he was undergoing a medical examination, while he was having his retinal pattern checked, he concentrated on a number of absorbing arrangements in space-time that served to keep his mood one of substantial mellowness. In particular, he dug a number of universals out of the toecap of his left boot or, more particularly, the hinge between the toecap and the rest of the boot. By the time he was allowed in to see his relation in the Wethouse, Otto had decided that for one skilled in the art, it would be possible to read from the creases in the hinge a complete history of all the journeys he had undertaken in this particular pair of boots. The right boot seemed somehow altogether more evasive about its history.

'Hullo, Father Palmer! Old Acid Head come to see you again. Remember me? It's been two years!'

The generations were a little mixed. Otto, in fact, was nothing less than great-great-great-great-grandson to Palmer Pommy's long dead brother, and the title 'Father' he used was therefore part honorary, part derisory. Despite his two hundred years and his zebra-striped effect, Palmer looked younger than the shaggy, whiskery Otto. Only in his voice was there a suggestion that he basked on considerably remoter shores than Otto would ever attain.

'You are my closest living relation, descended by six generations from my brother. Your name is Otto Jack Pommy. You have shaved since I saw you last.'

Otto broke into affectionate laughter. 'Only you'd be able to detect it!' He stretched for a hand and gripped Palmer's; it had a blubbery feel and was cold, but Otto did not flinch. 'I love you damned old Immies – you're so funny! I wonder why the hell I don't come to see you more often.'

'You're more faithful to the principle of inconsistency than to any individual, that's why. Also, you don't like the climate of the Wethouse.'

'Yeah, that's a consideration – though it's not one I had considered.' He stopped talking, absorbed in meditation on Palmer's face. It was a cartographic face, he came to the

conclusion. Once the marks of senility, the wrinkles and pits
and folds, had been as real as irregularities in hilly ground;
now they were abstracts merely, like contours. 'You got a
cartographic face,' he said.

'It is not a map of me: I don't wear my heart on my face.'

'Of time, then? Marked out in isobars or secobars or
something?' His attention was wandering. He knew why
everyone hated the Immortals, why nobody wanted to become Immortals, although their great contributions to life
were so obvious. The Immies were too different, strange to
look at, strange to talk to – except that *he* did not find them
so. He loved them: or he loved Palmer.

It was the Wethouse he could not bear, with its continual
gouts of water. Otto was an anti-water man. He and Palmer
were talking now – or staring at each other in a dream, as
was their custom – in one of the guest rooms, where no water
was in evidence. Palmer was garbed in a wrap-round towelling robe from which his ancient tattooed head and striped
legs protruded like afterthoughts. He was smiling; over the
last hundred years, he had smiled as widely perhaps once
every six years; he liked Otto because Otto amused him. It
made him proud of his long-dead brother to look at his
great-great-great-great-grandson.

'Are you managing this session pretty painlessly without
water?' Otto asked.

'It doesn't hurt for a while. The hurt doesn't hurt for a
while.'

'I've never understood your whole water-orientation – or
for that matter whether you Immies yourselves understand
it.'

Palmer had momentarily lost contact. 'Difference between
hurt and harm. A term should be inserted between them
meaning "benevolent pain stimulus".'

'Water-orientation, Father.'

'No, that doesn't ... Oh, water-orientation ... Well, it de-
pends what you mean by understanding, Otto. Life renews
itself in wetness and slime. The central facts of existence –

at least until my kind arrived – were bathed in moisture. The vagina, semen, womb – goodness me, I've almost forgotten the realities those terms represent ... Mankind comes from the sea, is conceived and born amid salty liquid, dissolves not into dust and ashes but slimes and salts. Except, that is, for us Immortals. We're up past our bedtimes and it seems to give us a terrible neurosis for water and the irreplaceable liquids that once belonged to our natural state.'

'Up past bedtime? Never thought of the grave as satisfying any particular craving of mine ... '

'Longevity is a nodal zone where thirsts partly metaphysical supplant most other desires.' He closed his ancient eyes, the better to survey the desert of non-death across which his kind journeyed.

'You talk as if you were dried up inside. Your blood still circulates as surely as the oceans of the world, doesn't it?'

'The blood still circulates, Otto ... It's below that level that the dryness starts. We need something we haven't got. It may not be extinction but it reveals itself as ever-rushing waters.'

'Water, that's all you see! You need a change of scenery.'

'I've forgotten your world, Otto, with its crowds and change and speed.'

Otto grew excited. He began to snap his fingers and a curious twitch developed in the region of his left cheek.

'Palmer, Palmer, you idiot, that's not my goddamned world any more than it's yours. I've opted out from the machine culture just as thoroughly as you. I'm an acid head – I know that rush of dark waters you mention pretty well myself. I love you, Palmer, I want to get you out of here. This place is like a damned prison.'

Palmer screwed up his eyes and looked slowly round the room, beginning to shudder, as if an ancient engine had started within his frame.

'I'm a captive,' he whispered.

'Only because you think there's nowhere to go. I've got a place for you, Father! Perfect place, no more than twenty miles away. Some friends of mine – bangers, every one of them, hopped high but gentle, I swear – we got hold of an old swimming pool. Indoor. Works fine. We doss in the cubicles. You could be in the shallow end. You'd be at home. Real home! People to talk to'd understand you. New faces, new ideas. Whole set-up built for you. I'll take you. Go right now!'

'Otto, you're mad! I'm a captive here!'

'But would you? Would you like to?'

His eyes were sometimes all surface and meaningless, like a patterned carpet; now they looked out and lived. 'Even if only for a little while … To be away … '

'Let's go then! You need nothing else!'

Palmer caught his hand pitifully. 'I keep telling you, I'm a captive. They'd never let us go.'

'The bosses? It's in the constitution! You're free to walk out whenever you want. The government pays. You don't owe anyone a damned thing.'

'In a century and a half, no Immortal ever walked out of the project. It would be a miracle.'

'We'll pray for a miracle!'

Shaking his head to show he would listen to not one more word of protest, Otto unstrapped his old secondhand shrine from his back and set it up before him on the table. He opened it, struck it when the altar light refused to glow, shrugged and assumed what Palmer took for a gesture of reverence. He began to pray.

'O Gods, sorry to bother you twice in one day! This is your old friend and trouble-maker Otto Jack Pommy in a proper fit of reverence. You'll recollect that when I was on to you first thing this morning, you were saying how arrogant I was. Remember?'

No answer came. Otto nodded in understanding. 'They have no small talk in heaven. Very proper. Of course you remember. Well, I'm never going to be arrogant again, and in exchange I beg of you, Almighty Gods, just one small miracle.'

From the darkness behind the altar, a level voice said, 'The Gods do not bargain.'

Otto cleared his throat and pointed an eyebrow at Palmer to indicate that this might be difficult. 'Quite right. Understandable in your position, O Gods. O Gods, I therefore pray you do me one small miracle without strings attached — wait, let me tell you — '

'There are no miracles, only favourable conjunctions of circumstances.'

'Very well put, O great Gods, in which case I pray you for one small favourable conjunction of circumstances, to wit, letting me get my dear old Father here out of this lousy project. That's all! That's all! And in return, I swear I will remain humble all the days of my life. Hear my prayer, O Gods, for thine is the power and the glory and we are in a genuine fix, for ever and ever. Amen.'

The Gods said, 'If you wish to remove the Immortal, then the time to go is now.'

'Ah!' Otto grabbed his shrine in both hands and fervently kissed the altar. 'You're lovely people to treat an old acid head so, and I swear I'll declare the miracle abroad and walk in truth and righteousness all the days of my life and get a new battery for the altar light. Amen in the highest, amen and out!'

Turning to Palmer with his eyes gleaming, he strapped the shrine back over his shoulder.

'There! What do you think of that? When the Gods work in our favour, there's nothing twenty-second century civilisation can do to stop us! Come on, daddy-o, and I'll look after you like a child.'

He pulled the Immortal to his feet and led him from the room. In confused excitement, Palmer in turn protested that he could not go and longed to leave. One arguing, one encouraging, they made their way down the extensive corridors of the project. Nobody stopped them, although several officials stared and looked hard after their eccentric progress.

It was when they got to the main door that their way was

blocked. Dean Cusak, imposing in his brown uniform, popped forward like a dummy and asked for their passes.

Otto showed his visitor's pass and said, 'As you'll probably recognise, this is one of the Immortals, Mr Palmer Pommy. He is leaving with me. He has no pass. He has lived here for the past 150 years.'

This was Cusak's big moment, and he painfully recognised it as such. Never having been face to face with an Immortal before, he felt, as many another man had done, the stunning impact of that encounter, which was invariably followed by a shock wave of envy, fear and other emotions: for here was a being already four times as old as himself, and due to go on living long after all the present generation was subsumed into ashes.

Cusak's voice came reedily. 'I can't let nobody through here without a pass, sir. It's the rules.'

'For the Gods' sake man, what are you? Are you going to be someone else's yes-man all your life? – A mere taker-of-orders? Look on this Immortal and then ask yourself if you have any right to offend his wishes!'

Cusak's eyes met Palmer's, and then dropped. It could have been that he was not even thinking of this present moment at all, or of these persons, but of some other time when someone else held the stage and a shriller voice made the same demands of him.

When he looked up, he said, 'You're quite right, sir. I pleases myself who I lets through here. I don't exist just to carry out Mr Darkling's orders. I'm my own man, and one day I'm going to run my own little farm. Carry on, gentlemen!'

He saluted as they went by.

Directly the two men were gone, Cusak began to suffer qualms. He dialled his superior, Zee Stone, and told him that one of the Immortals had left the project.

'I'll deal with it, Cusak,' Stone said, snapping off the doorman's flow of apology. He sat for a moment staring into vacancy, wondering what to do with this interesting piece of news. It was his only for a while; by evening, if he let the Immy go, it would be all over the planet. The news value was colossal; no Immortal had ever dared leave the project before. Certainly the news would bring the project under close investigation and no doubt a number of secrets would come to light.

In particular, it would bring Jaybert Darkling under investigation. He would probably get the sack. So, for that matter, might Zee Stone.

'I don't care!' he said. 'I'd be free to write, to suffer as a writer should ... '

The old vision was back with renewed strength. Only he could not quite get it in focus. It wasn't fiction exactly he wanted to write – the characters were too difficult in fiction. It was ... it was ...

Well, he could settle that later. Meanwhile, he could settle the hash of his beloved boss, Darkling, if he played his cards right.

Darkling's moustache twitched as Stone entered.

'I won't detain you a minute, sir. A little matter has just arisen that I'm sure you can deal with.'

His tone was so unusually pleasant that Darkling knew something horrible was about to emerge.

'I'm expecting a call from the Extrapolation Board at any second, so you'd better be brief.'

'Oh, I will be brief. You were telling me this morning, sir – I was very interested in what you said – about how you disapproved of the policy of the board of governors of this project.'

'I hardly think I am likely to make such a comment to my subordinates, Stone.'

'Oh, but you did, sir. I mean, we all know how the project exists to milk the Immortals of their strange ideas and turn them into practical applications for the benefit of mankind. Only it also happens to benefit the governors as well, and so although the Immortals began as free men here, the project

merely providing an ideal environment, they've come to be
no more than prisoners.'

'I said – '

'And you said that if one of them escaped, you'd back him
against the governors.'

'Well, yes, maybe I did say something like that.'

'Sir, I wish to report that one of the Immortals has just
escaped.'

Darkling was on his feet in an instant, his fingers on the
nearest buzzer.

'You fool, Stone, why shillyshally? We must get him back
at once! Think of the publicity ... ' His face was white. He
faltered to a stop.

'But, sir, you just said – '

Darkling cut him off. 'Circumstances alter cases.'

'Then this *is* a prison, sir.'

Darkling rushed at him, arm waving. 'You crafty little
bastard, Stone, get out of my office! You're trying to trick
me, aren't you? I know your kind – '

'It was just what we were saying about hypocrisy – '

'Get out! Get out at once and never come in here again!'

He slammed the door after Stone's retreating back. Then
he leant on the door, trembling, and rubbed the palm of his
hand over his forehead. He knew the Gods were looking
down on him; he knew that they, in their infinite cunning,
had sent Stone to him for a scourge. This was his time of
testing. For once he would have to stand by what he had
represented to be his own true feelings, or else be forever
damned in his own eyes.

If he let the Immy go, the governors would surely have
his blood. If he hauled the Immy back – and the matter was
urgent, or he would be lost in the city – Stone would see he
was morally discredited, perhaps even with the governors.
Either way, he was in trouble; his only policy was to stand
by what he had said – said more than once, he recalled
faintly.

From somewhere came an unwonted memory of someone

jokingly defending hypocrisy in his presence by saying, 'Hypocrites may be scoundrels, but by their nature they sometimes have to live up to the fine feelings to which they pretend.' Darkling had wanted to tell the idiot that he failed to understand the essential thing about a hypocrite: that their nature was genuinely mixed, that the fine feelings were there all right, that it was the will that was weak ... well, now the will was trapped by circumstance.

He would have to let the Immy go.

'You win, Gods!' he cried. 'I've been a better man today, and it'll probably ruin me!'

Shakily, he went behind his desk. As he sat down, a bright idea came to him. A smile that Stone might have recognised as sly and dangerous played on his face. There was, after all, a way in which he could defend himself from the wrath of the governors – by enlisting the big battalions on his side.

His eyes went momentarily upwards, in silent thanks for the hope of release.

Pressing the secretarial button on his desk, he said crisply, 'Get me World Press on the line. I wish to tell them why I have seen fit to release an Immortal from this institution.'

He occupied the time pleasantly, while waiting for the call to come through, in summoning the doorman, Cusak, to make financial arrangements with him for his co-operation, and in dropping Stone a note demanding his resignation.

By the side of the old swimming pool a crowd gathered. A few women sprawled among the men, their hair as lank and uncombed as their mates'. Such garments as were worn were nondescript; some of the younger men went naked. Everyone moved in a gentle, bemused manner.

Palmer Pommy did not move. He lay on a couch erected in the shallow end of the pool so that his striped body was awash. Some of the shower equipment had been reassembled so that he was perpetually sprayed with warm water. He was laughing as he had not done for many decades.

'You bangers are on my wave-length,' he said. 'We

Immies can't take the thoughts of ordinary short-span people – they're too banal. But you lot think as daft as me.'

'We take a shot of immortality occasionally,' one of the crowd said. 'But you're as good as a dose, Palmer – the impact of meeting you loops me double, like a miracle.'

'Gods sure sent him,' another said.

'Hey, what do you mean, Gods sent him? *I* brought him,' Otto said. He was lounging by the poolside in an old chair while one of the more repellent girls stroked his neck. 'Besides, Palmer don't believe in Gods, do you, Father?'

'I invented them.'

They all laughed. A blonde girl said, 'I invented sex.' They turned it into a game.

'I invented feet.'

'I invented knee-caps.'

'I invented Pommy Palmer.'

'I invented inventions.'

'I invented me.'

'I invented dreams.'

'I invented you all – now I disinvent you!'

'I invented the Gods,' Palmer repeated. He was smiling but serious now. 'Before any of you were alive, or your parents. That's what we Immies are for, thinking up crazy ideas because our minds aren't lumbering with ordinary thoughts, else they'd kill us off because the immortality project didn't turn out as they hoped – it wasn't fit for all and sundry.

'The Gods were more or less in existence. Vast computers were running everything, comsats supplied instantaneous communication, beamed power was realised, psychology was a strict science. Mankind had always regarded computers half-prayerfully, right from their inception. All I did was think of hooking them all up, giving everyone a free communicator or shrine, and there was a new power in the world: The Gods. It worked at once, thanks to the ancient human need for gods – which never died even in scientific societies like ours.'

'Not mine, dad-o!' one of the men cried. 'I'm no robot-bugger! And say, if you invented the Gods, who invented the theology to go with them? Did you servo that too?'

'No. That came naturally. When the computers spoke, each of the old religions fell into step and adapted their forms. They had to survive: like none of them ever could stand up against personalised answer to prayers. Cranky notion ... but war's died since the Gods ruled.'

'Who's Waugh?' someone asked.

'That was a miracle. There've been others. Ask Otto. He claims that getting me out of the project was a miracle.'

Otto wriggled and removed his nose from the repellent girl's navel.

'I don't know about that. I mean I'm not so sure,' he said, scratching his chest. 'It was just that old fool doorman was bluffed into letting us out. No, I did it – I'm the miracle worker.'

'You told me different,' Palmer said, looking searchingly from the pool.

'You think I'm being arrogant. You could be right. But I reckon what I really feel, Father, is that there isn't any such thing as a miracle – just favourable conjunction of circumstances, that's all.'

There was a slender girl in the crowd who leant forward anxiously and tapped Palmer's zebra arm.

'If you've really handed us over into the power of the machines, isn't there a danger they will end by ruling us completely?'

Palmer looked slowly about the echoing chamber before deciding what to reply. He looked at the lounging group about him, most of whom had already recovered from the novelty of his presence and were interesting themselves in each other. He looked long at Otto, who had unstrapped his old shrine for comfort and was now cuddling the repellent girl in a purposeful way. Then his face crinkled into a grin.

'Don't worry, girlie! Men always cheat their gods,' he said.

A Spot of Konfrontation

The ketch moved of its own accord, engine purring, lights out. A glimmer of false dawn drifted like oil slick among thin cloud, as the boat slid beyond the West Mole into La Reine Pomare Harbour.

To one side of the harbour, old warehouses protruded over the water; beneath these the ketch found its way. Its motors died. It was home now, safe from the prying eyes of the Politzei.

Three men climbed out into the darkness, moored the boat, and ascended a slippery stair, pushing through a trap-door into a secret store. The light went on.

They were a motley collection. One was a slender brown man with nervous gestures; one was small and shaped like a crate, with a head of stubble; one was a black giant with massive shoulders.

The most human of the three, the man with nervous gestures, said, 'Phew, dies temperturo! That's enough work for one night! Let's get home before anyone's about ... ' Gunpat Smith was his name.

His companions nodded, preparing to depart, both pocketing revolvers. Gunpat Smith picked up a plastic sack and found his way into the street, where the temperature was several degrees lower than in the go-down.

The dawn wind was rising. Smith hurried along a lane of souvenir stalls. He halted by one, through whose sealed windows plastic grass skirts and battery-driven toy war-canoes were visible, and peered anxiously back the way he had come. Satisfied, he moved on. They were not following him.

He went through an alley stuffed with closed tourist shops – closed, in many cases, until the winter season brought back the tourist herds next month – and across de Bougainville Square, where the mammoth hotels began. They stood in ranks, the Ambassador, Bristol, Hilton, Florida, Antibes, Grande, Tropicana, Ritz, Concorde, all the traditional names, all alike in belching stale air and a whiff of cooking oil into the streets.

Beyond the hotel belt, the pseudo-smartness of Papeete City died at an unfinished inner ring road. Great grey apartment blocks piled here stood at all angles among scrub and bare earth, slatternly and uninviting. Gunpat was glad to slip into the Napoleon. The lift was working, though at slow pace, powered by yesterday's sunlight. It took him to the fifth floor, and he let himself into his apartment.

It was called a Tourist Town Flat – a polite way of hinting that it was very small.

The kitchen served as hall. He loaded a squid, still in its plastic sack, into the fridge. At least Flavia, being Italian, knew how to cook squid!

The living room was stuffy. Last night's bottle of wine stood on the fake-bamboo table. Smith kicked his shoes off and crossed to the bedroom, no great distance, preparing to smile.

She was not there. Her unreliability was such a blemish – and so inevitable in the circumstances! The bed had been slept in. He went over and smiled hard at it, squeezing the back of his neck with one hand where it throbbed. There was a small blood stain on the sheet, but it was old. The tele-phone by the side of the bed was shuttered, the Orgstar at the head of the bed, its electrodes dangling, still accusingly showed their latest orgasm-rating; 3.4.

Smith stood there for some while, massaging his neck, before he saw a note lying folded on the room's only chair.

He took it and went to lie down before opening and reading it.

The note was in SPEEC, the only language Smith and Flavia had in common.

'Helo, Gunny! Jeg exita. Apologio fur absenso. Too much temperturo in dies rummet fur somno, als eterno. Jeg reviendra par middago. Somna vohl! Amor, Flavia.'

Friendly as usual. And her usual excuses ... She would be working for Hakabendahassi. Light was filtering through the jammed jalousie. He closed his eyes and let his head throb in comfort. Soon he drifted off to sleep.

He was having a nightmare about the police trying to break into his room. They were using spiked metal chains. He awoke and found the blind rattling savagely and the door banging. The west wind was blowing again. Smith lay absolutely still, trying to decide whether he could bear to get up off the bed; he saw by his watch that he had been asleep for under two hours.

The effort had to be made. How few actions in this world were voluntary! Pulling himself up, he secured the door and went to look out of the window. Below the angle of the jutting blind, he saw that Papeete was now about its usual business, with taxis and tramcars snarling through the streets. Few people were walking because of the wind. It blew steadily and constantly out of a clear blue sky, never deviating or dropping. This was the fifth day it had blown without ceasing. It surprised Smith to find the Pacific contained so much wind without rain.

He went and rinsed his face and neck, slowly and with loving thoroughness, under the cold tap. Then he shaved. There was no point in going back to bed. This was Thursday, the day when his fate was to be decided.

He dawdled over coffee. The British Consulate did not open until ten, and they never really welcomed callers before 10.30. As far as they could be said to welcome callers at all. Smith tried to tell himself that he had begun to grow to like Mr Skinner. 'He's a man of the old school,' he said aloud, striving for conviction in his voice. 'A man of the old school.'

In honour of Mr Skinner, Smith put on his light blue nylon jacket over his sweat shirt. He studied himself in the mirror, collected his briefcase off the table, said to the room in general, 'You'd rialto better be back by middago, my girl!' and left the apartment.

Wind hit him as he entered the street, and went on hitting him in one continuous blow. It roared at him, pushed, jostled, and dried out his skin. He put on a painful smile to show how much he was enjoying the tropics, and hurried for the nearest alleyway. The alley acted as a funnel between the Alhambra and the South Seas; the wind bellowed down it.

Well, the wind was an excuse for a drink. At Cythera Corner, by the garish curry-and-chip stands, he staggered into the Kon-Tiki Bar, gasping for breath, and ordered a beer mai tai.

The locals were already there, throwing it down, mainly Tahitians and French, together with a couple of silent Japanese. Smith knew several of them by sight, but they shunned him, recognising him for some sort of tourist in trouble. Only the barmaid spoke to him. She was a big majestic woman, with dyed blonde hair straggling round a broken Polynesian face. As she slid the foaming mai tai across to him, she said, in broken SPEEC, 'Common' geht, Mister Smeet? Okay to-dago?'

'I'm okay, danke. And vous, Rosie? Cheers!' He lowered his mouth to the glistening stuff.

'Vous geht zuruck to U.K. to-dago, by la mambo-jet?'

'If I'm lucky, Rosie. Ven jeg fortunato!'

'Unt Flavia – elle restera hier in Papeete?'

Smith gulped at his drink. 'I couldn't possibly get mileage-allowance for Flavia. I'm having totaal trouble getting a ration for myself.'

'U.K. lange wego from Tahiti.'

'Very lange wego,' he agreed, smiling. It was a pleasure to talk to anyone, his two partners-in-crime always excepted.

Rosie glanced round at the other men in the bar and then asked, 'Common' vous amora Tahiti, Mister Smeet?'

'Oh, jeg mucho amora. Rialto wunderbar.'

Perhaps she was surprised. 'Unt dies vesto vento?'

'Ooh, lovely warm wind, rialto! Jeg high-rise to be here.' He bared his teeth to her.

She laid a hand momentarily over his. 'Ven vous reviendra to Papeete nexta jahr, 2074, jeg findera vous wunderbar young mam'selle, virgo, rialto dock-strike!' She gave a lightning impression of breasts and virginity in the air before her. 'Common' vous amorera, Mister Smeet?' When he hesitated, she added, significantly, 'Nix whore, rialto good filly. Mine little daughter! Jeg kenna vous rialto amora etwas go-go sex, nix?' She winked.

He drained his jar and gave Rosie his practised smile. 'Das is mine gross konfrontation,' he said, ruefully. Earth, who knew, he might be fool enough to get co-opted onto the Tahiti holiday rota again next year. In which case – he had no illusions about himself – he might well be glad to take up Rosie's offer. But not if his wife was with him. Couldn't let poor old Valerie down two years running in the same way.

The alcohol had done him no harm. He waved airily to Rosie before slipping through the air-lock doors and into the wind again.

On the front it was unyielding. To be out and about at all, one had to bend to the prevailing wind. The deserted pleasure boats rocked at their moorings. Spray was whipped from the nearby waters and piled against one end of the harbour, which looked revoltingly like a vast beer mai tai. Beyond the harbour, the Pacific was flecked with white. The sky was the hard, unlikely blue of a picture postcard.

The British Consulate stood up a side street off the harbour, two lofty palms lending dignity to its plain stucco exterior. Smith was hurried in by the wind and gave a dazzling smile to the doorman, whom he disliked.

'Mr Skinner's office, please.'

He knew his way. There were already several people waiting in the outer office, not speaking, and looking at each other only covertly. Smith tried to catch someone's eye and smile, but it would not work; there were no eyes to be caught this morning.

At last it was his turn to see the Vice-Consul.

Mr Skinner's office was small but neat; only his desk top was extremely untidy, proclaiming to all who entered that they were not the only pebbles on the consular beach. On the wall hung the usual portrait of the British president, with a holograph of some chaps at somewhere that could well have been Eton.

It was at such moments that Gunpat Smith remembered he was undersized, was rather drab in colour, had never been any good at games, and moreover lacked an attractive personality. These realisations came on him every time he entered the presence of Mr Skinner, who was well-built, well-dressed, pink, and obviously marvellous with men and horses.

'The wind is persisting again today.'

'Terrible stuff. It's absolutely overkill put paid to the regatta this afternoon.'

'A very dry wind for an oceanic wind, don't you think?'

'Well, let's get down to business, Mr Smith. I'm terribly sorry to say that we've still got a spot of konfrontation with your excess-mileage application.'

Despite himself, Smith let out a wail of despair, correcting it quickly with a huge smile.

'You know my situation, Mr Skinner. I am penniless here and I must get home. I am relying on you overkill!'

'I'm doing all that's possible. The airport closure delayed matters – '

Smith leant over the desk. 'Please, Mr Skinner, understand my plight! Today is Thursday. I have to be back at work at my desk in the U.K. by Monday, or I shall lose my job by being a month overdue from holiday-leave. Do you know what it means to lose your job if you are just a middle-echelon clerk like me? It means cancellation of classification, a cut in state pay, loss of ration privileges, dent in pension, curtailment on interior-travel allowance, debarrment from lotteries, maybe even getting matrimonial benefits struck off ... And the situation will grow worse every extra day I'm stranded here on Tahiti!'

Mr Skinner gazed kindly on the chaps at somewhere like Eton. 'I do realise you have an interface, old man. Believe me, it would make me terribly high-rise to be able to sort things out. I've done my best. But these things take time. Besides, you did get yourself into this spot of konfrontation, didn't you?'

Skinner had never actually said this before, although he had looked it on several occasions. The remark signified a deterioration in their relationship. Smith tried a hearty, fellow-Etonian manner.

'Chaps on holiday traditionally have a go at the native girls. It's all part of the sport of holiday. Trouble is, my wife Valerie found out. She's an unstable woman, rialto, and how was I to know that she would make such a sammy-davis and catch the next mambo home with the two children? An impossible act ... '

The back of one of Mr Skinner's hands demanded close attention. As he examined it, he said, 'I know we live in a bureaucratic age and all that – have to, on account of all the people in the world – but on that point the rules and thatchers are perfectly radar. Citizens can't just swan round the globe undocked. As a "C" Grade clerk of One Two status with two offspring, your annual personal travel-mileage allowance is twelve thousand miles, doubled when the children are with you. Since your two offspring are no longer with you, and you exhausted eighty-five per cent of your allowance just fluging out here, you cannot return to the U.K. until we get clearance from Brussels for an excess-mileage allowance. And that takes time.'

The Vice-Consul made his speech in a slightly sing-song voice, to denote that its content was familiar to both parties.

'In a whole month, stranded here, nothing has gone forward at all!'

'That's not entirely true. We've had acknowledgments from Brussels.'

'Acknowledgments!' He smiled.

'You cannot expect the Brussels Out-Tourist Departement to pay particular attention to any one individual case. And unfortunately, you've picked the month when most of the Central EEC administration is on holiday. Not to mention a month when the other Market States are applying Communication Sanctions against the U.K. over the CEB payments ... '

'So I'm supposed to rot here, talking SPEEC to the natives ... ' Even the smile failed to conceal Smith's bitterness.

'As for that, you may have heard the news that the U.S.S.R. and Greece are applying to join the Market States ... SPEEC could become a lot more complex than it is now.'

Smith brushed the remark aside. 'Meanwhile, I'm supposed to taiwan here!'

Laying his hand carefully on the desk, as if it were to be filed away, Skinner said, 'The Out-Tourist Departement may have run into a bit of irregularity in your papers, via Whitehall. Mr Smith, your great-grandfather arrived in the U.K. as a young Asian immigrant, isn't that so?'

'That was over a century ago. You can read it in my documents. My great-grandfather married a half-English lady, and our family has lived in the U.K. ever since. What is the point of referring to long-past history as dead as private cars?'

'Nothing at all, nothing at all. As far as I know everything is absolutely dock-strike. It was just that there was some doubt about the *legality* of your great-grandfather's entry into the U.K.'

Smith stood up. 'You make me despair of help, Mr Skinner. I will plead no more. You know where I live if you have any good news for me.'

The Vice-Consul also stood up, looking Smith manfully in the eye. 'Don't worry, everything will turn out koestler. It's overkill possible we'll have news *after* the weekend, when of course I'll be in touch. Meanwhile, perhaps it would be advisable if I hang on to your passport – just in case anything sputniks meanwhile.'

'Why do you need my passport? For goodness ache!'

'Mere thatcher. Just in case anything sputniks.' He held out his hand.

Staring fixedly at the hand, the hand of authority, Smith unzipped his briefcase, removed his passport, and placed it in the waiting palm. As he did so, a desperate need to placate this solid official overcame him.

'Mr Skinner, I feel some of my remarks to you have not been sufficiently genial. You must excuse me – it is because of this insoluble interface I'm in. Let me make amends and invite you as my honoured guest to a dinner of calamari I am giving this evening. Fresh-caught squid! A delight to have your friendly British company!'

Without moving a muscle or altering his expression, Mr Skinner managed to give the impression that he was constructed of wood. A non-squid-eating wood.

'I have to dine with the Governor at the Jockey Club tonight,' he said. 'Thank you.'

'Uh – oh, well, that's a rialto nixon. Never mind – uh, some other time ... '

He left the building, glad to get into the scorching wind again.

On his way back to the Napoleon Apartments, Gunpat Smith slipped into the Gauguin A-Go-Go, where a bottomless waitress served him two Rye Whiski Ananas mit Creme. He stared moodily at her pubic wig all the while, and did not speak. His life-alternatives were social degradation in the U.K. after next week, or exile in Tahiti for ever!

At last he pushed himself back to the Napoleon Apartments. On all of Ancien de Gaulle, that tavern-loaded avenue, only the Gauguin A-Go-Go was open at this low season. In another six weeks the thoroughfare would again be choked with thousands of hapless tourists from all the Market States.

He knew that Flavia had returned before he opened the door; the tele-phone was blaring hawaiian-zigane, the latest thing in pap music. As Smith entered the kitchen-hall, the band was giving out with 'Elle Donata Me Blow fur Blow' – apparently an overkill hit throughout the Pacific Urbanizacion.

She was in the shower. Abe Hakabendahassi himself was sitting in the living room in a mock-bamboo chair, drinking the last of Smith's red wine. Although the Japanese-Germano-Tahitian was Flavia's protector, although he had provided Smith with work of a sort, that did not necessarily make the little bandit welcome to Smith; indeed, his presence reminded Smith forcibly of his mistress's trade. But he smiled somehow, feeling his cheeks creak, and said, 'Hello, Abe, nice to see you again so soon. Prettig to videora vous. Nix somna?'

He stretched out for the wine bottle, but changed his mind at the last moment and grabbed the mineral-water bottle instead.

'Common' geht?' he asked, still grinning.

'Zo-zo,' Hakabendahassi said.

Smith took a swig of mineral water and headed for the bathroom, bottle in hand. He managed to shuck his nylon jacket as he went. Was the ugly little man checking up on Flavia or him? Or both?

> 'Ven jeg sensera alto or elle sensera low
> Elle donata me blow fur blow ... '

Flavia was towelling herself, slowly and luxuriously. Full-breasted, she beamed at him.

'Ah, mine overkill caro liebling! Common' geht to-dag?'

'Flavia, jeg mussa speec mit vous. Rialto gross konfrontation! Die Konsulat ha mine passeport getaken. No, what's the bloody word? Gehefta. Mine passeport is komandeert! Die Politzei mussa be on mine numbero.'

She arranged the towel about her loins and looked seriously at him. She was a handsome girl, with heavy blonde hair, dark eyes, and a commanding nose. Her hips and thighs were growing rather ponderous. On impulse, glad to see her taking him seriously, Smith leant forward, put one arm round her neck, and gave her a kiss. Flavia stuck her tongue into his mouth. Part of the stock-in-trade.

'Vous mussa raconta alles to Abe. Abe kenna waz-wot in Papeete.'

'Mais, Flavia, vous kenna radar jeg nix konfidenza in dies man Hakabendahassi.' He smiled furiously at the very mention of her protector's name. She immediately began to wave her arms and swear at him in Italian. In the end, Smith allowed himself to be rounded up and marched before Hakabendahassi with Flavia, insecurely draped, behind him. By way of protest, he flipped off the tele-phone as they passed it.

He explained to them both how the latest interview at the Consulate had gone, and how Mr Skinner had casually confiscated his passport. He omitted mention of the invitation to dinner.

'Is es totaal doomwatch?' Flavia asked Hakabendahassi, who sat stolidly at the table drinking and saying nothing.

'Rialto serios. The Politzei maj ha suspekta dies Schmit as Displaced Tourist. Feleich they shadowa Schmit.'

Although Smith resented being referred to in the third person, he felt compelled to say, 'Then they must know about you, too, Abe. What are we going to do about it then? Speel me, was tun wir?'

Sitting rigidly in his chair, Hakabendahassi went into a long harangue about the powers of the Tourist Police and the Secret Police and the Politie Arme, the Market States police, as they applied to Tahiti, together with the bribes needed to pay them off. The complications were not helped by Hakabendahassi's bad SPEEC, which was heavily over-

loaded with German words. Anxious though he was to take
it all in, Smith could not help pining for the simple British
conversations he was used to: 'Sorry, we're closing'; 'The
St John's Wort has done very well this year'; 'I'm afraid
the tramplane is late again today'. There were many dis-
advantages to be set against the one central advantage of
living with a whore, and he longed for his sedate, law-abiding
wife, not to mention the sedate, law-abiding life that went
with her.

When the harangue was done, Smith said despondently,
'It's all too complicated for me, Abe. I only came in with you
to earn some shekkels to keep myself alive. This whole mess
wasn't of my choosing! The best thing I can do is to go back
to the Consulate and give myself up, if you really think
they're on to me. I'll keep you out of it.'

Hakabendahassi thumped a fist on the table. 'Englisch nix
speec! Speec sPEEC!'

Smith went through it all again in stumbling sPEEC.

At the end of it Hakabendahassi grabbed his wrist and
stood up. 'Wir nix kaput yet, Schmit! Kom! Wir transportera unser kommodities nach ein neu hide-out. Politzei
nix find. Okay?'

'Jeg kenna die rialto perfecto hide-out!' Flavia said. 'Zu
votre fratello villa nach Vaitoto.' To Smith she explained,
'Abe ha ein brudder, Hans, in Vaitoto. Die kommodities
restera fail-safe in Hans' villa. Gang mit Abe unt assistera
cargo die schip. Jeg restera hier unt dekoyera die Politzei.
Common' overkill!' She laughed.

It seemed he had no option but to go. 'Where is this
Vaitoto?'

Vaitoto was at the other end of the island, in a remote
area still comparatively undeveloped for tourism, where it
appeared there were no police.

'I put a squid in the fridge,' he said. 'Cook it up with oil,
Italian-fashion – I'll be hungry when I get back. Calamari
als jeg reviendra. Savvy?'

'You funny English boy,' she said. 'Chow!'

Her cooking was good, when she bothered. That was another point in her favour, Gunpat Smith decided, indulging in his life-long hunt to discover consolations for his current situation. The cuisine on Tahiti was rialto horrible. In the Trade Winds Hotel, the 'C' Grade hotel in Taapuna, a suburb of Papeete, to which Smith and his family had been allocated, the food was virtually inedible. He and Valerie had quarrelled over it. It was while he was eating a sausage tutti-frutti on the front – alone and sulky – that he had spotted Flavia flaunting her limbs at the next-door ice-lolly kiosk. Encouraged by her glance, he had followed her among the souvenir stalls, knowing that she knew ...

Ah, the perpetual excitement of the hunt! Perhaps it was more blessed to chase than to capture!

As for the local cooking, there were historical reasons for its badness – or so all the tourists had been eager to assure each other. The island had suffered mild commercial exploitation in the early twentieth century. Then the French had instituted their series of nuclear tests in the Pacific. Thousands of French technologists and their families had been lodged in Tahiti, disrupting its fragile economy and bringing the inflation, unemployment, alcoholism, and crime rates which usually attend the interpenetration of an inferior culture by a superior one.

But the coming of jumbos and, later, mambos – the mammoth jumbos – had solved a lot of problems. Gigantic hotels for tourism were built, and the Tahitians co-opted to staff them. Their traditional love of fun, their idleness, their inability to cook anything more complex than a sprat in vine-leaves, and the rascality they had learnt from their masters, quickly made their standards of tourist hospitality a legend among the holiday-makers of the Western world.

Or that was how the tourists in the Trade Winds told it, over a warm wine late at night, unable to sleep for prickly heat, talking loud to combat the beat of the Fletcher Christian Ten ...

'I'm rialto glad I came,' Smith said to himself determinedly, following Abe Hakabendahassi through town. 'It's another world.'

It had been a disappointment at first to discover that Flavia was also just a Displaced Tourist, not a native girl. But the native girls were mostly four thousand miles south, decorating the new resorts along what was now called the Sunny Amundsen Sea. Flavia had been Displaced a year back, when her husband had walked out on her, much as Valerie had walked out on Smith. But Flavia had certain talents which ensured her survival. Smith had not realised precisely what those talents were that first evening, when he had taken her on the funicular up Le Diadème. There, on the spectacular ridge, in brilliant moonlight, with moths like bats wheeling above their interlocking bodies, he had found out.

Dock-strike! What a girl! None of the ghastly things that had happened since could take that experience away from him!

Despite all his prudent intentions, Smith had not managed to limp back into the Trade Winds until after petit fruhstuck next morning. Valerie had already reported his absence to the Politzei; the boys were out combing the beaches – calling their father's name laughingly, no doubt!

That day they were booked for a hydrocruise to the Disappointment Isles. How dismally significant the name had proved! Valerie had prised the whole story of the previous night from him, had so avidly enquired for all the intimate high-rise details, that finally he had exploded and accused her of lesbian tendencies.

He must have hit the nail on the head. Just as soon as she could, Valerie and the boys caught the next mambo home, leaving him stranded with no mileage allowance.

Smith smiled tooth-wrenchingly to himself. Life wasn't always so full of incident. You could say that. Wasn't even Hakabendahassi's company better than the daily U.K. stint among his fellows in the Ministry of Geriatry?

By now the two men had fought their way through the wind down to La Reine Pomare Harbour. With a grunt of relief, the Japanese pushed his way into a small warehouse and slammed the door behind them.

It was dark and sinister in the warehouse. Many things creaked.

'Informera wir Cancer Thouars?' Smith asked. Thouars was Hakabendahassi's partner-in-crime. He ought to know what they were doing.

A hideous expression resembling a grin blanketed the expanses of Hakabendahassi's countenance. 'Feleich wir donatera Cancer die cut-out dopple-cross! Alles profit surly-mon fur uns, vous unt jeg! Ja?'

'Cancer wouldn't like that!' Smith said, aware that they stood in Cancer's warehouse.

'Cancer nix kenna until alles kommoditie geht! Nix konfrontation! Kom, Schmit, wir arbeit schnell, rapido!'

'Cancer is a dangerous man,' Smith said, curling his lips and shaking his head. But he followed Hakabendahassi into the gloom. A crate stood against one wall. Between them, they shuffled it over far enough to enable them to push through a concealed door behind.

Hakabendahassi shut the door and switched on a dim light. To one side lay a trap door leading down to the ketch and the oily waters of the harbour. Piled about them were smuggled goods, half of which they had brought in only a few hours before. Smith yawned automatically at the sight of them.

It was a tough life being a smuggler! He went over and opened one crate. Inside lay piles of Tahitian cuckoo clocks, the numerals on their plastic faces surrounded by war canoes and chocolate-coloured girls with flowers in their hair. All carefully designed to tempt the tourist! Prominently along the base of each clock ran the legend: MADE IN TAHITI. Smith, with his superior and dreadful knowledge, understood that the mechanisms were manufactured in the Market States, the plastic cases in Korea, the little wooden cuckoos

— despite sanctions! — in the United White States, and the whole assembled illegally by cheap Croat labour in Australia. Cancer had told him as much, gloatingly, when they were fetching the last delivery off the Indonesian submarine lying two miles out to sea.

'Okay! Schnell, rapido, vite! At the double, Schmit!'

He kicked open the trap door, peered down at a gleam of water, and turned to the crates. With a great effort, his entire head turning brick-red, he heaved a crate on to one of his massive shoulders and staggered down the steps to the boat.

'That squid's going to be good after all this,' Smith told himself.

He managed to drag a crate to the trap and angle it down the steps one at a time. Dragging it up the little ramp into the boat almost killed him. He staggered back upstairs out of Hakabendahassi's way, and sat down to pant.

While he was doing that, he saw the door opening. In terror, he slid down behind the remaining crates. The Politzei? Mr Skinner?

Even worse — Cancer Thouars! The expression on the black Frenchman's face was enough to freeze blood a metre deep. Once he was in the store, he made no effort to be silent, running in his boots from one side to another, perhaps relying on the constant bellow of the wind to cover his movements. He carried a terrifying object in one enormous hand, a revolver with a long barrel, which he held before him in the manner of one strangling a cobra. Smith prayed frantically for a heart attack.

Cancer wasted only a moment dancing about the store — his gaze was too insane to spy out the crouching Englishman.

'Abe! Vous schweinhund!' he bellowed, and ran to the trap door. He fired downwards.

Smith hugged the floor. The noise seemed to go on for ever.

At last he picked himself up, wondering if he were dead.

Cancer was dead.

The big man had staggered back against one of the crates. It had broken under his weight, and he sprawled in bowers of shattered plastic and goggling cuckoos, still bleeding. The enormous gun lay against one wall. Smith stood petrified, watching the man's faded yellow vest turn a dismal red.

'Abe, don't shoot,' he whispered, going towards the trap door. 'Nix bang-bang!' His hearing was still distorted; the wind sounded like roaring voices.

Hakabendahassi made him no answer. Gingerly, Smith felt his way down the steps as fast as his trembling legs would take him. His head was filled with the idea that they would have to carry Cancer Thouars out to sea and dump him overboard. Poor fellow, what wretched luck it was to be born with a quick temper!

He stood by the boat and was calling 'Abe!' again, when he saw Abe. Hakabendahassi was floating face down in oily water. Although his arms were outspread, he did not look at all alive. Smith stood clasping the back of his neck and watching for several minutes to see whether he might decide to come climbing out, dripping water and blood. Abe made no further move. He had shot Cancer as he died.

Only when he observed little fish gathering round Abe's ears did Smith determine to go back to Napoleon Apartments and phone Mr Skinner.

Flavia had to pour several brown gins into him, and prime him repeatedly on what story to tell, before Smith could bring himself to call Mr Skinner's number.

'Oh, you managed to outwit them yourself, eh?' Mr Skinner said, a note of scepticism strong in his voice. 'Dock-strike for you, Smith! Certainly the Politzei will be interested in collecting the remains of both gentlemen. Of course, it places you in rather a spot ... Half the underworld of Polynesia will be after your blood now. I'll have to speak to the Consul about terminating your stay in Tahiti immediately, what!'

'I never wanted to come here in the first place,' Smith

said, smiling with an agonised frown at Flavia, to indicate that the remark was not aimed at her.

'That's hardly an excuse for the konfrontation into which you have managed to nasa yourself,' Mr Skinner said. 'You know as well as I do that a month's tourism somewhere in the Third World is compulsory every year for every member of the Market States. It maintains GTB – Global Trade Balance, in case the term is not familiar to you.' His sarcasm was plain now. The manager of men and horses was enjoying himself as he watched Smith cringe on the screen. 'You were lucky to be posted to Tahiti. It could so easily have been the Cape Verdes, the Anderman Islands, or Amundsen City. After all, it is the duty of the richer nations ... '

Despite his fearful respect for Mr Skinner, not only in his own person but as consular representative of his country, Smith found his attention wandering. A delicious smell was permeating the room. He ceased smiling in order to savour it. By Earth, she was frying the squid!

'Flavia, vous caro, wunderbar, perfecto filly!' he said.

She made a face at him round the kitchen door. Never had she looked more high-rise. The understanding came to him – she was nothing but glad that her friend and protector Hakabendahassi was dead!

He took in a little of what Mr Skinner was saying.

'Flav! Die Konsulat flugera me zuruck to U.K. by mambo, unter arrest. Savvy? In chains!' Absent-mindedly, he switched Skinner off in mid-sentence.

She came running to him from the kitchen, wearing extraordinarily little, her face full of concern. 'Unter arrest?'

'Mais Skinner nix transportera me till morgen,' he said.

He couldn't help laughing. They could spend all night together. Count your state blessings!

'Unt jeg ha ein rialto prettig cuckoo-clock fur vous,' he said, smiling.

The Soft Predicament

I Jupiter

With increasing familiarity, he saw that the slow writhings were not inconsequential movement but ponderous and deliberate gestures.

Ian Ezard was no longer aware of himself. The panorama entirely absorbed him.

What had been at first a meaningless blur had resolved into an array of lights, gently drifting. The lights now took on pattern, became luminous wings or phosphorescent backbones or incandescent limbs. As they passed, the laboured working of those pinions ceased to look random and assumed every appearance of deliberation – of plan – of consciousness! Neither was the stew in which the patterns moved a chaos any longer; as Ezard's senses adjusted to the scene, he became aware of an environment as much governed by its own laws as the environment into which he had been born.

With the decline of his first terror and horror, he could observe more acutely. He saw that the organisms of light moved over and among – what would you call them? Bulwarks? Fortifications? Cloud formations? They were no more clearly defined than sandbanks shrouded in fog; but he was haunted by a feeling of intricate detail slightly beyond his retinal powers of resolution, as if he were gazing at flotillas of baroque cathedrals, sunk just too deep below translucent seas.

He thought with unexpected kinship of Lowell, the astronomer, catching imaginary glimpses of Martian canals

– but his own vantage point was much the more privileged.

The scale of the grand, gay, solemn procession parading before his vision gave him trouble. He caught himself trying to interpret the unknown in terms of the known. These organisms reminded him of the starry skeletons of terrestrial cities by night, glimpsed from the stratosphere, or of clusters of diatoms floating in a drop of water. It was hard to remember that the living geometries he was scanning were each the size of a large island – perhaps three hundred kilometres across.

Terror still lurked. Ezard knew he had only to adjust the infra-red scanners to look much deeper into Jupiter's atmosphere and find – life? – images? – of a different kind. To date, the Jupiter Expedition had resolved six levels of life-images, each level separated from the others almost as markedly as sea was separated from air, by pressure gradients that entailed different chemical compositions.

Layer on layer, down they went, stirring slowly, right down far beyond detection into the sludgy heart of the protosun! Were all layers full of at least the traces and chimerae of life?

'It's like peering down into the human mind!' Ian Ezard exclaimed; perhaps he thought of the mind of Jerry Wharton, his mixed-up brother-in-law. Vast pressures, vast darknesses, terrible wisdoms, age-long electric storms – the parallel between Jupiter's atmospheric depths and the mind was too disconcerting. He sat up and pushed the viewing helmet back on its swivel.

The observation room closed in on him again, unchanging, wearily familiar.

'My god!' he said, feebly wiping his face, 'My god!' And after a moment, 'By Jove!' in honour of the monstrous protosun riding like a whale beneath their ship. Sweat ran from him.

'It's a spectacle right enough,' Captain Dudintsev said, handing him a towel. 'And each of the six layers we have surveyed is over one hundred times the area of Earth. We are recording most of it on tape. Some of the findings are being relayed back to Earth now.'

'They'll flip!'

'Life on Jupiter – what else can you call it but life? This is going to hit Russia and America and the whole of Westciv harder than any scientific discovery since reproduction!'

Looking at his wristputer, Ezard noted that he had been under the viewer for eighty-six minutes. 'Oh, it's consciousness there right enough. It stands all our thinking upside down. Not only does Jupiter contain most of the inorganic material of the system, the Sun apart – it contains almost all the life as well. Swarming, superabundant life ... Not an amoeba smaller than Long Island ... It makes Earth just a rocky outpost on a far shore. That's a big idea to adjust to!'

'The White World will adjust, as we adjusted to Darwinism. We always do adjust.'

'And who cares about the Black World ... '

Dudinstev laughed. 'What about your sister's husband that you're always complaining about? He'd care!'

'Oh, yes, he'd care. Jerry'd like to see the other half of the globe wiped out entirely.'

'Well, he's surely not the only one.'

With his head still full of baffling luminescent gestures, Ezard went forward to shower.

II Luna

Near to deep midnight in Rainbow Bay City. Standing under Main Dome at the top of one of the view-towers. The universe out there before us, close to the panes; stars like flaming fat, distorted by the dome's curvature, Earth like a chilled finger-nail clipping. Chief Dream-Technician Wace and I talking sporadically, killing time until we went back on duty to what my daughter Ri calls 'the big old black thing' over in Plato.

'Specialisation – it's a wonderful thing, Jerry!' Wace

said. 'Here we are, part-way to Jupiter and I don't even know where in the sky to look for it! The exterior world has never been my province.'

He was a neat little dry man, in his mid-thirties and already wizened. His province was the infinitely complex state of being of sleep. I had gained a lot of my interest in psychology from Johnnie Wace. Like him, I would not have been standing where I was were it not for the CUFL project, on which we were both working. And that big old black thing would not have been established inconveniently on the Moon had not the elusive hypnoid states between waking and sleeping which we were investigating been most easily sustained in the light-gravity conditions of Luna.

I gave up the search for Jupiter. I knew where it was no more than Wace did. Besides, slight condensation was hatching drops off the aluminium bars overhead; the draughts of the dome brought the drops down slantingly at us. Tension was returning to me as the time to go on shift drew near — tension we were not allowed to blunt with drink. Soon I would be plugged in between life and death, letting CUFL suck up my psyche. As we turned away, I looked outside at an auxiliary dome under which cactus grew in the fertile lunar soil, sheltered only slightly from external rigours.

'That's the way we keep pushing on, Johnnie,' I said, indicating the cacti. 'We're always extending the margins of experience — now the Trans-Jupiter Expedition has discovered that life exists out there. Where does the West get its dynamism from, while the rest of the world — the Third World — still sits on its haunches?'

Wace gave me an odd look.

'I know, I'm on my old hobby-horse! You tell me, Johnnie, you're a clever man, how is it that in an age of progress half the globe won't progress?'

'Jerry, I don't feel about the Blacks as you do. You're such an essential part of CUFL because your basic symbols are confused.'

He noticed that the remark angered me. Yet I saw the

truth as I stated it. Westciv, comprising most of the Northern Hemisphere and little else bar Australia, was a big armed camp, guarding enormously long frontiers with the stagnating Black or Third World, and occasionally making a quick raid into South America or Africa to quell threatening power build-ups. All the time that we were trying to move forward, the rest of the over-crowded world was dragging us back.

'You know my views, Johnnie – they may be unpopular but I've never tried to hide them,' I told him, letting my expression grow dark. 'I'd wipe the slate of the useless Third World clean and begin over, if I had my way. What have we got to lose? No confusion in my symbols there, is there?'

'Once a soldier, always a soldier ... ' He said no more until we were entering the elevator. Then he added, in his quiet way, 'We can all of us be mistaken, Jerry. We now know that the freshly charted ypsilon-areas of the brain make no distinction between waking reality and dream. They deal only with altering time-scales, and form the gateway to the unconscious. My personal theory is that Western man, with his haste for progress, may have somehow closed that gate and lost touch with something that is basic to his psychic well-being.'

'Meaning the Blacks are still in touch?'

'Don't sneer! The history of the West is nothing to be particularly proud of. You know that our CUFL project is in trouble and may be closed down. Sure, we progress astonishingly on the material plane, we have stations orbiting the Sun and inner planets and Jupiter – yet we remain at odds with ourselves. CUFL is intended to be to the psyche what the computer is to knowledge, yet it consistently rejects our data. The fault is not in the machine. Draw your own conclusions.'

I shrugged. 'Let's get on shift.'

We reached the surface and climbed out, walking in the direction of the tube where a shuttle for Plato would be ready. The big old black thing would be sitting waiting by the crater terminus and, under the care of Johnnie Wace's team, the other feeds and I would be plugged in. Sometimes I felt lost in the whole tenuous world that Wace found so congenial, and in all the clever talk about what was dream, what was reality – though I used it myself sometimes, in self-defence.

As we made for the subway, the curve of the dome distorted the cacti beyond. Frail though they were, great arms of prickly pear grew and extended and seemed to wrap themselves round the dome, before being washed out by floods of reflected electroluminescence. Until the problem of cutting down glare at night was beaten, tempers in Main Dome would stay edgy.

In the subway, still partly unfinished, Wace and I moved past the parade of fire-fighting equipment and emergency suits and climbed into the train. The rest of the team were already in their seats, chattering eagerly about the ambiguous states of mind that CUFL encouraged; they greeted Johnnie warmly, and he joined in their conversation. I longed to be back with my family – such as it was – or playing a quiet game of chess with Ted Greaves, simple old soldier Ted Greaves. Maybe I should have stayed a simple old soldier myself, helping to quell riots in the overcrowded lanes of Eastern Seaboard, or cutting a quick swathe through Brazil.

'I didn't mean to rub you up the wrong way, Jerry,' Wace said as the doors closed. His little face wrinkled with concern.

'Forget it. I jumped at you. These days life's too complex.'

'That from you, the apostle of progress!'

It's no good talking ... 'Look, we've found life on Jupiter. That's great. I'm really glad, glad for Ezard out there, glad for everyone. But what are we going to do about it? Where does it get us? We haven't even licked the problem of life on Earth yet!'

'We will,' he said.

We began to roll into the dark tunnel.

III Ri

One of the many complications of life on Earth was the dreams of my daughter. They beguiled me greatly: so much that I believe they often became entangled with my fantasies as I lay relaxed on Wace's couch under the encephalometers and the rest of the CUFL gear. But they worried me even as they enchanted me. The child is so persistently friendly that I don't always have time for her; but her dreams are a different matter.

In the way that Ri told them, the dreams had a peculiar lucidity. Perhaps they were scenes from a world I wanted to be in, a toy world – a simplified world that hardly seemed to contain other people.

Ri was the fruit of my third-decade marriage. My fourth-decade wife, Natalie, also liked to hear Ri's prattle; but Natalie is a patient woman, both with Ri and me; more with Ri, maybe, since she likes to show me her temper.

A certain quality to Ri's dreams made Natalie and me keep them private to ourselves. We never mentioned them to our friends, almost as if they were little shared guilty secrets. Neither did I ever speak of them to my buddies sweating on the CUFL project, nor to Wace, nor the mind-wizards in the Lunar Psyche Lab. For that matter Natalie and I avoided discussing them between ourselves, partly because we sensed Ri's own reverence for her nocturnal images.

Then my whole pleasure at the child's dreams was turned into disquiet by a casual remark that Ted Greaves dropped.

This is how it came about.

I had returned from Luna on the leave-shuttle only the previous day, more exhausted than usual. The hops between Kennedy and Eastern and Eastern and Eurocen were becoming more crowded than ever, despite the extra jumbos operating; the news of the discovery of life on Jupiter – even the enormous telecasts of my brother-in-law's face burning over every Westciv city — seemed to have stirred up the ants' heap considerably. What people thought they could do about it was beyond computation, but Wall Street was registering a tidal wave of optimism.

So with one thing and another, I arrived home exhausted. Ri was asleep. Yes, still wetting her bed, Natalie admitted. I took a sauna and fell asleep in my wife's arms. The world turned. Next thing I knew, it was morning and I was roused by Ri's approach to our bedside.

Small girls of three have a ponderous tread; they weigh as much as baby elephants. I can walk across our bedroom floor without making a sound, but this tot sets up vibrations.

'I thought you were still on the Moon feeding the Clective Unctious, Daddy,' she said. The 'Clective Unctious' is her inspired mispronunciation of the Collective Unconscious; wisely, she makes no attempt at all at the Free-Living tail of CUFL.

'The Unctious has given me a week's leave, Ri. Now let me sleep! Go and read your book!'

I watched her through one half-open eye. She put her head on one side and smiled at me, scratching her behind.

'Then that big old black thing is a lot cleverer and kinder than I thought it was.'

From her side of the bed, Natalie laughed. 'Why, that's the whole idea of the Clective Unctious, Ri — to be kinder and wiser than one person can imagine.'

'I can imagine *lots* of kindness,' she said. She was not to be weaned of her picture of the Unctious as a big black thing.

Climbing on to the bed, she began to heave herself between Natalie and me. She had brought along a big plastic talkie-picture-book of traditional design tucked under one arm. As she rolled over me, she swung the book and a corner of it caught me painfully on the cheek. I yelled.

'You clumsy little horror! Get off me!'

'Daddy, I didn't mean to do it really! It was an acciment!'

'I don't care what it was! Get out! Go on! Move! Go back to your own bed!'

I tugged at her arm and dragged her across me. She burst into tears.

Natalie sat up angrily. 'For god's sake, leave the kid alone! You're always bullying her!'

'You keep quiet – she didn't catch you in the eye! And she's peed her bed again, the dirty little tyke!'

That was how that row started. I'm ashamed to relate how it went on. There were the tears from the child and tears from Natalie. Only after breakfast did everyone simmer down. Oh, I can be fairly objective now, in this confession, and record my failings and what other people thought of me. Believe me, if it isn't art, it's therapy!

It's strange to recall now how often we used to quarrel over breakfast ... Yet that was one of the calmest rooms, with the crimson carpet spread over the floor-tiles, and the white walls and dark Italian furniture. We had old-fashioned two-dimensional oil paintings, non-mobile, on the walls, and no holoscreen. In one corner, half-hidden behind a vase of flowers from the courtyard, stood Jannick, our robot house-maid; but Natalie, preferring not to use her, kept her switched off. Jannick was off on this occasion. Peace reigned. Yet we quarrelled.

As Natalie and I were drinking a last cup of coffee, Ri trotted round to me and said, 'Would you like to hear my dream now, Daddy, if you're really not savage any more?'

I pulled her on to my knee. 'Let's hear it then, if we must. Was it the one about warm pools of water again?'

She shook her head in a dignified manner.

'This dream came around three in the morning,' she said. 'I know what the time was because a huge black bird like a starving crow came and pecked at my window as if it wanted to get in and wake us all up.'

'That was all a part of the dream, then. There aren't any crows in this stretch of Italy.'

'Perhaps you're right, because the house was sort of dirtier

than it really is ... So I sat up and immediately I began
dreaming I was fat and heavy and carrying a big fat heavy
talkie-book up the hill. It was a much bigger book than any
I got here. I could hardly breathe because there was hardly
any air up the hillside. It was a very *plain* sort of dream.'

'And what happened in it?'

'Nothing.'

'Nothing at all?'

'Nothing except just one thing. Do you know what? I saw
there was one of those new Japanese cars rushing down the
hill towards me – you know, the kind where the body's inside
the wheel and the big wheel goes all round the body.'

'She must mean the Toyota Monocar,' Natalie said.

'Yes, that's right, Natalie, the Toyta Moggacar. It was
like a big flaming wheel and it rolled right past me and went
out.'

'Out where?'

'I don't know. Where do things go out to? I didn't even
know where it came from! In my dream I was puzzled about
that, so I looked all round and by the roadside there was a
big drop. It just went down and down! And it was guarded
by eight posts protecting it, little round white posts like
teeth, and the Moggacar must have come from there.'

Natalie and I sat over the table thinking about the dream
after Ri had slipped out into the courtyard to play; she had
some flame- and apricot-coloured finches in cages which she
loved.

I was on her small imaginary hillside, where the air was
thin and the colours pale, and the isolated figure of the child
stood clutching its volume and watched the car go past like
a flame. A sun-symbol, the wheel on which Ixion was cruci-
fied, image of our civilisation maybe, Tantric sign of sympathetic fires ... All those things, and the first unmanned
stations now orbiting the Sun – one of the great achievements of Westciv, and itself a symbol awakening great
smouldering responses in man. Was that response reverberat-
ing through the psyches of all small children, changing them,

charging them further along the trajectory the White World follows? What would the news from Jupiter bring on? What sort of role would Uncle Ian, the life-finder, play in the primitive theatres of Ri's mind?

I asked the questions of myself only idly. I enjoyed popping the big questions on the principle that if they were big enough they were sufficient in themselves and did not require answers. Answers never worried me in those days. I was no thinker. My job in Plato concerned feelings, and for that they paid me. Answers were for Johnnie Wace and his cronies.

'We'd better be moving,' Natalie said, collecting my coffee cup. 'Since you've got a free day, make the most of it. You're on frontier duty with Greaves again tomorrow.'

'I know that without being reminded, thanks.'

'I wasn't really reminding you – just stating a fact.'

As she passed me to go into the kitchen, I said, 'I know this house is archaic – just a peasant's home. But if I hadn't volunteered for irregular frontier service during my off-duty spells, we wouldn't be here. We'd be stuck in Eastern or some other enormous city-complex, such as the one you spent your miserable childhood in. Then you'd complain even more!'

She continued into the kitchen with the cups and plates. It was true the house had been built for and by peasants, or little better; its stone walls, a metre thick, kept out the heat of summer: and the brief chill of winter when it rolled round. Natalie was silent and then she said, so quietly that I could scarcely hear her where I sat in the living room, 'I was not complaining, Jerry, not daring to complain ... '

I marched in to her. She was standing by the sink, more or less as I imagined her, her dark wings of hair drawn into place by a rubber band at the nape of her neck. I loved her, but she could make me mad!

'What's that meant to mean – "not daring to complain"?'

'Please don't quarrel with me, Jerry. I can't take much more.'

'Was I quarrelling? I thought I was simply asking you what you meant by what you said!'

'Please don't get worked up!' She came and stood against me, putting her arms round my waist and looking up at me. I stiffened myself and would not return her gaze. 'I mean no harm, Jerry. It's terrible the way we row just like everyone else — I know you're upset!'

'Of course I'm upset! Who wouldn't be upset at the state of the world? Your marvellous brother and his buddies have discovered life on Jupiter! Does that affect us? *My* project, CUFL, that will have to close down unless we start getting results. Then there's all the disturbances in the universities — I don't know what the younger generation thinks it's doing! Unless we're strong, the Thirdies are going to invade and take over —'

She was growing annoyed herself now. 'Oh yes, that's really why we came to live down here in the back of beyond, isn't it? Just so that you could get an occasional crack at the enemy. It wasn't for any care about where I might want to live.'

'Unlike some people, I care about doing my duty by my country!'

She broke away from me. 'It's no part of your duty to be incessantly beastly to Ri and me, is it? Is it? You don't care about us one bit!'

It was an old tune she played.

'Don't start bringing that up again, woman! If I didn't care, why did I buy you that robot standing idle in the next room? You never use it, you prefer to hire a fat old woman to come in instead! I should have saved my money! And you have the brass nerve to talk about not caring!'

Her eyes were wild now. She looked glorious standing there.

'You don't care! You don't care! You hurt your poor little daughter, you neglect me! You're always off to the Moon, or at the frontier, or else here bullying us. Even your stupid friend Ted Greaves has more sense than you! You hate us! You hate everyone!'

Running forward, I grabbed her arm and shook her.

'You're always making a noise! Not much longer till the end of the decade and then I'm rid of you! I can't wait!'

I strode through the house and slammed out of the door into the street. Thank the stars it was frontier duty the next day! People greeted me but I ignored them. The sun was already high in the South Italian sky; I sweated as I walked, and rejoiced in the discomfort.

It was not true that I bullied them. Natalie might have suffered as a child, but so had I! There had been a war in progress then, the first of the Westciv-Third wars, although we had not thought of it in quite those terms at the time, before the Cap-Com treaty. I had been drafted, at an age when others were cutting a figure in university. I had been scared, I had suffered, been hungry, been wounded, been lost in the jungle for a couple of days before the chopper patrol picked me up. And I'd killed off a few Thirdies. Even Natalie would not claim I had *enjoyed* doing that. It was all over long ago. Yet it was still with me. In my mind, it never grew fainter. The Earth revolved; the lights on that old stage never went dim.

Now I was among the hills above our village. I sat under the shade of an olive tree and looked back. It's strange how you find yourself thinking things that have nothing to do with your daily life.

It was no use getting upset over a husband-wife quarrel. Natalie was okay; just a little hasty-tempered. My watch said close to ten o'clock. Ted Greaves would be turning up at the house for a game of chess before long. I would sit where I was for a moment, breathe deep, and then stroll back. Act naturally. There was nothing to be afraid of.

IV Greaves

Ted Greaves arrived at the house at about ten-fifty. He was a tall fair-haired man, dogged by ill-luck most of his military career and somewhat soured towards society. He enjoyed playing the role of bluff old soldier. After many years in the service, he was now Exile Officer commanding our sector of the southern frontier between Westciv and the Blacks. As such he would be my superior tomorrow, when I went on duty. Today we were just buddies and I got the chess board out.

'I feel too much like a pawn myself to play well today,' he said, as we settled down by the window. 'Spent all the last twenty-four hours in the office filling in photoforms. We're sinking under forms! The famine situation in North Africa is now reinforced by a cholera epidemic.'

'The Third's problems are nothing to do with us!'

'Unfortunately we're more connected than appears on the surface. The authorities are afraid that the cholera won't respect frontiers. We've got to let some refugees through tomorrow, and they could be carriers. An emergency isolation ward is being set up. It's Westciv's fault – we should have given aid to Africa from the start.'

On the Rainbow-Kennedy flight, I had bought a can of bourbon at a duty-free price. Greaves and I broached it now. But he was in a dark mood, and was soon launched on an old topic of his, the responsibility of the States for the White-Black confrontation. I did not accept his diagnosis for one minute, and he knew I didn't; but that did not stop him rambling on about the evils of our consumer society, and how it was all based on jealousy, and the shame of the Negro Solution – though how we could have avoided the Solution, he did not say. Since we had been mere children at the time of the Solution, I could not see why he needed to feel guilt about it. In any case, I believed that the coloured races of

Third were undeveloped because they lacked the intellect and moral fibre of Westciv, their hated Pinkeyland.

So I let Greaves give vent to his feelings over the iced bourbon while I gazed out through the window to our inner courtyard.

The central stone path, flanked by a colonnade on which bougainvillaea rioted, led to a little statue of Diana, executed in Carrara marble, standing against the far wall. All the walls of the courtyard were plastered in yellow. On the left-hand side, Ri's collection of finches chirped and flitted in their cages. In the beds, orange and lemon trees grew. Above the far wall, the mountains of Calabria rose.

I never tired of the peace of that view. But what chiefly drew my eyes was the sight of Natalie in her simple green dress. I had loved her in many forms, I thought, and at the end of the decade it would not come too hard to exchange her for another – better anyhow than being stuck with one woman all life long, as under the old system – but either I was growing older or there was something particular about Natalie. She was playing with Ri and talking to the Calabrian servant. I couldn't hear a word they said, though the windows were open to let in warmth and fragrance; only the murmur of their voices reached me.

Yes, she had to be exchanged. You had to let things go. That was what kept the world revolving. Planned obsolescence as a social dynamic, in human relationships as in consumer goods. When Ri was ten, she would have to go to the appropriate Integration Centre, to learn to become a functioning member of society – just as my other daughter, Melisande, had left the year before, on her tenth birthday.

Melisande, who wept so much at the parting ... a sad indication of how much she needed integration. We were all required to make sacrifices; otherwise the standard of living would go down. Partings one grew hardened to. I scarcely thought of Melisande nowadays.

And when I'd first known Natalie. Natalie Ezard. That was before the integration laws. 'Space travel nourishes our deepest and most bizarre wishes.' Against mental states of maximum alertness float extravagant hypnoid states which colour the outer darkness crimson and jade and make unshapely things march to the very margins of the eye. Maybe it is because at the heart of the richness of metal-bound space-travel lies sensory deprivation. For all its promise of renaissance, vacuum-flight is life's death, and only the completely schizoid are immune to its terrors. I was never happy, even on the Kennedy-Rainbow trip.

Between planets, our most *outré* desires become fecund. Space travel nourishes our deepest and most bizarre wishes. 'Awful things can happen!' Natalie had cried, in our early days, flinging herself into my returning arms. And while I was away, Westciv passed its integration laws, separating parents from children, bestowing on ten-year-olds the honourable orphanage of the state, to be trained as citizens.

It all took place again before the backdrop of our sunlit courtyard, where Natalie Wharton now stood. She was thinner and sharper than she had been once, her hair less black. Some day we would have to take the offensive and wipe out every single Black in the Black-and-White world. To my mind, only the fear of what neutral China might do had prevented us taking such a necessary step already.

'You see how old it is out there!' Ted Greaves said, misreading my gaze as he gestured into the courtyard. 'Look at that damned vine, that statue! Apart from lovely little Natalie and your daughter, there's not a thing that hasn't been in place for a couple of hundred years. Over in the States, it's all new, new, everything has to be the latest. As soon as roots begin forming, we tear them up and start over. The result – no touchstones! How long's this house been standing? Three centuries? In the States it would have been swept away long ago. Here loving care keeps it going, so that it's as good as new. Good as new! See how I'm victim of my own clichés. It's better than fucking new, it's as good as old!'

'You're a sentimentalist, Ted. It isn't things but other people that matter. People are old, worlds are old. The Russo-American ships now forging round the System are bringing home to us just how old we are, how familiar we are to ourselves. Our roots are in ourselves.'

We enjoyed philosophising, that's true.

He grunted and lit a flash-cigar. 'That comes well from you, when you're building this Free-Living Collective Unconscious. Isn't that just another American project to externalise evil and prune our roots?'

'Certainly not! CUFL will be an emotions-bank, a computer if you like, which will store – not the fruits of the human intellect – but the fruits of the psyche. Now that there are too many people around and our lives have to be regimented, CUFL will restore us to the freedom of our imaginations.'

'If it works!'

'Sure, if it works,' I agreed. 'As yet, we can get nothing out of our big old black thing but primitive archetypal patterns. It's a question of keeping on feeding it.' I always spoke more cheerfully than I felt with Greaves: to counteract his vein of pessimism, I suppose.

He stood up and stared out of the window. 'Well, I'm just a glorified soldier – and without much glory. I don't understand emotion banks. But maybe you overfed your big black thing and it is dying of over-nourishment, just like Westciv itself. Certain archetypal dreams – the human young get them, so why not your newborn machine? The young get them especially when they are going to die young.'

Death was one of his grand themes; 'the peace that passeth all standing,' he called it once.

'What sort of dreams?' I asked, unthinking.

'To the nervous system, dream imagery is received just like sensory stimulae. There are prodromic dreams, dreams that foretell death. We don't know what wakefulness is, do we, until we know what dreams are. Maybe the whole Black-White struggle is a super-dream, like a blackbird rapping on a window pane.'

Conversation springs hidden thoughts. I'd been listening, but more actively I'd wondered at the way he didn't answer questions quite directly, just as most people fail to. Someone told me that it was the effect of holovision, split attention. All this I was going through when he came up with the remark about blackbirds tapping on windows, and it brought to mind the start of Ri's latest dream, when she was unsure whether she woke or slept.

'What's that to do with dying?'

'Let's take a walk in the sun before it gets too stinking hot. Some children are too ethereal for life. Christ, Jerry, a kid's close to the primal state, to the original psychological world; they're the ones to come through with uncanny prognoses. If they aren't going to make it to maturity, their psyches know about it and have no drive to gear themselves on to the next stage of being.'

'Let's go out in the sun,' I said. I felt ill. The poinsettias were in flower, spreading their scarlet tongues. A lizard lay along a carob branch. That sun disappearing down Ri's hill – death? And the eight teeth or posts or what the hell they were, on the edge of nothing – her years? The finches hopped from perch to perch, restless in their captivity.

V Sicily

Almost before daybreak next morning, I was flying over Calabria and the toe of Italy. Military installations glittered below. This was one of the southern points of Europe which marked the frontier between the two worlds. It was manned by task forces of Americans, Europeans and Russians. I had left before Ri woke. Natalie, with her wings of dark hair, had risen to wave me goodbye. Goodbye, it was always goodbye. And what was the meaning of the big black book Ri had been carrying in her dream? It couldn't be true.

The Straits of Messina flashed below our wingless fuselage. Air, water, earth, fire, the original elements. The fifth, space, had been waiting. God alone knew what it did in the hearts and minds of man, what aboriginal reaction was in process. Maybe once we finished off the Thirdies, the Clective Unctious would give us time to sort things out. There was never time to sort things out. Even the finches in their long imprisonment never had enough time. And the bird at her window? Which side of the window was in, which out?

We were coming down towards Sicily, towards its tan mountains. I could see Greaves's head and shoulders in the driver's seat.

Sicily was semi-neutral ground. White and Black world met in its eroded valleys. My breakfast had been half a grapefruit, culled fresh from the garden, and a cup of bitter black coffee. Voluntary regulation of intake. The other side of the looming frontier starvation would have made my snack seem a fine repast.

Somewhere south, a last glimpse of sea and the smudged distant smoke of Malta, still burning after ten years. Then up came Etna and the stunned interior, and we settled for a landing.

This barren land looked like machine-land itself. Sicily – the northern, Westciv half – had as big a payload of robots on it as the Moon itself. All worked in mindless unison in case the lesser breeds in the southern half did anything desperate. I grabbed up my gas-cannon and climbed out into the heat as a flight of steps snapped itself into position.

Side by side, Greaves and I jumped into proffered pogo-armour and bounded off across the field in giant kangaroo-leaps.

The White boundary was marked by saucers standing on poles at ten-metre intervals; between saucers, the force barrier shimmered, carrying its flair for hallucination right up into the sky.

The Black world had its boundary too. It stood beyond our force field – stood, I say! It lurched across Sicily, a ragged wall of stone. Much of the stone came from dismembered towns and villages and churches. Every now and again, a native would steal some of the stone back, in order to build his family a hovel to live in. Indignant Black officials would demolish the hovel and restore the stone. They should have worried! I could have pogoed over their wall with ease!

And a wall of eight posts ...

We strode across the crowded field to the forward gate. Sunlight and gravity. We were massive men, three metres high or more, with gigantic boots and enveloping umbrella-helmets adding to our stature. Our megavoices could carry two kilometres. We might have been evil machine-men from the ragged dreams of Blacks. At the forward gate, we entered and shed the armour in magnetised recesses.

Up in the tower, Greaves took over the auto-controls and opened his link with Palermo and the comsats high overhead. I checked with immigration and isolation to see that they were functioning.

From here we could look well into the hated enemy territory, over the tops of their rusted towers, into the miserable stone villages, from which hordes of people were already emerging, although fifty minutes had yet to elapse before we lowered the force-screens to let any of them through. Beyond the crowds, mountains crumbling into their thwarted valleys, fly-specked with bushes. No fit habitation. If we took over the island – as I always held we should – we would raise desalination plants on the coast, import topsoil and fertiliser and the new plus-crops, and make the whole place flow with riches in five years. Under the status quo, the next five would bring nothing but starvation and religion; that was all they had there. A massive cholera epidemic, with deaths counted in hundreds of thousands, was raging through Africa already, after moving westwards from Calcutta, its traditional capital.

'The bastards!' I said. 'One day there will be a law all over the world forbidding people to live like vermin!'

'And a law forbidding people to make capital out of it,' Greaves said. His remark meant nothing to me. I guessed it had something to do with his cranky theory that Westciv profited by the poor world's poverty by raising import tariffs against it. Greaves did not explain, nor did I ask him to.

At the auxiliary control panel, I sent out an invisible scanner to watch one of the enemy villages. Although it might register on the antiquated radar screens of the Blacks, they could only rave at the breach of international regulations without ever being able to intercept it.

The eye hovered over a group of shacks and adjusted its focus. Three-dimensionally, the holograph of hatred travelled towards me in the cube.

Against doorways, up on balconies decked with ragged flowers, along alleys, stood groups of Blacks. They would be Arabs, refugee Maltese, branded Sicilians, renegades from the White camp; ethnic groups were indistinguishable beneath dirt and tan and old non-synthetic clothes. I centred on a swarthy young woman standing in a tavern doorway with one hand on a small boy's shoulder. As Natalie had stood in the courtyard under the poinsettias, what had I thought to myself? That once we might have propagated love between ourselves?

Before the world had grown too difficult, there had been a sure way of multiplying and sharing love. We would have bred and raised children for the sensuous reward of having them, of helping them grow up sane and strong. From their bowels also, health would have radiated.

But the Thirdies coveted Westciv's riches without accepting its disciplines. They bred. Indiscriminately and prodigally. The world was too full of children and people, just as the emptiness of space was stuffed with lurid dreams. Only the weak and helpless and starved could cast children on to the world unregulated. Their weak and helpless and starved progeny clogged the graves and wombs of the world. That laughing dark girl on my screen deserved only the bursting seed of cannonfire.

'Call that scanner back, Jerry!' Greaves said, coming towards me.

'What's that?'

'Call your scanner back.'

'I'm giving the Wogs the once-over.'

'Call it back in, I told you. As long as no emergency's in force, you are contravening regulations.'

'Who cares!'

'I care,' he said. He looked very nasty. 'I care, and I'm Exile Officer.'

As I guided the eye back in, I said, 'You were rough all yesterday too. You played a bum game of chess. What's got into you?'

But as soon as I had asked the question, I could answer it myself. He was a bag of nerves because he must have had word that his son was coming back from the wastes of the Third World.

'You're on the hook about your anarchist son Pete, aren't you?'

It was then he flung himself at me.

In the dark tavern, Pete Greaves was buying his friends one last round of drinks. He had been almost three weeks in the seedy little town, waiting for the day the frontier opened; in that time he had got to know just about everyone in the place. All of them – not just Max Spineri who had travelled all the way from Alexandria with him – swore eternal friendship on this parting day.

'And a plague on King Cholera!' Pete said, lifting his glass.

'Better get back to the West before King Cholera visits Sicily,' a mule driver said.

The drink was strong. Pete felt moved to make a short speech.

'I came here a stupid prig, full of all the propaganda of the West,' he said. 'I'm going back with open eyes. I've become a man in my year in Africa and Sicily, and back home I shall apply what I've learned.'

'Here's your home now, Pete,' Antonio the barman said. 'Don't go back to Pinkeyland or you'll become a machine like the others there. We're your friends – stay with your friends!' But Pete noticed the crafty old devil short-changed him.

'I've got to go back, Antonio – Max will tell you. I want to stir people up, make them listen to the truth. There's got to be change, got to be, even if we wreck the whole present set-up to get it. All over Pinkeyland, take my word, there are thousands – millions – of men and girls my age who hate the way things are run.'

'It's the same as here,' a peasant laughed.

'Sure, but in the West, it's different. The young are tired of the pretence that we have some say in government, tired of bureaucracy, tired of a technocracy that simply reinforces the powers of the politicians. Who cares about finding life on Jupiter when life here just gets lousier!'

He saw – it had never ceased to amaze him all his time in Blackeyland – that they were cool to such talk. He was on their side, as he kept telling them. Yet at best their attitude to the Whites was ambivalent: a mixture of envy and contempt for nations that they saw as slaves to consumer goods and machines.

He tried again, telling them about Student Power and the Underground, but Max interrupted him. 'You have to go soon, Pete. We know how you feel. Take it easy – your people find it so hard to take it easy. Look, I've got a parting gift for you … '

Drawing Pete back into a corner, he produced a gun and thrust it into his friend's hand. Examining it, Pete saw it was an ancient British Enfield revolver, well-maintained. 'I can't accept this, Max!'

'Yes, you can! It's not from me but from the Organisation. To help you in your revolution. It's loaded with six bullets! You'll have to hide it, because they will search you when you cross the frontier.'

He clasped Max's hand. 'Every bullet will count, Max!'

He trembled. Perhaps it was mainly fear of himself.

When he was far from the heat and flies and dust and his ragged unwashed friends, he would hold this present brave image of himself, and draw courage from it.

He moved out into the sun, to where Roberta Arneri stood watching the convoy assembling for the short drive to the frontier gate. He took her hand.

'You know why I have to go, Roberta?'

'You go for lots of reasons.'

It was true enough. He stared into the harsh sunlight and tried to remember. Though hatred stood between the two worlds, there were areas of weakness where they relied on each other. Beneath the hatred were ambiguities almost like love. Though a state of war existed, some trade continued. And the young could not be pent in. Every year young Whites – 'anarchists' to their seniors – slipped over the frontier with ambulances and medical supplies. And the supplies were paid for by their seniors. It was conscience money. Or hate money. A token, a symbol – nobody knew for what, though it was felt to be important, as a dream is felt to be important even when it is not comprehended.

Now he was going back. Antonio could be right. He would probably never return to the Third World; his own world would most likely make him into a machine.

But he had to bear witness. He was sixteen years old.

'Life without plumbing, life with a half-full belly,' he had to go home and say. 'It has a savour to it. It's a positive quality. It doesn't make you less a human being. There's no particular virtue in being white of skin and fat of gut and crapping into a nice china bowl every time the laxatives take hold.'

He wondered how convincing he could make it sound, back in the immense hygienic warrens of Westciv – particularly when he still longed in his inner heart for all the conveniences and privileges, and a shower every morning before a sit-down breakfast. It had all been fun here, but enough was enough. More than enough, when you remembered what the plague was doing.

'You go to see again your father,' Roberta diagnosed.

'Maybe. In America we are trying to sever the ties of family. After you get through with religion, you destroy the sacredness of the family. It encourages people to move to other planets, to go where they're told.'

He was ashamed of saying it – and yet half-proud.

'That's why you all are so nervous and want to go to war all the time. You don't get enough kisses as little kids, eh?'

'Oh, we're all one-man isolation units! Life isn't as bad as you think, up there among the wheels of progress, Roberta,' he said bitterly. He kissed her, and her lips tasted of garlic.

Max slapped him on his shoulder.

'Cut all that out, feller – you're going home! Get aboard!'

Pete climbed on to the donkey cart with another anarchist White who had recently sailed across to the island from Tunisia. Pete had arrived in the mysterious Third World driving a truck full of supplies. The truck had been stolen in Nubia, when he was down with malaria and dysentery. He was going back empty-handed. But the palms of those hands were soft no longer.

He shook Max's hand now. They looked at each other wordlessly as the cart-driver goaded his animal into movement. There was affection there, yes – undying in its way, for Max was also a would-be extremist; but there was also the implacable two-way enmity that sprang up willy-nilly between haves and have-nots. An enmity stronger than men, incurable by men. They both dropped their gaze.

Hiding his embarrassment, Pete looked about him. In his days of waiting, the village had become absolutely familiar, from the church at one end to the broken-down bursts of cactus in between. He had savoured too the pace of life here, geared to the slowest and most stupid, so that the slowest and most stupid could survive. Over the frontier, time passed in overdrive.

Across the drab stones, the hoofs of the donkey made little noise. Other carts were moving forward, with dogs following, keeping close to the walls. There was a feeling — desperate and exhilarating — that they were leaving the shelter of history, and heading towards where the power-house of the world began.

Pete waved to Max and Roberta and the others, and squinted towards the fortifications of his own sector. The frontier stood distant but clear in the pale air. As he looked, he saw a giant comic-terror figure, twice as high as a grown man, man-plus-machine, bound across the plain towards him. Bellowing with an obscene anger as it charged, the monster appeared to burn in the sun.

It came towards him like a flaming wheel rushing down a steep hill, all-devouring.

VI Ego

Ted Greaves was my friend of long-standing. I don't know why he flung himself on me in hatred just because I taunted him about his son. For that matter, I don't know why anger suddenly blazed up in me as it did.

My last spell on CUFL had left me in relatively poor shape, but fury lent me strength. I ducked away from his first blow and chopped him hard below the heart. As he doubled forward, grunting with pain, I struck him again, this time on the jaw. He brought his right fist up and grazed my chin, but by then I was hitting him again and again. He went down.

These fits had come over me before, but not for many years. When I was aware of myself again, I was jumping into the pogo-armour, with only the vaguest recollections of what I had done to Greaves. I could recall I had let the force barrier down.

I went leaping forward towards the hated land. I could hear the gyros straining, hear my voice bellowing before me.

'You killed my daughter! You killed my daughter! You shan't get in! You shan't even look in!'

I didn't know what I was about.

There were animals scattering. I overturned a cart. I was almost at the first village.

It felt as if I was running at 150 kilometres an hour. Yet when the shot rang out, I stopped at once. How beautiful the hills were, if one's eyes never opened and closed again. Pigeons wheeling white above tawdry roofs. People immobile. One day they would be ours, and we would take over the whole world. The whole world shook with the noise of my falling armament and dust spinning like the fury of galaxies.

Better pain than our eternal soft predicament ...

I was looking at a pale-faced boy in a cart, he was staggering off the cart, the cart was going from him. People were shouting and fluttering everywhere like rags. My gaze was fixed only on him. His eyes were only on me. He had a smoking revolver in his hand.

Wonderingly, I wondered how I knew he was an American. An American who had seized Ted Greaves's face and tugged it from inside until all the wrinkles were gone from it and it looked obscenely young again. My executioner wore a mask.

A gyro laboured by my head as if choked with blood. I could only look up at that mask. Something had to be said to it as it came nearer.

'It's like a Western ... ' Trying to laugh?

Death came down from the Black hills until only his stolen eyes were left, like wounds in the universe.

They disappeared.

When the drugs revived me from my hypnoid trance, I was still plugged to CUFL, along with the eleven other members of my shift, the other slaves of the Clective Unctious.

To the medicos bending over me, I said, 'I died again.'

They nodded. They had been watching the monitor screens.

'Take it easy,' one of them said. As my eyes pulled into focus, I saw it was Wace.

I was used to instructions. I worked at taking it easy. I was still in the front line, where individuality fought with the old nameless tribal consciousness. 'I died again,' I groaned.

'Relax, Jerry,' Wace said. 'It was just a hypnoid dream like you always get.'

'But I died again. Why do I always have to die?'

Tommy Wace. His first name was Tommy. Data got mislaid.

Distantly, he tried to administer comfort and express compassion on his dried-up face. 'Dreams are mythologies, part-individual, part-universal. Both de-programming dreams and prognostic-type dreams are natural functions of the self-regulating psychic system. There's nothing unnatural about dreaming of dying.'

'But I died again ... And I was split into two people ... '

'The perfect defence in a split world. A form of adaptation.'

You could never convey personal agony to these people, although they had watched it all on the monitors. Wearily, I passed a hand over my face. My chin felt like cactus.

'So much self-hatred, Tommy ... Where does it all come from?'

'Johnnie. At least you're working it out of your system. Now, here's something to drink.'

I sat up. 'CUFL will have to close down, Johnnie,' I said. I hardly knew what I said. I was back in the real world, in the abrasive lunar laboratory under Plato – and suddenly I saw that I could distinguish true from false.

For years and years – *I'd been mistaken*!

I had been externalising my self-hatred. The dream showed me that I feared to become whole again in case becoming whole destroyed me.

Gasping, I pushed Wace's drink aside. I was seeing visions. The White World had shed religion. Shed religion, you shed other hope-structures; family life disintegrates. You are launched towards the greater structure of science. That was the Westciv way. We had made an ugly start but we were going ahead. There was no going back. The rest of the world had to follow. No – had to be led. Not shunned, not bullied. Led. Revelation!

Part of our soft predicament is that we can never entirely grasp what the predicament is.

'Johnnie, I don't always have to die,' I said. 'It's my mistake, our mistake!' I found I was weeping and couldn't stop. Something was dissolving. 'The Black-and-White are one, not two! We are fighting ourselves. I was fighting myself. Plug me back in again!'

'End of shift,' Wace said, advancing the drink again. 'You've done more than your stint. Let's get you into Psych Lab for a check-up and then you're due for leave back on Earth.'

'But do you see –' I gave up and accepted his beastly drink.

Natalie, Ri ... I too have my troubled dreams, little darling ...

My bed is wetted and my mattress soaked with blood.

Johnnie Wace got one of the nurses to help me to my feet. Once I was moving, I could get to Psych Lab under my own power.

'You're doing fine, Jerry!' Wace called. 'Next time you're back on Luna, I'll have Jupiter pinpointed for you.'

Doing fine! I'd only just had all my strongest and most emotionally-held opinions switched through 180 degrees!

In the Psych Lab, I was so full of tension that I couldn't let them talk. 'You know what it's like, moving indistinguishably from hypnoid to dream state – like sinking down through layers of cloud. I began by reliving my last rest period with Natalie and Ri. It all came back true and sweet, without distortion, from the reservoirs of memory! Distortion only set in when I recollected landing in Sicily. What happened in reality was that Ted Greaves and I let his son back through the frontier with the other White anarchists. I found the revolver he was trying to smuggle in – he had tucked it into his boot-top.

'That revolver was the symbol that triggered my nightmare. Our lives revolve through different aspects like the phases of the Moon. I identified entirely with Pete. And at his age, I too was a revolutionary, I too wanted to change the world, I too would have wished to kill my present self!'

'At Pete Greaves's age you were fighting *for* Westciv, not against it, Wharton,' one of the psychiatrists reminded me.

'Yes,' I said. 'I was in Asia, and handy with a gun. I carved up a whole gang of Thirdies. That was about the time when the Russians threw in their lot with us.' I didn't want to go on. I could see it all clearly. They didn't need a true confession.

'The guilt you felt in Asia was natural enough,' the psychiatrist said. 'To suppress it was equally natural – suppressed guilt causes most of the mental and physical sickness in the country. Since then it has gone stale and turned to hate.'

'I'll try and be a good boy in future,' I said, smiling and mock-meek. At the time, the ramifications of my remark were not apparent to me, as they were to the psychiatrist.

'You've graduated, Wharton,' he said. 'You're due a vacation on Earth right now.'

VII Clective

The globe, in its endless revolution, was carrying us into shade. In the courtyard, the line of the sun was high up our wall. Natalie had set a mosquito-coil burning; its fragrance came to us where we sat at the table with our beers. We bought the mosquito-coils in the local village store; they were smuggled in from the Third World, and had MADE IN CAIRO stamped on the packet.

Ri was busy at one end of the courtyard with a couple of earthenware pots. She played quietly, aware that it was after her bedtime. Ted Greaves and Pete sat with us, drinking beer and smoking. Pete had not spoken a word since they arrived. At that time I could make no contact with him. Did not care to. The ice floes were still melting and smashing.

As Natalie brought out another jar and set it on the rough wood table, Greaves told her, 'We're going to have a hero on our hands if your brother flies over to see you when he gets back from Jupiter. Do you think he'll show up here?'

'Sure to! Ian hates Eastern Seaboard as much as most people.'

'Sounds like he found Jupiter as crowded as Eastern Seaboard!'

'We'll have the Clective Unctious working by the time he arrives,' I said.

'I thought you were predicting it would close down?' Greaves asked.

'That was when it was choked with hate.'

'You're joking! How do you choke a machine with hate?'

'Input equals output. CUFL is a reactive store – you feed in hate, so you get out hate.'

'Same applies to human beings and human groups,' Pete Greaves broke in, rubbing his thumb nail along the grain of the table.

I looked at him. I couldn't feel sweet about him. He was right in what he said but I couldn't agree with him. He had killed me – though it was me masquerading as him – though it had been a hypnoid illusion.

I forced myself to say, 'It's a paradox how a man can hate people he doesn't know and hasn't even seen. You can easily hate people you know – people like yourself.'

Pete made no answer and wouldn't look up.

'It would be a tragedy if we started hating these creatures on Jupiter just because they are there.'

I said it challengingly, but he merely shrugged. Natalie sipped her beer and watched me.

I asked him, 'Do you think some of your wild friends from over the frontier would come along and feed their archetypes into CUFL? Think they would stand the pace and the journey?'

Both he and his father stared at me as if they had been struck.

Before the kid spoke, I knew I had got through to him. He would not have to go quietly schizoid. He would talk to Natalie and me eventually, and we would hear of his travels at first-hand. Just a few defensive layers would have to be removed. Mine and his.

'You have to be joking!' he said.

Suddenly I laughed. Everyone thought I was joking. Depending on your definition of a joke, I felt I had at last ceased joking after many a year. I turned suddenly from the table to hide a burning of my eyes.

Taking Natalie by the arm, I said, 'Come on, we must get Ri to bed. She thinks we've forgotten about her.'

As we walked down the path, Natalie said, 'Was your suggestion serious?'

'I think I can work it. I'll speak to Wace. Things have to change. CUFL is unbalanced.' The finches fluttered in their cages. The line of sun was over the wall now. All was shadow among our orange trees, and the first bat flying. I loomed over Ri before she noticed me. Startled, she stared up at me and burst into tears. Many things had to change.

I picked her up in my arms and kissed her cheeks.

Many things had to change. The human condition remained enduringly the same, but many things had to change.

Even the long nights on Earth were only local manifestations of the Sun's eternal daylight. Even the different generations of man had archetypes in common, their slow writhings not merely inconsequential movement but ponderous and deliberate gesture.

So I carried her into the dim house to sleep.

Non-Isotropic

The boy was first seen as a distant figure across sand. Behind him was water, then hills, green and tan. Beyond them, mountains, fading to blue, teased by cloud.

The boy was running wildly about a deep pool. As the viewpoint neared, it could be seen that he was laughing in excitement. He had a net which he jabbed inexpertly at the water. He jumped into the pool, to emerge shrieking with laughter.

The viewpoint moved remorselessly nearer, across the bare, wet sand. The boy stooped to make a trawl with his net. So close was the viewpoint that the serrations of the boy's backbone showed, white-knuckled. He straightened, lifting high a crab for the inspection of the hidden viewer.

Research Vessel *Truganini* hung just beyond Home Galaxy, its antennae probing forward into the non-isotropic fault. It resembled a malformed spider, with its one extended leg housing delicate instruments protected from the artificial magnetosphere of the ship. Like certain kinds of spider, the *Truganini* trailed a web. The web was designed to catch the fossil microwave radiation which powered it.

A lay brother switched the latest compread-out to the screen before which Priest Captain Shiva Askanza stood, talking with his chief navigator, Varga Bergwein. Captain and navigator briefly scanned the figures.

'We're at the extreme limit of safety,' Askanza said.

'There's the fault ahead of us. Nothing for it but to send out the drone and see where it gets us.'

'If it can locate Cellini before it becomes inert, we're in God's luck.'

Askanza bent over his panel and activated the auxiliary systems which controlled Drone A. The picture on the big screen jumped, and began to yield drone-oriented data as the machine nosed its way forward into space from its homing tube.

From the germanium brain of the drone came a simulation of the non-isotropic fault, writhing in concentric radiation contours shaped roughly like ram's horns. The fault was only some eighty light years long at its longest, and fifty across. Its depth could not be estimated; conflicting readings suggested infinite depth. It was the first NIF to be discovered, and as shattering an event in its way as the discovery of the Expanding Universe two millennia ago.

The astrophysicist Rufort Cellini had developed the dislocation theory and the math behind it which postulated the existence of NIFs; he had gone out in a research vessel, ranging beyond the undetectable walls of the galaxy, and had verified his hypothesis – firstly, by finding the NIF, secondly by disappearing into it.

Drone A nudged forward from the *Truganini*, scattering a trail over Askanza's screen. The scatter cleared, the readings resumed, the simulation switching automatically from microwave to long wave to equivalent temperature to hadron to lepton to photon plot. The picture built up of a customary space trellis with average particle activity for such quadrants.

Askanza muttered a prayer. He found himself breathing more tightly as he watched the drone make its approach to the NIF. It took up a position almost stationary in relation to the fault, and then began to wind in sideways in response to Askanza's remote command.

The figures changed. The readings fell, all except the proton count. The temperature reading dropped to only a few decimal points off zero K.

Varga Bergwein grunted. Askanza shot him a glance, and by so doing almost missed the flash of red on the margin of the screen. It was there, it was gone.

The drone moved up against the fault in a shower of plummeting figures. It entered the fault. Readings and simulation ceased. A brilliant flash. The screen went dead. The drone had ceased to exist in relation to the isotropic universe.

In his ordinary voice, Askanza said into the phone, 'Rerun of that please, and the photo-record.'

The photo-record came up first, corrected for visual frequencies. Clear through the fault, the viewers could see the shapes of two distant galaxies. The picture was steady, the NIF did not show. It had no refractive index, light travelled it unimpeded.

When the re-run appeared, Askanza slowed the picture and switched an auxiliary screen to infra-red. When the flash of red showed again, he stopped the film and brought up magnification. There was no fuzziness. Limned in blue, there was the spider-shape of the *Poseidonian.*

'That's Cellini's ship right enough,' said Bergwein. 'There he is, but can we get him out?'

'Photons at least have the same properties in or out of non-isotropic space. Whatever goes on in there, we can see the ship. We can capture it and bring it and ourselves out again – provided our shield holds.'

'You think Cellini will be alive, Captain?'

'Cellini was the theorist, the man with the hypotheses. Let's worry about him first and the hypotheses later.'

He turned to the phone. 'Switch on external amplifiers. Tell the crew to stand by. We are preparing to enter the NIF.'

The boy had walked far across the stretch of sand. So low was the tide in the estuary that the channel of the river could hardly be seen from its banks. Several veins of water meandered through the sand, but the boy had now reached the deepest channel.

He was lost in thought. The viewpoint went to look over his bare shoulder and found him dredging pebbles out of the water and arranging them on the sharply defined edge of the sand. The water gurgled. A gull cried overhead.

He looked up and said, 'It's glory here. I'd like to come here every holiday, really get to know the play of the tides, see how the sand patterns changed with the season. I just wish you could be here too, Father, to enjoy it with me ... '

The man said, 'I'm sorry. I'm still sorry. Forever sorry ... ' He switched off the cube and sat with it under his palm. After a moment, he mastered himself and switched it on again.

The boy planted a big stone half in the river and against the bank, so as to watch the swirl of water undercut the sand, sharpening the miniature cliff. 'Too bad you have to be away in space so long. I don't understand your dislocation theory too well – I guess I'll have to be older to do that. Right now, I don't ever want to leave Earth. It's so – it's so inexhaustible. I mean, just look at the dislocation I have here at this bank, between liquid and solid. One day I suppose I will understand the formula for this kind of thing, what makes solids solid and liquids liquid. I mean to understand if I can.'

'Yes, yes, you mean to – for your father's sake,' the man said, looking down with furrowed brow at the contents of the cube.

'I wish you were here to play with me,' said the boy.

The man switched the holocube off. For a long time he sat staring blankly ahead. A tap at the door made him sit up and collect himself, instinctively covering the cube with one broad hand.

A messenger looked in.

'Captain Askanza, we are ready to ferry down to Earth if you're ready.'

Askanza nodded curtly without speaking.

Omega was a mere chunk of inert rock some four hundred kilometres long and half as thick. It suited Rufort Cellini.

He anchored his vessel and set up some instruments on the rocky surface. The thickness of Omega cut out some of the background galactic radiation. He made observations. When he felt like it, he walked and thought. Cellini made a point of exercise, and derived pleasure from taking a stroll on the very edge of the galaxy.

When he walked in one direction, the cosmic night was there, intermittently lit by distant other galaxies. When he turned about and walked in the opposite direction, the great wheel of the Home Galaxy reared up, diamond bright and cruel, every nearer light with a cutting edge. From that wheel he received signals older than any light received from the most distant of galaxies to his rear.

Inter-galactic space, he felt instinctively, was a gulf that mankind would never cross; there were burdens of distance too great for organic matter to shoulder. The galaxies had separated as thought separates, to further unity. All would become functions in his formulae. There was a solution to every mystery – even the Great Why itself – the solution that Rufort Cellini had set himself to discover, many years ago.

Certain basic equations had moved into his mind at the same time as the computer of the Congregation to which he belonged offered him the opportunity of a year's marriage.

Intellectual curiosity moved him to take up the year. He enjoyed sexual intercourse, he found the woman pleasant; but he experienced with her the same impatience he felt with his male friends: he could not bear idle conversation – and for Cellini most conversation was idle. He left her before the year had expired, but not before she became pregnant. It was social intercourse Cellini could not stand.

He had seen the child since then, spent time with it on his three visits back to Earth. The child he could tolerate. Growing organisms held some interest as a process, particularly when seen in temporal cross-section, as he saw his son. Unfortunately the child showed him affection and that was a claim Cellini was not prepared for. Only his work had his love.

That work, his lifetime's work, was now justified.

Reading his instruments, looking ahead into inter-galactic space, Rufort Cellini trembled. He saw as clearly into his own brain as he saw into the universe ahead; indeed, the two views were disconcertingly parallel.

The insight brought recollections. He saw again the first nebulous intimations he had received in his teens that man's plan according to which the universe had been mapped held a dislocation, a fatal dislocation which prevented comprehension alike of the macroscopic and the microscopic and their extraordinary inter-relationship: that the courses of the stars as well as the motions of the particles which constituted sub-nuclear physics were plotted according to a misapprehension that was almost fundamental to the mind of man. He remembered that fear, the burden of that knowledge which set him on a course further and further apart from his fellow humans. To him was given the task of correcting the misapprehension – and with it the basic comprehensions of mind.

Only gradually did Cellini perceive that the dislocation could be expressed in mathematics. But the mathematics which served to carry men in metal ships across their home galaxy was itself a product of the dislocation, and perpetuated the dislocation. He had to return to beginnings and invent a new mathematical language, the Cellini system, to formulate the divergences he began to see more and more clearly.

How lucid his brain had become, isolated despite his colleagues at the institute, despite his marriage period. It had worked without cease. Even the dream periods of sleep were oriented about his one central preoccupation, and were so oriented that they abolished the untidiness of normal human dreams.

Only in space, free of the irritating radiations of terrestrial life, had Cellini managed to complete his computations. He travelled in the *Poseidonian* at near light speed, willing his own generation left behind to age and die, seeing in their death his freedom from all emotional and human ties.

A new enlightenment overtook him. Remotely, he regarded the word 'enlightenment' with sardonic amusement; it had been coined unknowingly long ago, specifically to describe his state of mind. For in his speeding brain photons themselves moved at a crawl: his thoughts travelled at near light speeds. There, his understanding and his Cellini system developed. Almost casually, he watched his computer spell out the syllables of the new equations that made the universe a different place.

Two voyages later he landed on Omega and set up his observatory. Confirmation in the real world of his abstractions was almost immediately forthcoming. He located a non-isotropic fault only a few light years away.

The Cosmological Constant on which all astronomy and physics had been founded was wiped away. The universe was non-homogeneous and non-isotropic. Its composition was of energy in three great phase transitions: matter and energy, which had long been recognised – and consciousness.

At length, Cellini turned away and went back into his ship. His face was expressionless.

Sitting in his favourite chair, he came to a decision. Before returning to the inhabited planets, he would investigate the alien space himself and determine its properties. There was no need for further speculation; he could investigate this mysterious fault, this consciousness, in person.

There was a certain pride in the decision. He recognised it for what it was, a remnant of human weakness. He smiled, idly picking up the glassite cube by his right hand.

Well, it was fun to be a child some times. He pressed the holocube. Briefly, a boy ran on damp sand, smiling and beckoning, hardly expecting a response.

Prayers were said in the *Truganini* before it moved forward into the NIF. The prayers were amplified and broadcast throughout the research vessel. Amplifiers on the outside of the ship caused the prayers to be broadcast through space, so that the ship was surrounded by a field of prayer.

Everyone prayed. Only Askanza and Bergwein and other essential priest officers were excused as the great vessel accelerated gently.

The navigation officer said, 'The holiness of this moment! If we survive, I shall go into isolation for the rest of my life, taking the Vow of Silence. Who can speak of such experience?'

Priest Captain Shiva Askanza was old. The hair on his head was sparse and grey, his shoulders were bent, but he straightened and said, 'Cellini delivered not just humanity but the universe itself from materialism. Beyond doubt he has proved that the explosion which began the universe happened in the mind of God. So the universe has always been non-homogeneous, contrary to assumptions. We ourselves, our bodies, are composed of the consciousness of God in a phase transition.'

'Quite. Consciousness, together with hydrogen, has been the basic building brick of the cosmos.'

With awe and rejoicing in their hearts, they fell silent. The volume of prayer about them rose as the vessel moved towards the NIF. The NIF showed like a pulsating green wall on the screens before them.

The *Truganini* entered the fault.

Science and religion became one.

The prayer-field acted like a shield. Most of the instrumentation went dead as they penetrated the non-homogenous matter. Photon-count remained steady; they had a visual fix on Cellini's lost ship and moved steadily towards it with grappling magnets ready.

Glory moved in them. They were penetrated harmlessly by the fault.

In them was no fault. All the ancient ancestral ideas of

God rose in their minds like birds from the surface of a lake. They were with God, with each other. Theirs was absolute comprehension. They traversed original undiluted godhead, which throughout the rest of the universe had been dispersed thinly. The Lord let his face to shine upon them.

Working in wonder, they reached the *Poseidonian*, matched velocities, secured it, brought it away.

The *Poseidonian* had had no prayer-shield. Cellini's mind had been burned out by glory.

He lay, a still youthful figure, sprawled on the floor of his cabin, clutching a holocube in his hand.

Safely back in normal space, back into the fringes of the Home Galaxy, Askanza and Bergwein reverently lifted the body out between them and carried it to the Captain's cabin. The crew, faces still transfigured, looked on.

Bergwein glanced from the youthful dead face to the gnarled old face of his priest captain. The resemblance prompted him to ask, 'Forgive me, but why did you not take your father's illustrious name of Cellini?'

Askanza set the body reverently down and retrieved the cube from the dead hand.

'It would have been prideful so to do. My mother's name was Askanza; she was the one who cared for me. My father could only find the Truth by neglecting all else.'

When he was left alone, and the *Truganini* had set its course for Earth, Askanza switched on the cube and watched his youthful self.

The boy had reached the remains of a wrecked ship. The bones of its hull curved out of the sand like ribs. It looked less like a vessel than the skeleton of a gigantic animal. The boy paced round it slowly.

After a while, he looked at the unseen viewer.

'I guess I should be able to grasp your dislocation theory or whatever you're going to call it. After all – solids and liquids, ships that don't make it home ... The world's full of such things ... '

He was silent a moment, before adding apologetically, 'And we two so far apart ... Another dislocation.' He sighed. 'We just haven't recognised the principle behind such things before. Like it's proved impossible for most people to imagine God, though he's all round us.'

The shallowest of waves lapped about his feet.

The boy looked embarrassed and prepared to flee.

'Maybe you don't even understand what I'm trying to say to you, Father. All these divisions ... Anyhow, I hope that this holocube will catch up with you some day and give you a bit of company on your way.'

Askanza switched off the cube and laid it beside his father's dead hand.

'Too late – as usual,' he said. Over most of the universe God was spread in fossil radiation, too old, too thin.

One Blink of the Moon

This is my story and the world's. Although its events have not yet happened, and will not till millions of years wheel away in their long faint tracks, their veracity may be checked against what has passed in previous millennia as easily as millionaires in their geometrical dwellings imagine themselves, in moments of hope and fear, going in rags, or as the poorest in the land dream that they consort familiarly with kings and queens.

It was high summer. My cousin Mike was with me. We had not seen each other for thirty years. During that time, he had travelled all over Africa and India as an agricultural adviser to emergent governments, while I had worked in Scandinavia, designing shopping centres and offices for prosperous socialists. We had met again over my father's, Mike's uncle's, coffin, and rediscovered a fellowship first enjoyed in childhood. To celebrate this reunion, we climbed into my car and spent some time exploring our native country, seeking out places which had remained unchanged by the years intervening since we had visited them in short trousers and plimsolls.

In particular, we rejoiced in a remote county where the population still remained sparser than before the visitation of the Black Death in the fifteenth century. In its lanes, heaths, marshes and beaches, we discovered a primitive force which refreshed us like bitter drink.

We left the car in the shade of a ruined church and took

to our own bare feet. Sun and heat ruled the land. By day we swam in shallow seas, by night we slept in dry ditches, savages only 150 miles from what for over a century had been the largest city on Earth.

I had taken along a sporting rifle. Among the dunes of Titcham Head we shot some rabbits. When I had gutted them, we carried them to the nearest farmhouse. The farmer proved to be an agreeable man who had farmed in Rhodesia and knew people Mike knew. He lent us two horses, a grey and a bay, and on them we rode at low tide all along the beach from Titcham Head round to Brunston Hard, thundering over dry sand. In the evening we returned slowly through the shallows. We slept that night in traditional fashion in the farmer's barn. Next day, we were in the sea at sunrise. Something untrammelled reawakened in us.

Finally we returned to the ordinary world and drove back to my home in the Midlands. As we approached home ground, we observed that everything was sodden. In the fields, golden harvests had been beaten flat by rain, parched earth had turned to sodden mud. As we slid down the long drive, the horse chestnuts dripped water on us. It was nightfall, ashes of rose and cyclamen still hung in the sky to the north-west.

My house was silent and unlighted.

Unlocking the side door, I gave a cheery hallo. No childish cries answered me, no calls from my wife or Mike's. All was still. Only the solemn tick of the clock in the hall. How beautiful and sad were the warm silences, different in every room, which greeted me as I walked through the house.

My wife had left a note. In the storm of the previous evening, lightning had struck the house and put the electricity out of action. The small children were alarmed, and so she was taking them all to stay with friends in a town some miles distant. They would be back in the morning.

'We don't need a light, the moon's coming up,' said Mike.

A letter lay in the front hall under the letter flap, an air mail envelope bearing foreign stamps. Opening the door, I stood on the porch and slit the envelope. Mike joined me, bringing two cans of beer with him.

The letter was from the United States, from a cheerful and mad scholar who had visited us in the early spring. No need to go into details, but he was compiling a definitive volume on architectural approaches to ideas of common territory and wished to incorporate some of my work. So bright was the moon, that generous August moon — it was at its full that night — that I could read his bold, dark handwriting by its light. My correspondent's handwriting was immaculate in its italianate style. His ability with a camera was rather less than his penmanship. He enclosed with the letter three photographs that he had taken when leaving. These snaps showed my wife and me standing with two of our children and my father (who was then living with us as we tended him in the early stages of his final illness) before the porch, between the four Ionic columns.

Because they had been taken rather distantly, these snaps showed our figures as if behind bars. When I puzzled them out in the moonlight, looking up at the actual later version of the scene depicted, I realised that the bars were spears of pampas which had got in the path of the camera lens. The pale spring sun on our living room window had the effect of blanking it out, as if a shutter had been drawn on the inside of the window. Over-exposure led to a pale moonlight effect in the three views — or so it appeared to me, examining them by real moonlight over my beer.

I passed them to Mike.

'You and Joyce are thin,' he said. He laughed. 'Did you diet over the winter?'

It was true that the tricks of light past and light present made both my wife and me look etiolated. Our children also appeared to have a wan passivity. Only my father, as far as I could determine, looked hale, ready for many more years of life. Here I was, as full of sun and wine as a grape, bursting with energy; the photographs might almost have come from the future rather than the past. Although I am not an imaginative man, a feeling of ghostliness overcame me, a sense of being insubstantial, a sense that even the house was insubstantial. Of a sudden, I was impatient with Mike's company, and wanted to see my wife and children again.

We walked in the moonlit garden, collecting vegetables. They were dying, killed by a long drought which the recent downpour had come too late to mend.

'I don't feel inclined to sleep in the house tonight,' I said.

He asked me where we should go. I pointed towards the south where, over the stone wall and the neighbouring fields, a line of hills could distantly be seen.

'We'll go on the downs, enjoy one last night sleeping in the open.'

We set out after a supper of bread, spring onions, lettuce, radish, cheese, and wine. The downs were no more than twelve miles away by road, or rather by the many winding roads which lay between our house and the hills. These byways formed a network between the main arterial road and the high ground, linking the villages whose names stood on frequent signposts: Kingstone Coombe, Letbourne Bowers, Waldrist Magna, Baybourne, Coxford Bassett, Coxford Regis, Piddlewalton, Upper and Lower Trindle, Childrey, Chaddle, Chorney, and the two Beauchamps, Compton and Winslow: names that were music in the swelling score of the countryside as it rose to its grand conclusion on the Waldrist Downs. We climbed Pulpit Hill and were upon the brow of the world.

Stopping the car and climbing out, we entered another age. Whilst the villages we had passed through had appeared lifeless, from the Down another picture emerged. We looked across a vale that was fairly seamed with lights. For anyone who cared, each village was identifiable as a patch of illumination in the night, as far as the distant towns of Didingford and Wanbury. Where we stood, no artificial lighting existed and Light itself reigned. Nothing stirred.

The great moon shone down from a southern sky unflawed

by cloud, making that sky a shield. All about us, it created silence over the land.

I took binoculars from the car and scanned the dark country below us, seeking a glimpse of my home. Dark clumps of trees, sodium lighting along a road, helped me pick it out. A gleam flashed through the eyepieces; the window which in the photographs appeared shuttered gave out a silver beam, reflected from the moon behind us. I read it as a signal; but what the signal meant I could not say.

I turned back towards the car. It had gone. My cousin had gone.

For a moment I believed myself blinded by the beam which had penetrated my eye. But the Down was still visible, the moon still steady in the sky.

Yet a change had come over them too. The moon appeared more flat, as if its craters and mountains had been obliterated, the sky more dark, the great hog-back of the Down more pallid, almost as if I were embedded in some faulty new photographic process being carried out on an astronomical scale.

Before I could recover from my astonishment, I saw that people were approaching along the wide track into which I had driven our vehicle. That track over the chalk, I should say, was the Ridgeway, and had existed since time immemorial. It formed an unhealing scar across the entire land, from the wild mountains in the west, down to the river estuary in the east. Throughout its length, it kept as much as possible to high ground, as if the first transhumance peoples who trod it, along with their sheep and thin-withered cattle, deliberately chose country that would remain – thanks to the thinness of its soils – forever uninhabited.

The group coming from the west showed as a dark, indeterminate feature against the pallor of moon-washed ground. They approached in silence.

As they emerged from translucent night, I saw they were many in number and I instinctively shrank back against a hawthorn bush growing in the hedge by the road. Among the walkers were cars and other machines, all moving silently and at walking pace. The first figures came level with me; they proved to be the leaders of a vast caravan stretching back down the old green track as far as eye could see.

The machines that accompanied them were familiar. There were cars and lorries, as well as machines which it was not inappropriate to find in country districts, such as harvesters and balers. Other machines were more out of place. There were cranes and many other objects not normally seen on the move. Great dams moved by like waves of concrete.

This inexplicable tide of human and inhuman continued steadily forward, moving in front of me from western horizon to eastern, always with the brazen moon behind it keeping it in silhouette. I watched a moving frieze.

Staring in a kind of stupefaction, I realised after a long time that the nature of the machinery was changing. It was growing bigger. Bigger, and more complex. Fewer of the items could I comprehend. The people were also changing, although less dramatically. They walked with a more automatic gait, scarcely swinging their arms. I fancied too that they were all now dressed more uniformly. Before this (the realisation dawned upon me), a few of them had been dancing.

This implacable caravan grew thicker. The entire Down became covered by black moving masses in which people could be distinguished progressing sluggishly at the bases of towering machinery. All the time the moon hung stationary in the sky above us. Everything in nature was unmoving.

The events of the previous week had made me harmonious to an unusual degree with the world of which I formed such a small part. I felt myself in tune with my present surroundings. My cousin had returned home through Europe, visiting many of its grander natural features, among them the volcanic pile, growing slowly from a period long before man emerged on the planet, which we call Mount Etna. Mike had been eloquent about this enormous abscess on the earth's surface, which the great Lyell described as a monument set to impress all the peoples of Europe with the vast distances of time.

Taken though I was with Mike's account of Etna, I still retained an immense respect for the distances of time as evidenced less flamboyantly by the downs on which I stood. For the Waldrist Downs, upon whose shallow soil I had often lain, was composed to a depth of many hundred feet of chalk made from the carapaces of myriads of tiny creatures, once alive, long dead, bearing witness to those same majestic processes which moved the minds of Lyell and Darwin, who had learned from Lyell's work.

I never walked on the Downs, savouring the sweetness of the air and of my own brief lifespan, without bearing in mind that continual double wonder: the processes of Earth and the processes of the human mind which, alone, is capable of interpreting and rendering Earth meaningful.

Now those processes were manifesting themselves in a new way – new but not entirely strange. Well, yes, strange – but we are more familiar than we care to admit with what is strange.

By degrees that strange procession became familiar. Without fatigue I watched the unending silhouette as it dragged from veiled horizon to veiled horizon ever larger machines, ever smaller people. The tempo became slower. The people marched in leaden step. Such was my emotional involvement that I seemed to travel about the Earth with them. I almost became part of them, as each tiny creature beneath our feet was part of the deep chalk. This I struggled against. I hated their defeat. Their shuffling presence was unbearable – they had lost human joy, human display. They walked under the bare sky as if imprisoned down a mine. They enacted a funeral of life.

The moon remained completely unaltered, unmoving. In time, something in the nature of the cavalcade altered. Slowly it dawned on me that although the machines were still increasing in size – they towered high into the sky, biting into its pale face as they passed – they were becoming fewer in number. The people grew yet more multitudinous. This was the order of things for so long that it seemed as if the procession had always been so constituted. The people became more featureless, leaning forward as if against a wind they could hardly endure.

Another change at last, gradual, gradual. There was a break in the ranks of the megamachines. Nothing but people filed past, monotonous, unending, glancing neither to left nor right. They flowed like a river without meander, coming from a hidden source towards an unknown destiny.

In the west a black object rose. For an age, it appeared like a black *doppelgänger* of the stationary moon, until its approach defined its outlines more clearly. It was shaped like the Great Pyramid of Egypt, was fully a match for that monument in size. It loomed steadily up from obscurity, grinding over the crescent of Waldrist Downs, dwarfing the attendants last at its base. For the first time I knew fear. I was unable to flee.

This terrible machine grew, slicing out larger and larger segments of sky. I can still feel that thing towering closer to me for ever, making its own night within night. It was horned at the top with bristling horns.

It made no noise. Yet its monstrousness created a kind of visual thunder.

In time – *in Time* – it too passed, lumbering down to its setting.

The moon was again revealed. Sane, mellow, familiar, bland, it shed its radiance as before. Now there was a mere trickle of people on which it shone.

And those people made their obscure journey bent almost double. Some threw up their arms in supplication. Some progressed on hands and knees.

This degradation seemed no worse than the robot-like march I had witnessed long before. Yet I grieved.

The stooped figures became fewer. A numb feeling of relief struggled up in my being – to be quenched by anguish.

Was this, I asked myself, the end of the great procession, the end of man's journey? Crippled, dumb, degraded, the last silhouette passed.

But no! More figures were on their way. A few more curved backs, then – a group, a group dancing! They came towards me down the ancient trackway. They pranced over the cretaceous hill. Although their movements were clumsy, they expressed joy – or did I read my own joy into them? I believe not.

More dancers arrived. They were always in groups, some small, some larger. Their costumes grew more decorative, their movements more graceful, their steps more intricate, so that I strained my ears, listening for a phantom music. How I would have loved to hear that music.

A sort of melody began to reach me, a music of action and graceful limbs. The human panorama was free now. Without its machines, it was recapturing something of the spontaneity that early man must have possessed in the world's wilds. Before my eyes new languages developed, couched in nudity and elaborate dress, in choreography and liquid gesture. For the first time, the frieze took on a genuine light-heartedness.

As time wore on, that light-heartedness grew to something more intense. A fresh mode was evolving; its rhythms were different from anything I knew. The people themselves were unknown, as if their bodies had developed new joints, fresh qualities of action. Their minds and thoughts had developed beyond my understanding.

One thing did awaken my sympathetic comprehension. The beautiful strangers flocking past were accompanied by animals. Large animals and small, wild or domestic, they cavorted among the human forms, playing a deliberate part in the ceremony. Monkeys and macaws rode on humans, men and women rode on tigers and horses.

This fantastic masque brought grave joy. Just to watch was to wish to watch for ever. Indeed, at the time it seemed to continue for ever. It girdled the world. All life had united. Life was a pageant. Slowly the players changed: some of the animal forms became large and fantastic, the bipeds more diverse in shape.

Epochs passed, while I could no longer comprehend what was happening. A kind of long ceremonial was played out before me, enacted by beings as like and unlike humans as elves. At length, like elves, they were taking to low darting flight. The argent night became full of wings and enchantments.

It was one thing I watched, a corporate thing made of many parts. The dark silhouette grew gradually dazzling. Elements blurred from my vision. The moon sizzled and blazed, sending out streamers of radiance that were not light. Everything was fading – no, not fading but gyrating, cascading – beyond access to my eyes. After a long, grand confusion, nothing remained but a sense of airy presence along the Ridgeway.

The moon died. Clouds blew over the bare back of hill, pulling thin curtains across its face. It shone out again at full strength, was again obscured.

I was released from my trance. Slowly, I turned about. Down in the vale, all lights had died. Not a village was to be seen, nothing but enfolding night. Nothing but one light. I recognised it by its position. It was the pale eye of my house, reflecting one blink of the August moon. Sheep bleated in a distant field.

My cousin was near by, and my car.

'Let's go home,' I said.

Space for Reflection

There once lived a man called Gordan Ivon Jefffris who achieved galaxy-wide fame at the age of five. This is his story.

Gordan Ivon Jefffris was born in a period when the major cultures of the galaxy were suffering from a combination of economic depression and spiritual uncertainty. The achievements of man, as he diversified on a million planets, were many and various. And yet, and yet ... among the thinking people everywhere – even among ordinary thoughtless people – grew the suspicion that achievement was somehow hollow, as if success were an apple that, once bitten, yielded no juice.

In an attempt to combat the disillusion, a consortium of leading planets which dubbed itself The Re-Renaissance Worlds arranged a curious competition. The terms of this competition were deliberately left vague. The winner was to be the man or woman who presented something that would contribute most to a fresh direction for mankind. The nature of the submission was left to the ingenuity of the entrants. The prizes were enormous.

This competition met with almost universal criticism. It was said that it would deflect useful endeavour into what was a dead end, that the idea of competition itself was one of the main concepts which required combating, that things philosophical were best left to philosophers, and so on.

Those who launched the competition were not deterred. They set no particular store by the idea of one outright winner; their hope was that the whole body of entries might together contribute the sort of vital injection of innovation for which they sought; and they believed that the kinds of entries they got would provide some consensus of opinion as to which way galactic culture was moving, as diagnosed by the best brains.

Unhappily, the best brains considered themselves above such a competition, and forbore to enter. Submissions were nevertheless almost countless, pouring in from every civilised planet. Some were works of art conceived to inspire; some were technical ingenuities designed to improve the daily lot of ordinary citizens; some were vast works of analysis; some were computerised plans for changing whole societies; some were projects for novel transmutations, for instance for transmuting light into food directly; some were syntheses of different disciplines, expressing gravity as music, or whatever; new languages, new media, new symbolic systems, were put forward; *und so weiter*.

In short, the organisers of the competition, and their committees and computers, were provided with much material over which to scratch their heads, much muddle from which they never, ultimately, achieved any significant order.

They bestowed first prize on a child of five, Gordan Ivon Jefffris, who presented the briefest entry of all. That entry was a sheet of plakin on which the boy had written in a childish hand, 'The universe has a dark corner, the human soul, which is its reflection.'

A fresh storm of almost universal criticism greeted the award. It was said that the thought was banal, that the concept of human souls was obsolete by about a million years, that the idea expressed was so pessimistic that it had no place in a competition designed to generate fresh directions, that there was no practical application, that in any case Ching Pin Jones's prospectus for mass producing suns was a thousand times more brilliant, *und so weiter*.

The organisers stuck to their guns. (They were old and stubborn, and in any case had nothing else to stick to.) They held that one of the things which had brought near-stagnation on a galactic scale was an insane optimism which lent a cloak to exploitation and tyranny in all their forms; that they were on the side of youth, even extreme youth; and that they admired the way in which the boy Jefffris had linked macrocosm and microcosm. *Und so weiter*.

Both competition and controversy ensured that livgrams of the five-year-old, his fair hair tousled and becoming, his round face smiling, were flashed to every planet in the galaxy. Fame had never been so universal.

Gordan Ivon Jefffris was brought from his backwoods planet and his parents' cloned-clatbuck farm and installed in the Institute for Creative Research on Dynderkranz, in the Minervan Empire at the heart of the galaxy. There, for twelve years, he specialised in non-specialisation, learning randomly from computers, superputers, and parent-figures.

The teaching was liberal (it was generally agreed that liberalism contributed to the decay of the Minervan Empire), and Jefffris was allowed to some extent to follow his natural bent. He was a perfectly normal child – a fact greeted with delight by half his teachers and dismay by the other half – while manifesting a tendency, evidenced in his prize-winning dictum, to regard man as a vital manifestation of the universe. He divided his study time between the phenomena of the external world and the phenomena of man and his culture.

The long training was only the preliminary part of Jefffris' prize. As his days at the Institute drew to a close, the superputer Birth Star, which now administered all his affairs, revealed that unlimited funds were at his disposal for the rest of his days, as long as he maintained an enquiring mind, moved about the galaxy, and reported reflections and findings back to the superputer.

There was no conflict between superputer's intentions and boy's ambitions. Jefffris' intellectual curiosity had been whetted. He longed to set out into the universe and experience its conditions for himself; the odyssey could last ten lifetimes for all he cared. With a male friend and two girls, competition-winners all, he set out in a superbly equipped flittership to travel whatever distances could be travelled.

'The universe has a dark corner, the human soul, which is its reflection.' The words had travelled round the known galaxy, together with the livgrams of the five-year-old face. The face had been forgotten for almost as long as Jefffris had outlived it; yet the words had not been forgotten. It could not be said that they changed anything, for a general decline continued. But it could be said that people discovered some mystery in them (if only the mystery in what is familiar) and were perhaps reminded that, for all the vastness of the humanised galaxy, it still rested upon the power of words to transmute formlessness into design. So it might be argued that the decline would have been faster had it not been for Jefffris' dictum.

However that might be, Jefffris and his companions travelled the civilised worlds without being recognised – fortified by the knowledge that he had lit a light, however tiny, in the skulls of almost everyone he ever met.

Everywhere he talked and listened, building up a picture of the spectre that had laid its spell over the galaxy.

'What is wrong with humanity is an ancient wrong,' said an ancient lady living on the core of a burnt-out sun. She had been an organiser in her day, and understood so much that most people became bemused just by gazing on her face. Consequently she wore a mask; but she removed it to speak to Jefffris.

'What is wrong with humanity is not what philosophers of this world commonly suppose,' she said. 'I mean, that man's involvement with technology, with its consequent divorce from what is called Nature, impoverishes him. True, that may be the cause, but if so it is merely a reflection of a deeper division in the human psyche, the division between intellect and the passions. The Babylonian invention of a written language, back on Earth so long ago, institutionalised a division that was already latent in the psyche of humanity.

Writing departmentalises, detaches. It bestows upon the ratiocinative faculties a dominance they should not have over the play of human emotions. The passions become feared, mistrusted.'

'Whole planets full of people have reverted to Nature, have abandoned literacy,' said Jefffris. 'The results have never been anything that responsible people would wish to copy. I visited one such planet, Bol-Rayoeo. Everyone's every breath was ruled by a maniacal belief in astrology, the human instruments of which were an iron priesthood. That priesthood had control over a series of holy factories in which machines were made – elaborate but non-functional machines. The machines were sacrificed on specific dates at specific hours. A paranoid mathematics was their language, yet such was their fear of a written alphabet that a mere glimpse of the letter A scrawled on a rock could kill them at once.'

'The first effect of a written literature,' said the ancient dame, 'is that it undermines the power of Continuers. In the Old World, Continuers were as vital to society as kings or slaves. They moved among all ranks and ages of society, conveying in their persons – in their gestures, their faces, their very breath – history, myth, story. Those elements that were alive, and lived through countless generations, became dead and impaled on a page, and the Continuers ceased. Records have been substituted for legend, the letter for life.

'You yourself, Gordan Ivon, may through fortune regard yourself as a free agent. Yet you are a slave of history. You are gathering facts, a profession which superseded hunting, a dusty parody of it, sans blood. The search for knowledge is too highly lauded.'

'You are yourself consulted as a repository of knowledge, madam.'

'The search for knowledge is an artificial goal – and, even worse, an achievable one. Eventually, all knowledge in the universe will be garnered, reduced to recorded impulses.

Which will mean the absorption of all that is real. Even our breathing will be codified. Classification will have supplanted diversification, all processes will terminate.'

He laughed. 'You speak as if it were a mystical process.'

'It is a mystical process. The further we go, the closer we come to our origins.'

'Nevertheless, I am sorry to find you so pessimistic.'

'Operative in each of us is the blind optimism of biological process; but you will appreciate from what I have already said that words themselves, in my view, tend towards the pessimistic, since they represent an energy-sink from life to abstraction.'

Jefffris was silent a while, picking his way among her statements. 'Is it mere coincidence that you speak more than once of breathing, as if it holds a special symbolism for you?'

'There is no "coincidence",' the ancient lady said, resuming her mask. 'Consciousness is the breath of the universe.'

Jefffris visited the system of Trilobundora, where the three central planets had been welded into one unit by means of transuranic metals. These enormous struts formed FTL roads for UMV traffic. Trilobundora was famed as one of the great industrial centres of the galaxy; in proof of this, all about it for many light years were impoverished planets, populated only by old and broken people. Trilobundora was a Mecca to which all went, hoping to be turned into gold.

He visited a great school on Primdora, where children were trained to be administrators from the age of two onwards. The children poured out after class, flocking at every level of the enormous tower to meet every sort of flying, leaping and wheeled vehicle which came to bear them away.

Plunging to the lowest level, Jefffris found a stooped man of middle age waiting at an entrance with his hands in his pockets. A gale blew, carrying rain with it, although the air was still and dry at higher levels.

'It's always like this here,' said the man. 'Something to do with the structure of the building, I guess. Creates its own storms.' His voice was neutral, passive. He never looked directly at Jefffris.

A small boy came running out of the entrance and stopped before he got to the stooped man. The man put out his hand, took the boy's, and, with a word of encouragement, started to walk away with him. Jefffris fell in beside him.

'Are you the only parent here who meets his child on foot?'

'I have to watch every cent. Besides, public transport doesn't run where we live. It's a slum district. I'm not ashamed; it's not my fault. You may have noticed I'm the oldest person to collect a child. I'm not this lad's father. I'm his grandfather. His parents were killed on their holiday, so now I look after him.'

The boy glanced up at Jefffris to see how he took this information but said nothing. Then he turned his pale face down again to his shoes.

'Is he a consolation?' Jefffris asked.

'He's a good enough lad.' The man had a listless way about him which seemed to have communicated itself to the boy. After a pause in which he appeared to weigh whether it was worth saying more, he went on, 'You see the trouble is that the accident which killed my daughter and her man occurred on the V lane of the FTLR between Primdora and Secdora. Their vehicle collided with a Secdora vehicle right at mid-point between planetary demarcations. Legislation could not decide which planetary government should pay compensation, Primdora or Secdora. The issue is still being heard in the courts. That's been the situation for five years now.

'Meanwhile, I couldn't work because I had to look after the boy. So I've forfeited my state pension. Now he has started school, I have a small morning job, which helps. I could have got someone in to look after him and worked myself, but that would have brought legal complications, since I am still not officially his guardian, and they might have taken him away into care. I want to be his official guardian, but I'm separated from my woman and she is litigating to become his guardian. I think she's only after the money which may accrue, so I fight back.'

'I don't want to go to Grandma,' said the boy. It was the first time he had spoken since leaving school. 'I don't know Grandma, she don't know me.'

'The uncertainty makes his life difficult,' said the man, ignoring the boy's remark. 'He can have no proper career without an official guardian or parent to sign forms – you have to sign forms every day on Primdora – and so he is getting sidetracked and will probably be E-graded. I do my best but I get sick of it all. Everywhere there's regulations. They keep bringing in more regulations. I just found today that they're restructuring the educational system, so he may be sent to another school further away. Then we'll have to move rooms. More expense. All these regulations, you can't escape them ... They're supposed to rationalise community life, aren't they? Instead, they're like a wall round you.'

'I hope the lad's a comfort to you,' Jefffris suggested.

'Who makes all these regulations? I can't understand how they get so complex. It didn't used to be like this. Where did they start, where do they stop? Do you know, I get a small supplementary family allowance for the boy which is taxed with my wage so that in reality I keep less cash than I would do if I didn't get the allowance?'

'Can't you forgo the allowance?'

'I went to see the computer about it. If I forgo the allowance now, I can never reclaim, and the tax structure might change next year in my favour. Then again, the rating scale comes into it – the amount of living space we can claim ... it's a headache.'

'Your grandfather has a lot of problems,' Jefffris said to the boy.

The boy nodded. 'He has a lot of problems.' He kept looking down at his shoes.

In the Beta arm of the galaxy, Jefffris rested with his companions on a delightful satellite called Rampan. It was a pastoral world, where a simple philosophy ruled and crime was almost unknown.

Wandering down a country lane by the sea one moonlit night, Jefffris encountered a slender man who appeared to be of no more than late middle age, yet claimed he was a million years old.

'Longevity and immortality are among the oldest dreams,' said Jefffris, 'and are likely to remain dreams. No biological structure is stable enough to remain intact over long periods of time.'

'A biological structure is only a highly organised state of inorganic material. All material carries the potential of life. The secret of continuous organisation was discovered right there on Argustal,' said the ancient youth.

He pointed up at the gibbous moon sailing over the treetops.

'If you've got time, stranger, I'll tell you a story about it.'

'I'd be glad to listen.'

'That's a rare talent, stranger,' said the slender man. His expression cheered slightly, and he launched into his story.

Argustal is the parent world of Rampam. Long ago, there lived on Argustal a regal young man called Tantanner. He possessed an equable temperament, and was content to let the years drift by in sport and laughter. Happiness came easily to him because he was married to a beautiful lady called Pamipamlar, whose nature was fully as sunny as his.

I have to pass over all their years of content together, for contentment has no history — it leaves its traces, indeed, but they cannot be described. Suffice it to say that one day Tantanner saw strange marks upon his beloved's face. He said nothing to her, so as not to alarm her, and imagined that the marks would fade away. Dawn followed dawn, and the marks did not fade. They deepened. He watched more anxiously. The times of snows came and went. The marks remained. They formed little lines upon Pamipamlar's forehead, below and beside her eyes, and about her pretty mouth.

Still he said nothing to her, but one dark night he rode out silently. Crossing a bleak moor, he went to where the last of a degenerate race of sub-humans eked out their existence in underground caves. These sub-humans – who, I've heard, are to be found on every planet in the early millennia of its development – were savage but cowardly; they fell back before Tantanner's royal insignia and, when he showed himself unafraid, they fawned upon him, as rabbits will try to charm a fox. He knew these untrustworthy creatures held old legends which the human race of Argustal had discarded, and so he demanded of them the meaning of the increasing marks upon the countenance of his beloved.

The sub-humans disputed among themselves, sometimes almost scratching each other's eyes out as they asserted and denied. Some maintained that the marks belonged to an ancient force called Illness, but eventually another point of view prevailed. A gnarled man with a face studded with hideous warts and hairs stood forth and addressed Tantanner where he stood beside his mount.

'Lord sire of the Upright Ones, when Knowledge recedes like an ocean, it leaves Names like shells upon the great beaches of History. We can only pick up these shells and offer them to your inspection, without ourselves understanding their contents.'

'Speak and tell me what ails my fair one.'

'Lord sire, her cheek of vellum is being inscribed by Age.'

'Age? What is Age?'

'A shell we pick up, Lord sire, knowing not its contents – except that one or two of us suppose that upon that spot*less* vellum you have discerned the faintest handwriting of Death.'

'Death? What is Death?'

'It is another shell, O Lord sire, lying half-buried in the vast sands of the Past.'

With that, Tantanner had to be content. He rode back to

the castle and settled by his fragrant Pamipamlar; but those
two dark shells, Age and Death, returned continually to his
mind.

Eventually they drove him from the castle, despite his
love's protests. He kissed her lined face and went forth. This
time he ranged far away, scouring the planet's distant places.
He enquired in the towns and hedgerows, in farms and on
highways, seeking someone or something to enlighten him.

No one knew much. A few people knew a little. Contentment had stuffed their heads with obliviousness, you see.
Once he met a solitary woman with a face like a bone who
farmed forty llamas in a desert region; she turned on him
savagely and said, 'Go home, let remain buried what has
remained buried! Lies at home are to be preferred to any
truth abroad. You will let loose a great evil on the world if
you meddle. Go home!'

But he went on. He went on, although he felt increasingly
the truth of what the woman with a face of bone had said.
For he was gradually piecing together the shreds of ignorance he collected, and making a garment of revelation for
himself.

He wandered into the periphery of a volcano which had
been an active sore on the face of Argustal since the world
was formed. By the coast, he halted at a spot called the
Green Grotto, where the sea steamed and vegetation grew
thick. Turtles slithered on the beach and birds scuttled
underfoot. A lizard-man and a blind youth came to see him
as he sat eating wild artichokes; he told them of his problem.

For a long time, neither lizard nor blind man spoke.
Then the lizard-man said, 'This region is named End Quest,
and I never understood why until now. It marks the end of
your quest. Like you, I have some shreds of knowledge.
They made no garment until joined with your shreds.

'For more years than can be told, I have wondered why
leaves remained on trees whether the sun shone or snow
fell for, according to legend from Olden Pretimes, trees went
bare half the year. I wondered also why birds hop naked

under our feet, when legends from Old Pretimes say they
flew with feathers far above the heads of men. Now I know
the answer.'

At these words, 'I know the answer', a great fear descended on Tantanner. He recalled the old lady with the face
of bone and he turned to run. There was no escape. Curiosity
got the better of him. He turned back and said, 'Speak,
lizard.'

The lizard-man said, 'Long, long ago, further than our
minds can stretch, a process was invented on this planet. It
was called continuous organisation. I cannot tell you what
it was – that's a secret for ever lost, I suspect. It worked
upon this planet, when set in motion by its masters, worked
as tirelessly as the weather machine which keeps air circu-
lating about us all. Under continuous organisation, all
biological processes remained intact as hitherto, no longer
subject to the previous ageing which led to a state of energy-
transference called Death. Death was feared, pale Death.
Continuous organisation guaranteed life. All biological
creatures have been immortal on this planet since that day.'

'We have not to fear Death?'

'Listen. Death had a second, rosier face called Birth.
When Death was banished, so went Birth. There was no
need of her. Everything alive lived. For replacements there
was no room. But those things which lived were subject to
the attrition of external factors. No trees shed their leaves
– and that original set of leaves is now made skeletal by the
action of winds and frost. Birds cannot die, but the elements
have eroded their feathers, so that they must go naked on
the ground, being no longer able to fly. The carapaces of our
turtles have worn thin as silk against the eternal sand. Many
more delicate creatures – insects – have simply been fined
away by the atmosphere.'

'And my Pamipamlar, what of her?'

The lizard-man looked down at the sand by his webbed
feet.

'Death is returning to its throne, my lord. Generation is

again needed; continuous organisation must itself die, its machineries run down.'

'Answer my question. What of Pamipamlar?'

'If you looked in a mirror at your own face, your question would be answered. The handwriting is set upon your cheek too. Death will call on you as surely as upon her.'

Tantanner swung into the saddle and turned for home. His bitterness towered to the heavens; perhaps he recalled the words of the sage who says that the human soul is a dark corner which reflects the whole universe. His questions were answered. Fear and regret rode with him, regret that he had neglected his beloved so long. And it was a long way home.

Alas, stranger, it was such a long way home that that foolish man arrived too late. Death had already claimed the one he loved. The world was in action again, the cycles of regeneration beginning again. But Tantanner's world had run down to a dead stop.

Jefffris sat silent, reflecting on the regenerative processes of the universe and looking up at the world of Argustal gleaming in Rampam's night sky.

'What brought you here?' he asked the solemn story-teller.

'I couldn't bear that world any more, with my beloved dead. Now I linger here in exile, waiting for Death to escort me home.'

After many years of travel, Jefffris came to the planet Earth. He had listened to countless profound comments, abstruse theories, and moving tales. All this he had reported back to the superputer.

At this stage in its history, Earth was a second league world in the Procyon Bloc. It called itself a republic and was ruled over by the Committee of Twenty-One, the President of which was Kuo Waung-Tang.

In a bar in a large city in Antarctica, Jefffris met a genial man who had served under Kuo Waung-Tang. He now called himself Dumb Dragon.

'Yes, I have served under the great Kuo Waung-Tang and much admire him,' admitted Dumb Dragon as he bought Jefffris a drink. 'I read his thoughts every night.'

'Yet he sent you into exile for ten years when you refused to serve on the Committee.'

'What else could Kuo do? I am grateful for that ten years. Now I have nothing to do with politics. I merely tell animal stories to anyone who cares to listen.'

'Thanks, not today. But I'd like to hear why you left politics.'

Dumb Dragon laughed engagingly. 'I simply discovered that mankind is not rulable although he perennially wishes to be ruled. Why? For a simple reason: because your perspectives change so radically when you make the transition from governed to governor. It's like a high tower – you can't see the top from the bottom, so you climb to the top, and then you can't see the bottom. It's hopeless. Ruler and ruled are almost different species.'

'The lust for power has a history as long as mankind.'

'Certainly. But I refer to something more complex. I really must tell you one of my latest animal stories. Do you mind very much?'

Jefffris enjoyed the man's company. 'Make me like it.'

'That's good. Story-tellers are brave men – they always battle with the listener's wish to dislike what they hear, for the listener wishes to be ruler of the story, although inwardly he longs to be dominated by it. Okay, this story is called "The Lion Who Had Ecology", bearing in mind that on Earth this year ecology and conservation are fashionable subjects. It probably means we are due for another big destructive war.'

He beamed at the wall, as if turning a smiling face towards the future no matter what happened, and commenced his story.

The last African lion was sitting comfortably under a deodar, reading the current issue of *Digest of World Lion Problems*, when a zebra of his acquaintance called Leopold galloped up and coughed expectantly (said Dumb Dragon, making lion and zebra faces as he went along.)

'Begging your pardon, sir,' said the zebra.

'What is it now?' asked the lion. He had a grudge against Leopold, just could not stand the zebra's airs and graces, and promised himself that he would eat him one day soon when it was not quite so hot.

'The animals would like to have a word with you, sir,' said Leopold. 'Looks like there's another ecological crisis brewing.'

The lion gave in with a bad grace and padded north across the game preserve with the zebra. Crowds of animals and birds of every variety – every remaining variety – were heading in the same direction. The leaders of this multitude had halted by a dried river bed and were staring across it, meanwhile uttering many cries of disgust, if not actual oaths. They stood back respectfully to let the lion through.

'Well, what seems to be the trouble this time?' he asked.

Nobody liked to thrust forward and answer, although a couple of jackals sidled up and said, 'We tried to get the mob to disperse but they wouldn't. Do you want us to try the skunk-gas on them?'

Ignoring them, the lion peered across the river bed. On the far side, a short distance away, some black men were working, unloading bricks from trucks and marshalling heavy machines. Nearer at hand other men were watching elephants pushing down large trees and dragging them away.

'Scabs! Blacklegs!' hissed the crowd, but the elephants ignored them and continued working.

'Oh, isn't it terribly awful!' exclaimed an ostrich called the Rev. Dean William Pennyfever, wringing his hands. 'Bang goes a slice more of the veld. They're putting up their simply nauseating little dwellings on the very spot where I emerged from the egg.'

'Dwellings, indeed,' exclaimed a giraffe, contemptuously. 'Putting up a whole bloody town, more like it, right where I enjoy a spot of necking. Perishing blacks! Dirty beasts!'

'Now then, remember they're victims of colonialism,' said the lion sharply. 'Besides, we don't *know* it's a whole town. We must get our facts right before we issue a complaint. Has anyone – you parrots – actually asked those men what's going on there?'

Silence fell, the animals shuffled about uneasily, not looking up at their leader.

'There you are then,' said the lion. 'Typical silly emotionalism. You moan and complain and you haven't a clue as to what is actually happening in the world. You're too parochial. Naturally, I share your anxiety about anything – anything at all – which encroaches on the amenities of the jungle, but statistically, let me assure you, those black chaps are having absolutely no effect on this continent's magnificent natural resources.'

Many animals, including hyenas, monkeys and snakes, clapped this fiery speech and shouted, 'Hear, hear.' But a bespectacled hippo, recently divorced, came up to the lion and spoke in a grumpy way. (Dumb Dragon put on a hippo face.)

'That's all very well as far as it goes, Mr Lion, but I represent the Amalgamated Mammal and Reptile Union, and the workers have vested in me the authority to ask you to do something positive about this latest infringement of our territory. We don't want words, we want action, right, lads?'

A great cry went up from the beasts, especially the rhinos, many of whom acted as shop stewards.

'We *all* want action,' the lion said impressively. 'I am much more anti any attempt to curtail living space than you are, because I am more aware of all the ecological factors involved. Nevertheless, it would be extremely unwise to let the sight of a few bricks precipitate us into a hasty move – a stampede or something silly, in which our weaker brethren might get trampled underfoot, or eaten, or even left destitute and incapacitated.'

'We'll go into the vexed question of sick benefits later, if you don't mind,' said the hippo, adjusting his spectacles. 'Meanwhile the workers have empowered me to demand immediate action in the shape of crossing yon river bed and eating up all the blacks on the building site. I am further empowered to demand that you take the tigers along, so that no feeble excuses like failing appetite can deflect you from our allotted task. As for your liberal-lackey remark about that being just a few bricks over there, it looks to me more like a whole frigging new suburb of Nairobi!'

The animals muttered and mewed in approval.

'This is entirely unconstitutional,' said the lion. 'If our nuclear commitment were up to strength, the situation might be different, but you opted for détente, remember. We must not offend the black men, or they will do us real harm, and then you workers will be the first to regret it. Don't they depend entirely on us for hides, horns, souvenirs of the chase, feathers, ivory, handbags, and leopard-skin rugs? Supposing they refuse to trade? As it is, we've got an adverse balance of payments because they're turning to plastic while we play hard to get. No, my friends, I know your business better than you do yourselves! Forget about that mangey scrap of ground, and let's get back to the veld.'

The animals all started milling about, undecided what to do. The hippos and rhinos conferred together, and Leopold said to the lion, 'I'm afraid we'll have to face the fact that this may mean the workers will try to depose you as king of the beasts.'

'Well, it's a democratic age,' said the lion weakly. 'I have political common sense on my side. Look, if we did as the hippos say, it would only encourage the young tigers; they cause enough disturbance as it is. All that's needed is a token gesture. Why don't you nip over on your own and kick a few black arses, just to show willing?'

Before Leopold could reply, a shot rang out across the

dried river bed. The animals who were looking in that direction could clearly see a man in a bush-hat standing on a truck, firing a rifle with telescopic sights. In the silence which followed, the lion collapsed, as leonine blood gouted from a hole in his forehead.

'A judgment from above!' said the Rev. Dean William Pennyfever. 'Let's get back to the veld before similar punishment strikes the entire congregation.'

'Piss off, you old fool!' shouted a hot-headed young rhino. 'Naked aggression! That just proves we were right. We've got to get those men before they get us. Let's have a show of hooves in favour of an immediate stampede.'

'Not so fast, not so fast!' said the bespectacled hippo. 'I'm in charge now. Let's not be rash.'

'But you were the one who suggested the charge in the first place,' said the young rhino in amazement.

'Circumstances alter cases. Pipe down – you're too free with your comments. Now the lion's dead, I'm managing things to see that we don't get another boss over us, and what I say goes.'

'But those men are building on our land.'

'They've got rights, same as us. Look, I know how you feel, but this needs a constitutional approach. Let's get back to the veld and talk things over in the light of this new development. Perhaps we can barney the men into a compromise.'

Everyone started trotting back towards the deodars. Leopold called out angrily, 'Are we going to forget our wise old leader just like that? Let's at least give him a decent burial with a copy of *Digest of World Lion Problems* beside him.'

But nobody paid any heed. They left the lion where he had fallen. It was too hot to bother, and only the jackals and vultures stayed with the body for the last obsequies.

Continuing on his travels, Gordan Ivon Jefffris visited representative planets all over the universe. A myriad viewpoints were presented to him for his consideration, all of which he sedulously reported back to Birth Star, the super-puter. He found every sort of philosophy, every sort of government, anarchies, hive-worlds, individualisms, utopias, some of which worked extremely well for a while, but none for ever. He spoke to men of action and men of contemplation, women who laughed and women who cried, old people and young people. He was confronted by an astounding diversity.

Gradually this diversity swallowed him up. He no longer sought answers. His companions left him, yet he went blindly on, almost unaware of what he was or why he did what he did. He was open to the whole universe, and in consequence less and less able to reach any conclusion about it. There was always something new; that something was age-old, yet at the same time it was new.

Jefffris himself grew old, despite constant rejuvenation shots.

Finally, the Institute recalled him and he sat in a comfortable geriatric chair before Birth Star itself.

'It is many years since you won the great competition. Have you reached any conclusions after your unique experiences?' asked the superputer.

'Experience ... how does anyone evaluate experience? I was born believing that humanity was a vital, not a freak manifestation of the greater universe, and nothing I have experienced has altered that view.'

'Have you reached any conclusions, then?'

'No. I began to consider that the universe itself was all-important. Its mere size ... Then, after a long time, I came to consider that human beings were all-important. Perhaps nothing is all-important ... '

He sank into a long silence from which the superputer finally roused him.

'Is that your conclusion?'

'What? No, certainly not. It is an error in logic to believe that nothing is all-important. That would only be possible in a universe of nothingness. At least I have come to believe that ideas, like the universe, like man, have their own validity, that they have a genetic structure of their own, that they are the link – no, not the link, the very medium, in which both universe and man's consciousness exist. I'm tired … '

'Go on, Gordan Ivon,' said the superputer. It played him reviving colours.

'Yes, ideas have a seminal fluid. They co-exist from the beginning of everything to the end of everything. They contain everything; that is why they appear to us, whatever we think of, to be at once fresh yet, on examination, very ancient. Such concepts carry us far beyond notions of pessimism or optimism; they carry us right to the heart of existence. And of course we have always been at the very heart of existence without knowing it. Whatever we are, whoever we are, whether young or old … '

The superputer let him ramble on, and said finally, 'So you have reached a conclusion.'

'No. Or yes.' He drew himself up. 'The human soul has a dark corner, the universe, which is its reflection. But I don't think I want to talk about it, thanks.'

Song of the Silencer

Noon of a summer day in a high latitude. Splendour from every corner of the city, and the squalid made splendid. Jubilation locally, celebration all round the planet, rejoicing throughout the solar system. The day of all days had come, the day of the Ultimate Machine.

Not on Earth alone did hooters wail and bells chime. On the planets and the satellites and asteroids of the system – wherever mankind had found a foothold – there also was a spirit of sober joy at the thought that Utopia had come at last. And come, undoubtedly, to stay.

From further afield, by space-warp and black hole, travelled mutated members of the human family who had forged a way into distant stellar systems; these distant cousins also returned to Earth or Moon, to be present at the scintillating birth of a new era for all mankind.

Reproduced everywhere, in the great 4-D cubes in public places or flat on arm-sets, were shots of the superb, the colossal, Ultimate Machine itself, as it was in space, awaiting activation this very day of days.

It was popularly known as the Ultimate Machine. So spoke the media. Its official designation was MOSRAB, but of this acronym, standing for Metafunctional Orbital Self-positing Replication Anthropoid Brain, the first and the last words only caught in the general fancy; Metafunctional Brain was the term frequently on the lips of the citizens of Moskoric, Parandam, Chicholo, and other vast metropolises.

Unfortunately, not all those citizens were capable of experiencing the same delight in this technological triumph as was felt by their leaders and advisers. A vanishingly small percentage – perhaps no more than a few hundred thousand desperadoes round the whole System – opposed the event about to be celebrated, the activation of the Ultimate Machine. A terrorist organisation, known as the Enemies of Knowledge, survived in the gutters and wastes, dedicating their perverted energies to destroying the Ultimate Machine.

The central event of this millennial day was to be the pressing of the key by the Interplanetary President which would activate MOSRAB and so change the course of human affairs for all time. This crucial key, with all the age-old symbolism attached to it, formed part of a terminal console on Earth linked by SUHF and PCM to the Brain in space, and was housed in the Palace of the Planets. For financial reasons, large structures like the Palace were nowadays generally situated in space, in a suitable energy-stable orbit; the Palace of the Planets was the largest building on Earth. Already men and women and children in their millions were flocking to it, on foot or in private corpsport.

Orderly though the crowds were, militia men were everywhere. Only a minute section of that concourse saw a brief scuffle involving uniformed men with immobilan guns. The gunmen ran after a black-clad youth, pursued him into one of the foyers of the subterraway, and shot him.

Half an hour later, the youth landed in an interrogation room. He lay in one corner where he had been dropped, a sardonic expression on his face, his spine curved backwards like a bow, so that only his heels and the crown of his head touched the floor. Visible effects of the immobilan drug were much like those of an extinct disease called tetanus. The militia had only to key their terminal for the solar computer – which stored complete biographies of the billions of billions of inhabitants of the system – to display appropriate data. This youth was Ben Michael Arazz, born Kubeer City, North Quadrant, Titan, 2015. A three-year criminal record of sabotage with the Enemies of Knowledge.

Judicious administration of the antidote to immobilan was in itself enough to extract information from Arazz. The EK were in the course of executing two plans to disrupt the great achievement about to be consolidated. Locally, one of their most notorious assassins, a young woman by the name of Gertheid Seribu-Chia, would assassinate the Interplanetary President just before he depressed the crucial key; while from a secret launching site on Luna, a kamikazi strike would be launched against the Ultimate Machine itself.

Arazz was given an immediate automated trial, and found guilty by the computer on thirty-eight of thirty-nine indictments. Before he was destructed, one more item of information was extracted from him. The insane fanaticism of the EK group was inspired in part by the intellectual teachings of one Ambrose Parblow, an ex-member of the system-wide Practical Philosophers Panel.

The PPP had been founded as an enlightened move by the first Interplanetary President, some twenty-six years ago. The PPP had infused superior wisdom into the hard governmental thinking of solar system politics; indeed, one of the PPP's earliest proposals had been for the establishment of an independent source of wisdom, to steer large issues of a philosophical nature touching the welfare of humanity as a whole. From this proposal had sprung the project of constructing an analogue of a human brain, as opposed to a mere computing machine, which had cumulated in MOSRAB.

The leading High-Philosopher, Ambrose Parblow, had opposed this grandiose scheme from the start. Despite the warnings of friends, he had insisted on voicing his reservations publicly; two years ago, when MOSRAB was nearing completion, it was found necessary to withdraw the High-Philosopher from office, in the interests of public confidence. He was at present incarcerated in one of the luxury confinement satellites in the so-called zeepees, or zodiacal planets, stabilised in a cislunar orbit.

The militia chief communicated his new findings to interested parties for immediate action, and decided himself to pay a visit to the High-Philosopher. The journey took only a few light seconds.

'Pray come in, gentlemen,' said High-Philosopher Ambrose Parblow. He stood back to allow the chief and his two escorting officers to enter the low room. 'I trust you have no trouble on your hands on this joyful day of all days.' He looked at them alertly, taking in their drab uniforms and beefy faces.

'We're expecting you to give us a few details of your opposition to the Ultimate Machine,' said the chief. The philosopher's irony was lost on him – as well it might be, for the video screens in the room were flooded with images of serious and glorious matters: space itself, with the great irregular shape of the Metafunctional Brain, and a view of the swelling congregation in the vast hall down on Earth. Small peripheral screens reinforced the general grandeur.

The High-Philosopher was a tall willowy man with a gaunt but lively face – 'a streamer of expressions fluttering in the wind', as it had once been poetically described by Parblow's dead mistress – white hair, and long articulate hands. He looked in many ways a typical ectomorph; on the Sheldonian scale he scored 1-2-7. He was a man whose nervous system was near the surface, and he glanced at the chief's helmet and held his tongue. For the chief wore a red-striped comhat, a reinforced metal transmitter that beamed whatever the chief saw and heard straight back to a subterranean headquarters on Earth.

The chief was a mesomorph, with enough of the endomorph to render him genial when the occasion demanded. His comrades were standard mesomorphs, with thick necks and big hands dangling at the ends of their uniformed arms.

'What precisely are your objections to the Machine?' asked the chief, after a silence.

'Well, you may recall – I'm sure you have such matters at your fingertips – that I published a volume a few years ago entitled *The Song of the Silencer* in which I set out –'

' "Precisely," Parblow, please.'

'I was not deviating from the question. You asked for my reservations. I have but one, yet it may strike you as complex. On the other hand, there is another reservation – not mine, but one registered by numerous technocrats and thinkers – which I can state succinctly in a three-word slogan which your people have done their best to suppress: "MOSRAB Never Sleeps".'

'Let's have that one first, then,' said the chief. He sat down, motioning the philosopher to do the same. 'And be quick about it. We're determined to wipe out the EK, so I need to know what you know, and I can't spend all day on it.'

'The day may indeed be shorter than you imagine.' The philosopher sat down on the arm of a sofa, crossing his long legs. 'That slogan, "MOSRAB Never Sleeps" means precisely what it says. The Metafunctional Brain is constructed as a replica of the human brain; its original architects designed it to function as a human brain functions, in so far as that is possible. Political pressure has swept away that consideration. For, think! To be cost-effective, the MOSRAB has been built in orbit, although it is designed to experience the circadian rhythm of the twenty-four hour day, as does every living thing on Earth. But its costs are met by taxation from all sources in the system. Communities on the most distant body – on the moon of Pluto – have contributed to the financing of this project. So they rightly claim an allocation of its real-time when it is functional. To meet that enormous demand, the MOSRAB must now work continually. No sleep periods. Ever.'

'That's logic,' said the chief. 'You don't suggest we should shut the machine down for nine hours of every twenty-four, a mechanical thing getting its shut-eye?' He laughed curtly.

The philosopher rose and paced up and down before the screens, his silhouette continually occulting the multi-coloured hemispheres of the Ultimate Machine.

'Chief, you bring me almost to my own reservation about this miraculous – for it is nothing less – instrument, the reservation for which I was dismissed from office. Will you please try and understand me if I speak my mind, for believe me I have much sympathy with your wish to serve the system's government, and with that government's wish to serve MOSRAB. I recognise that your intentions, and the intentions of the government, are good. That you have become tainted by power is inescapable. Such is human nature. Power warps imagination.'

'Cut the verbosity!'

'That is my endeavour. I'm nervous, can't you see?' He exhibited his hands, which he had been clasping and unclasping. 'I believe that this is a day of doom – to what extent no man can determine – for the human race, the death of its aspirations and not their fulfilment. You see, although your *intentions* may be well enough, your basic *assumptions* are totally incorrect.'

He lifted a hand commandingly, to silence the militia chief.

'Take this question of sleep. You think mechanically, your attitude to life is exploitive, as it is in all who seek power. You view hours spent sleeping as mere wastage. That is mistaken. Sleep – the balm of hurt minds, in Shakespeare's fine phrase – is a reservoir of new life and insight in which we need to bathe our psyches every day. In sleep, we commune with our deeper selves, with a permanent part of our selves which is beyond fear or ambition or envy. Even the vilest bully and torturer in your employ, even a Genghis Khan or a Joseph Stalin, escapes his terrible appointed role for a third of his life. All positive things arise from sleep and the oases of sleep we call dreams. Deprive a man of sleep – your inquisitors will tell you, sir – and he suffers from hallucinations within three days, and becomes mad after ten. Yet MOSRAB, the replication of a human brain, on whose sanity the system must soon depend, is sentenced to chronic insomnia. It cannot rest or gain insight or recuperate. I would think that is a formidable enough reservation for anyone. Yet it has been set aside, in the interests of democracy and revenue.'

While he spoke, the events as depicted on the screens

behind his slender back were going forward. The greatest
moment was not far away.

The Ultimate Machine rode in a lunar orbit, a quarter of a
million miles from Earth. It was as large as the Moon, although its mass was less. The elements and energies used in
its construction had been found by the cannibalisation of
Uranus. It gleamed in the eternal energy output of the Sun,
half in light, half in shadow. So greatly had it influenced
the minds of men that the entire surface of cladding which
shielded the artificial brain within had been decorated —
decorated in a thousand ways, according to the desires of the
communities who had played their part. Among many ab-
stract panels were representational views of terrestrial landscapes, reproductions of Rembrandt canvases ten miles high,
Chinese poems with characters larger than whales, and many
other brilliant inspirations which indicated how fully this
space-born leviathan bore the hopes of mankind. From a
certain distance, the vast artefact resembled a randomly
tattooed human face.

Gathering round it like sprats — like whole shoals and
fleets of sprats — were countless police- and pleasure-craft,
moving as near as permitted to gain a close-up view of this
innovation at such an inspiring moment. The militia chief,
failing to concentrate on what the High-Philosopher was
saying, scrutinised the craft like a hawk. Something in his
helmet checked them off for him. He responded into a throat
mike.

Among the multitudinous space vehicles lurked the enemy,
the kamikazi vessel operated by the EK. A signal came
through the helmet. The space militia had identified it.

With a grunt of triumph, the chief ran forward and altered
the magnification of the philosopher's main screen. The viewpoint, from being distant, rushed in on the target, so that
ships seemed to scatter from all sides of the vision. Now only
a few craft could be seen, the magnification making them
appear as if made of wool. One was a bright yellow, sharp-
edged against an enormous bas-relief of Eva Peron's face.

Its hull became blackened: it glowed momentarily, then disintegrated like a spent firework. The space militia had got their man.

The chief's two beefy escorts cheered.

While the chief communicated with his helmet, High-Philosopher Parblow went to stare moodily at another screen. It showed a scene almost as spectacular as the view of space, for the Palace of the Planets was covered down the full length of its façade with banners and flowers.

Slowly, impressively, the viewpoint swung in under the high central archway, moved into the great auditorium, over the heads of the multitude, to focus on the podium and the figure, as yet minute in the distance, of the grey-haired Interplanetary President of the United Solar System.

As if sight of that figure spurred him to talk, the philosopher said, 'Yes, *The Song of the Silencer* – that's the man, your beloved President, who banned my book and had me confined here like Ariel pent in an oak. I believe he genuinely could not understand the explanation I gave him of the dangers that MOSRAB represents. Some men must always destroy what they do not understand.

'He could not understand the true nature and function of the human brain. Few can. We think, yes, *cogitamus ergo sumus*, but as yet *homo sapiens* is too immature to understand what thought is. We think, but cannot think about thought. In much the same function, our ancestors sailed the oceans of the round globe, believing it flat. MOSRAB has been built as a perfect model of the brain – yet with complete misunderstanding of the nature of both brain and universe.'

The chief had finished communicating with an unseen ally. He turned to his escort and said. 'They've discovered that Seribu-Chia is somewhere in the auditorium, armed to assassinate the President. They've got her alpha/omega graph in the scanner, so we should have her any moment.'

He turned to the philosopher to cut him off, but something the President was saying made him hesitate and listen.

'This is the moment in history which will make all history

until today seem like prehistory,' declared the President to the multitudes. He was a large, solid man with a thick neck and heavy folded jowls, yet with a touch of what men term nobility in his carriage: a typical mesomorph with more than a touch of ectomorph in his make-up. 'The brain of *homo sapiens*, the improved cerebrum, is the instrument which has brought Man in such a brief time from the status of just another ape to his present condition, where he can look upon the Universe and not be dismayed.'

'And not comprehend what he sees!' interjected the philosopher.

'Yet, as we know, that brain has led mankind into a long history of war and cruelty and strife. When I press the key of this console before me, that bloodthirsty story will cease. We shall have the power of pure thought, the thought of the Metafunctional Brain, to guide us. An exponential increase in knowledge will cloak us.'

The philosopher gave a sob, pressing a long hand to his throat. 'It's not knowledge we lack. We have the knowledge, you kakistocrat, more than we can deploy! What we need is the dream-qualities, wisdom and imagination – the imagination that can make knowledge effective for good.'

The image of the man on the screen raised a finger just above the level of its skull. 'Mankind's adolescence, the long age of confusion, is over. This justly named Ultimate Machine marks the point where history, religion and politics – yes, and art – all converge.'

'But it's a mistake!' cried the philosopher. He turned beseechingly to the militia chief, whose eyes were searching the crowded levels of the auditorium. 'He subscribes to the orthodox thinking, the politically correct line, that the human brain originates thought. How can that be so for one minute? The thought we experience, the thoughts that guide migratory birds, the thoughts that tell the lowliest flower when to blossom, the micro-organism when to divide – they come from without, from the Universe!'

'The Universe *thinks*?' asked the chief.

'Yes, yes, we are all one of God's thoughts, or the Universe's, as every dolt knows who ever paid attention to his dreaming self!'

But the President on distant Earth continued in even tones, surrounded by the presidents and chairmen and advisers from many worlds and satellites.

'My friends, you know that human lives for many centuries – and especially for the last three centuries – have been marred by a great war between religion and politics and science. They are three of the great constants that demarcate the boundaries of the modern human situation. In MOSRAB, they become one. We cannot deny that the Ultimate Machine has a godlike power, or that it in future will resolve our destinies. We shall, for the first time since the cerebrum drove us from the dim comfort of the Pleistocene jungles, become at one with the Universe.'

The philosopher clutched at his narrow skull. 'That's precisely what we will not become, you deluded man! Such hubris! You know nothing! We are about to be isolated from the Universe.' With a sigh, he turned to the chief. 'Sir, understand – stop this grotesque performance, phone through and stop it. Say there's been a technical hitch. Listen, the brain does not originate thought. It is a censor, the world's best silencer. That's what I said, that's why they banned my book, why I was expelled from office. The Universe booms and echoes with thought – radiation, it's called – so loud no one could cope with it. Mankind has gained supremacy because our brains act as baffles, suppressors, admitting only a trickle of that great sound. The thoughts of which we are so overweeningly proud are really snatches of the universal song at a volume we can tolerate.'

He grasped the chief's shoulder to make him listen, but the chief's eyes were darting over the screen as he called to base. 'Yes, yes – great, keep tracking! Yes, wait – yes, I have her now!'

He threw himself forward, twisting the controls. One of the topmost galleries came into focus. From the back row of seats, a black-clad girl rose and aimed a shoulder-missile at the distant figure standing on the podium.

'Oh, shoot, Gertheid, shoot, for the love of humanity, shoot!' cried the philosopher.

Calmly the voice of the Interplanetary President continued. 'As we have always dreamed of God in our different races and creeds, so, at last, through the power of science and politics working in unison, we have been able to invent Him. The guidance we have forever sought is at hand. We have merely to listen in humility, when I have pressed this switch –'

'That damned thing orbiting out there is a monster silencer, not the voice of God!' shouted the philosopher. 'Gertheid, shoo- ohhhh!' He subsided as one of the escort men caught him behind the ear with a row of knuckles.

' – this simple plastic key before me,' continued the calm voice of the President, reaching out his hand.

Under the chief's hand, the screen zoomed in on the black-clad girl as she squinted down her sights.

The crucial key was depressed beneath the President's finger. Along the equator of the Ultimate Machine, lights fluoresced. The High-Philosopher pulled himself to his knees, to his feet, as the screens went berserk.

The girl assassin was frozen with the weapon at her shoulder. The President stood oddly hunched over the console. The militia chief, his assistants, remained leaning forward, staring blankly at nothing.

Over the great auditorium, stillness fell. Everyone was silent. The viewpoint settled on them.

The High-Philosopher sank to his haunches. He glared ahead. Days passed, and hair sprouted from the unmoving viewers. Bony protruberances grew from their joints and foreheads. Weeks passed, and drifting dust settled on them. It was impossible to see that anyone stirred. Years passed.

About the equator of the Ultimate Machine, lights glowed steadily, but still not a soul anywhere moved.

The Universe sang to them. Sang sweetly and in vain.

Indifference

The nearest civilised planet lay eighty of God's light years away as the church swung into orbit about Bormidoor.

The church computed itself a landing site and commenced descent. The great mesh of particles called space withdrew, rushed back like a tide before the banks of atmosphere. Inside the church, time started again, and the ache of human consciousness.

Every time a church moved through space, something was changed, to the farthest reaches of the web.

Night reigned. Bormidoor had no moon. Hurrying cloud permitted an occasional glimpse of stars. In this hemisphere there were stars to be seen; in the other none or almost none. The church stood on a stretch of low-lying coast with its spire pointing to heaven. From its cabin a midnight ocean could be glimpsed, dark, with only an occasional glimmer betraying its restless motion. The ocean was interfacial. The humans looked out at it occasionally as they went through their exercises and prayers, restoring themselves to life in preparation for the labours ahead.

When the pallor of dawn arrived, the humans left the church and stepped out upon unfamiliar soil. They bowed in unison towards the quarter of sky in which Creation had begun, repeating gestures of an age-old ritual.

There were three humans, the Erlauries, accompanied by

a large doglike animal, a berund, which lumbered friskily about their heels. In the throat of a great cloud that was piled above the ocean lay a chill spring of light. It lit their three faces. Their faces were identical. They were neuclones, sent to Bormidoor as missionaries for the dissemination of Theomanity.

During that first day they did no work. They walked about the land and the dunes. They ventured down upon the beach to stand and look at the great sea that pounded the sand. They kept their cloaks from its spray. Only the berund ventured close enough to get splashed. Very few were the words they exchanged.

On the second morning, after their rituals were completed, they made a start upon the labours, which they knew might take years. The timing of their arrival on Bormidoor had been carefully planned by savants of the Theomane Church back on Earth – savants who, under the laws of relativity, were in their graves by now. Although they had ample time for the completion of their task, that time was not infinite. Bormidoor was now past the perihelion of its long elliptical orbit about the sun, Dooriz; its northern hemisphere was enjoying full-blown summer. Ahead lay the long ripe decay of autumn and then a thousand Earth-years of winter as the planet laboured round its distant point of apogee. Before that infinite winter closed in, the Theomane Centre would be finished and functioning, the neuclones would have gone away.

The summer days were coolish and wet. Bormidoor was a primitive planet, with little vegetation and no animal life; it was a world hostile to intelligence. It abounded in insects, a few species of which were as big as sea birds. They flew rejoicing while the bright year lasted.

Undeterred by climate, uncaring about the insects, the three humans went about their programme, consulting the church computer at every step. First they built about the church a large, barnlike building of light monomolecular metals, so that the spire of the former rose up from the central point. Inside this barn they began to assemble machines.

When they had assembled and launched a stratokite, their power source was assured. The great foil wings of the kite rode fifteen kilometres above them, beaming down all the energy they required for the present.

They assembled a robot factroid in the barn. The factroid built a land vehicle and an air vehicle. The chief neuclone rode off in the land vehicle, the second took off in the air vehicle. The third stayed in the barn with the berund. The berund galumphed in small circles, catching insects.

Both the new vehicles mapped the territory surrounding the landing site. Geological samples linked with aerial photographs gave a comprehensive picture of the terrain. Veins of metallic ore lay close to the surface only eleven kilometres from the site.

Mining equipment was driven to the site. Two of the neuclones worked there, day in, day out, keeping in touch with the church by radio. It was a hard, primitive way of obtaining metals; but they were on the very frontiers of the Church.

One bright morning the two miners left their foil hut to offer up their daily ritual. They had chosen a site by a river. The river followed a meandering course through a shallow sandy valley. A couple of bends away down-river a wooden boat with a sail was approaching. The cries of the men aboard told the clones that they had been seen. The two crouched by their machines, watching anxiously; they had no defences.

Before the boat was moored, armed men jumped ashore and marched up the bank.

The Erlauries were born not on Earth, but on Vladimir. Vladimir was one of the artificial zodiacal planets which specialised in the creation of cloned neuter families. Only the memory banks of the Church could tell how many identical members of the Erlaurie family there were.

At the age of five the Erlauries were designated to tasks according to their abilities. Even mass-produced objects vary from one another. The scrupulous psychic profiles taken of every neuclone enabled them to be delegated to life-work which fitted and enhanced their capacities.

After a period of field-work on a remote planet, the least efficient Erlauries were despatched to Reconstitution Centres, and the rest formed into groups of three. From now on, for the remainder of their lives, they would work as three-man teams. The life-span of the Erlauries had been determined before birth; since they were destined for missionary work out in the galaxy, most of their existence would be passed in spaceflight. They were accordingly given a middle-longevity, gamma on the Belov scale.

The team chosen for Bormidoor were Aprav, Nupor, and Ovits Erlaurie. They were sent from Vladimir to Earth, where they spent a year in the Religious Academy of Korovsk on the Kola Peninsula. The Academy was a great stone building of many levels. Aprav, Nupor and Ovits were clad in rich monastic garb. For the first time in their lives, they wore fur-lined boots, ate nonsynthetic food, listened to live music, and associated with the ancient non-cloned type of human being. They were grounded intensively in the religious sciences, Cosnizance, which formed the basis of the beliefs of the universal Theomane Church. Then they were despatched to the uninhabited planet of Bormidoor, on the rim of the known universe.

The leader of the marauders from the boat was a gaunt, hard man who stood a full head taller than his men. His face was composed of a few harsh planes. It was hairless. The pupils of his eyes were of such a light blue-grey that they appeared almost white. His manner, while quiet, suggested that he was accustomed to immediate obedience.

'Tie them up,' he ordered.

Aprav and Nupor offered no resistance. They were bound and secured to the support of the shelter they had constructed for the mine.

The leader and his henchmen walked round the site before returning to the captives.

'Any more of you people here?'

'No.' As always, Aprav spoke for the Erlauries.

'Where's your base?'

'On the coast.'

The leader looked at his henchmen. 'As I said.' Turning back to Aprav, he said, 'We saw your ship come down from space. It's taken us a week of days to get here. Who are you and where are you from?'

While Aprav answered these questions simply, without fear or concealment, Nupor bowed his head. The leader's men, ten in number, prowled about the camp, opening crates, spilling contents from boxes.

'Enough.' The leader interrupted Aprav. 'No more of your damned religion. What do you think we're doing, living on this desert of a planet, if not to escape from Theomanity? But we'll not hurt you and it's certain you can't hurt us. All we want's some of your equipment and maybe a few things else. Keep quiet and you'll come to no harm. We're not murderers, like your masters.'

All this, and the looting that followed, Nupor heard and watched, his eyes furtively scanning under lowered brows. Fear was in his heart, but the fear was banished as he saw a further person approaching from the direction of the boat.

It was a woman.

Nupor saw her through the fuzz of his eyebrows, watched her arrival between moving men, between coarse shrubs, behind posts and machinery.

Like the leader, she was tall. Something of the bleakness of his face was echoed in hers. Her skin was pale, her hair was long and dark, straggling about the lines of her neck. Her eyes were grey. Her lips were of a red Nupor had once glimpsed in the wing of a winter bird. She wore a tight-fitting blouse with a jerkin over it which revealed the outline of her breasts. Her skirt reached to mid-calf. On her feet were black boots.

Her expression was neutral, mysterious.

Nupor had never seen a woman before, except in pictures. He knew what she was, knew instinctively that she was non-cloned and belonged to the leader.

She came among the men, who gave way to her, and looked about.

'Earth clones?' she said interrogatively to the leader, and under his brows Nupor watched her lips move, glimpsed her teeth.

'Aye, so-called missionaries. Neuters, straight from the hive.'

'It's still buzzing then.' She turned on the two bound humans a look of contempt and – perhaps pity, perhaps fear. Nupor caught it, and she caught his glance. Unable to face her eyes, he looked hastily at the ground.

She and the leader stood where they were, issuing the occasional instruction while the others worked. It took them an hour to amass what they wanted. They seized half the food supplies, some tools, and the radio. These they loaded into the land vehicle. One of the men practised driving the vehicle. He could not grasp the simple principle of the drive; Aprav was untied to demonstrate it to him.

The thieves were ready to leave. One or two staggered towards the boat with their loot.

'Keep to this part of the world and we may not molest you again,' said the leader, directing his white stare at them. As Aprav and Nupor bowed their heads, he turned, touched the woman's elbow, and they walked away, following the loaded vehicle.

That day and the next, Dooriz shone, the sky was free of cloud. Aprav decided that they must return on foot to the church to reorganise their limited resources before mining was resumed. Nupor could only agree.

The way to the coast seemed almost impassable. For much of the route, the ground was marshy and treacherous. Large insects lived in the reeds which grew everywhere. Step by step, the Erlauries were assailed by giant flying things. They were forced to follow higher ground and, by the evening of the second day, they were lost.

They made camp for the night as best they could. The water in pools nearby was brackish, but they boiled and drank it. Nupor caught some hopping insects and prepared to grill them over a fire.

'We may die of eating those things,' said Aprav. 'Better to starve a little. Tomorrow we will be back at the church.'

'I see no guarantee of that,' replied Nupor. 'I will eat them if you will not. I feel weak and need nourishment.'

'You were always weak,' said Aprav.

'That's true. I'm sorry about it.'

'No reason to poison yourself,' said Aprav. He waited a moment to see if Nupor threw away the grilling insects. When Nupor merely crouched over the fire, Aprav rose and kicked the grill into the bushes.

Nupor made no protest. Secretly, he was glad of Aprav's action. The smell of the insects cooking nauseated him and, after Aprav's warning, he was scared to eat them in case they did prove poisonous.

'Let's pray, Nupor. The consciousness of God is all about us and we must raise it to a higher level to survive.'

Next dawn they woke to find the world enveloped in fine mist. They rose. Aprav led, Nupor followed. They waded through a shallow pool, climbed two dunes, and there was the spire of their church, its solitude reinforced by the hollow pounding of the sea.

The camp was in a great muddle. The barn still stood about the church, but goods and equipment had been strewn everywhere. Of Ovits Erlaurie and the berund there was no sign.

Tracks running over the dunes indicated clearly what had happened. The marauding gang – perhaps just the leader and his lady – had driven here in the stolen land vehicle and taken as much equipment as they could carry back to their boat.

Nupor stood in a kind of daze while Aprav marched about, exclaiming.

After the initial period of dismay, they began working in an orderly fashion as they had been trained to do. To be indifferent to circumstance was one of the articles of their creed. Circumstances were no more than the noise of cosmic consciousness.

By the time they had restored order and checked to see what was missing — mainly food and grain and seed of various kinds — they were exhausted. Only then did Aprav allow them to enter the church, remove their wet garments, and relax with a nourishing broth.

Whilst they were eating, Ovits and the berund appeared.

Ovits had a neat, small face with the small nose and narrow mouth that characterised all the Erlauries. He was pale and wet; his dishevelled hair dripped down his cheeks. The great berund was also sodden. It came to Nupor and rested its chin on his lap, panting.

'Where were you?' asked Aprav, looking sternly at his fellow neuclone.

'Aprav, I was so frightened. I saw our vehicle approaching. Two strangers were in it, and one a female. In that moment, I believed you and Nupor must have been killed. Why did the savants of Cosnizance not warn us there were enemies on this globe? Of course I ran away, and Plovol came with me. We hid in the dunes. Will they come back?'

Aprav continued to sup his broth. Ovits and Nupor looked at him anxiously, awaiting his answer.

'Of course they will be back,' he said. 'They need machines for their ungodly purposes as we need them for our godly ones. They will return for the kite and the factroid, mark my words. We must fortify this place.'

In the period that followed, the three Erlauries worked all waking hours, indifferent to the elements.

They drew up a list of priorities. The original plan had

been first to secure supplies of minerals and oil. Now their primary aim was to defend the perimeter.

After some argument, they agreed not to cannibalise their air vehicle. They used it every day to fly over the camp and observe nearby territory, so that they would never be taken unawares again. By removing panels from the church, they collected material enough for a digger; the factroid had a programme for a digger, and so a digger was built.

Prolonged study of their home-made photographic map convinced them that they could best defend an area of some ten hectares, shaped like a crescent with its straight side bounded by the sea. The curve of the perimeter followed dunes and a river bank to the west and east, and a marshy pool to the south.

Metal stakes were driven into the pool, in a line running roughly parallel with the shoreline. The river was then made to flood into the pool until a lake was formed too deep to ford. The stakes just below the lake's surface made an obstacle which would wreck any boat.

With the aid of the digger, further excavations improved the height of the river bank. The dunes posed more of a defensive problem. Wood was lacking. The computer advised the planting of trees. From their pillaged horticultural store, the Erlauries retrieved seeds of a fast-maturing strain of Corsican pine. The seeds were planted along the headland, protected by netting and brush, and nurtured by prayer.

As a stop-gap measure, the dunes were rigged with electrified wire. It was the only defensive weapon the church possessed.

Meanwhile, the agricultural programme went ahead. This was particularly urgent because their food supplies had been so depleted. Caprine genetic material was inserted into the womcubator, and miniature goats were soon frisking about the stockade, consuming the harsh grasses of Bormidoor. Cereals and vegetables were planted. When the first paired leaves appeared green in rows above the soil the goats broke in and ate them all. More were planted.

Work continued in rain and fine. Between the hard physical world and the subatomic world of God's consciousness stood the human brain, God's lens. The three human brains occupied themselves with labour, and with prayer at dawn and dusk; Nupor thought of the woman with dark hair and red lips, but said nothing.

Perhaps prayer had its effect. Months passed. No intruders appeared. The daily reconnaissance aloft revealed only the chequered brecklands of the planet.

Still their real task, the ordained command to build a self-controlled Theomane centre, could not be embarked on.

'We have to return to the mining camp,' said Aprav. 'Without sufficient metals, we cannot commence work on the centre.'

'We are in danger at the camp. Here we are reasonably safe,' said Nupor. He heard the weakness in his own voice.

'Safety is not the first factor of importance. We must go back. Nupor, you and I will go as before. Ovits, you stay here with Plovol. Every morning you will fly over us and see that we're safe.'

'Weapons. That's what we need,' Ovits said. 'Why were there no weapons in our supplies?'

'Shame,' said Nupor. 'Our task is the promotion of consciousness, not its extinction.' To make his clone-brother feel bad made him feel better.

Ovits cast his gaze to the dusty ground and did not reply.

When Aprav and Nupor returned to the mine, a season of bad weather set in. Their machines became bogged down and they could do nothing but wait in their flimsy shelter, sitting out the storms, watching the rain assail the distant river. To eke out their rations they caught the large jumping insects, which made a pleasant supplement to the diet when grilled. Nothing more was said about being poisoned.

When the weather improved, the neuclones returned to work.

They had been there for many days, and accumulated great

piles of ores, when the air vehicle came over one morning, buzzed them, and rolled its wings three times. Aprav and Nupor climbed to the eminence above the mine. Far down the meandering river, a sail was visible, yellow against yellow.

'Here we have a weapon,' said Nupor. 'Our laser drills can be set up on the breast of this rise. We can direct them at anyone who comes and kill them.'

Aprav stared at him without expression.

'Now you are arguing for extinguishing consciousness.'

'If these marauders steal our mining equipment, we cannot establish a permanent Theomane consciousness. Isn't that true, Aprav? Isn't Theomane consciousness of a higher order than the consciousness of this outlaw gang?'

Aprav said nothing, staring ahead for such a long time that Nupor grew restless; yet he dared not ask his question again. Finally, Aprav said, 'Would you have the stomach to turn our lasers on a non-cloned human?'

It was Nupor's turn to fall silent. He thought of the woman with the dark hair and lips of the red of a bird's underwing. 'You could do that,' he said at last.

And what was in Aprav's answering silence? he asked himself. Resentment, or just a brutish durance?

The boat appeared to make little progress. They stared at it until their eyesight blurred.

By evening the boat was no nearer. They tried to keep watch turn and turn about during the night. Stars wheeled overhead and their eyelids drooped. Nupor fell asleep during the drab hours when it was his spell of watch.

He woke with Aprav's boot in his ribs. As he sat up, he saw that a chilly dawn was breaking. He clutched his pained side, putting on a look of injury.

'We could have been killed through your laziness.'

'You despise me, Aprav, don't you?'

'Get up. Time for prayer.' Aprav turned away.

The boat was nearer.

They set the machines to work and then lay watching the vessel for hours as it made its tardy approach. At last they decided that there was only one human on board, and that he must be sick. The air vehicle flew over, dipped its wings, and returned to the church. They stood up and went cautiously down to the river, Aprav leading.

The young man in the boat was called Tom. He was not so much sick as weak, having pulled through the worst of his illness. Two companions who had set out with him had both died of the plague which afflicted their settlement.

Tom told Aprav and Nupor that he had been sent by the leader to secure their assistance. After the raid on the church, when the party of marauders had returned to their settlement, disease had broken out. There were two dramatic deaths as they stepped off the boat. Soon half the population had been struck down with terrible fevers and ulcers all over their bodies. Many had died. The scourge was seen as a visitation, because of the robbing of the church.

The settlers sent Tom and two others to beg the neuclones to come with modern medicines and help cure the sick. Their goods would then be returned, they would be troubled no more. The name of the settlement was New Union, and the leader feared that many more deaths would cause it to disintegrate.

'How many people in New Union?' asked Nupor.

'Until the outbreak of this pestilence, we were 215 men, women and children.'

Nupor marvelled to himself ... all with black hair and red lips? Children? He had never seen a natural-born child. The idea was obscene and exciting.

They took Tom to the mine and fed him whilst discussing what should be done. Aprav brushed away Nupor's faltering suggestion that he should go to New Union.

'*You* must go with medicines, while Ovits and I work here,' said Aprav. 'We have enough ore to start smelting. We'll continue with the programme while you are away.'

'I can't go alone. Suppose it is a trap?'

'Don't be foolish, Nupor. You can tell that it is no trap

by the condition of this man, Tom. It would give you the chance to see that woman again.'

Aprav's words made Nupor blush deep crimson, so deep that his cheeks smarted an hour afterwards. He had no idea that Aprav, whom he regarded as insensitive, had observed him so searchingly. To cover his confusion, he said, 'It is not part of our programme that we go on such a mission.'

Contemptuously, Aprav kept silence. To recover their essential equipment, particularly the land vehicle, and possibly to convert the population of the settlement to the Theomane Church, were praiseworthy goals, well within the terms of their objectives. The characteristically uneasy dumbness that lived between them was there again, as real as a wall. It was as if whoever spoke next, against the stiff breeze of silence, had lost a battle of wills.

'You must go, Aprav,' said Nupor. 'Not I.'

Aprav stood up. 'I'll go.'

Nupor blushed again, this time with regret that he had passed over such an opportunity. Children, women, lips as red as a bird's underwing ...

Sometimes the weather was better, sometimes worse. Always, in the background, Ovits and Nupor were aware that the fluctuations in temperature had to be set against a slow decline. Bormidoor's orbit was taking it far away into the darkness; the summer would endure yet awhile, but, with increasing rapidity, winter approached. For the lifetimes of many men, Dooritz would be but a distant star. All would die. The atmosphere of the planet would fall as snow upon the land. Only the Theomane centre they were installing would survive, plugged into the warming mantle of the world.

Metal poured blazing from the furnace, was cooled, shaped according to the blueprint. Delicate parts were turned upon lathes, burnished. All was laborious labour. This was the way the Church liked things done. Not too much reliance on machines. Labour intensive: more brains: more brains, greater God. Humans were born only to labour and to worship. Nothing was easy. Men must be as hard as the universe to which they gave meaning. Endurance was the one great principle. God was good and he endured.

When things went wrong, they did so in order to challenge the capacity for endurance.

The day before Ovits and Nupor were to harvest their first cereal crop, a great storm arose. They feared the church was about to blow over. The structure rocked when the gusts of wind were at their height, tearing in across a waste of ocean. Instead, the winds roused great tides which broke through the dunes. Most of the fortified area was inundated. The crop was washed away. Many of the goats were drowned, while others escaped and were lost. The young Corsican pines were mostly washed away.

When the storm was over, Nupor walked on the beach alone and looked at the turbulent grey sea. It cared not what it had done. It was Interfacial. For a moment he glimpsed God there, and flinched.

Ovits and Nupor set to work immediately to clear up the damage. They replanted, they caught and tethered some of the goats that survived. But the salt water spoiled the poor soil for many a long month, so that they had to break new ground for agriculture beyond their fortifications. They prayed and worked. The weather remained indifferent. Aprav did not return.

The boy Tom had proved too frail to return to New Union in the boat. Aprav had sailed up the river to the settlement alone. When Tom was stronger, the two Erlauries tried to persuade him to help with the work. He had no talent for it. Instead, he sat all day by the river, angling, and brought them good fat fish for supper.

After prayers each night, before they slept, Nupor and Ovits educated Tom in theological history, hoping eventually to convert the lad to Theomanity.

'The difference between man and the animals preceding him is that man has a large brain. That brain told human beings that they had a purpose. What the purpose was had to be discovered. That's clear enough, isn't it?' Nupor said.

'I suppose so,' said Tom. He showed no interest, but apathy in most things was one of his notable talents.

'Two of the leading characteristics of the brain should have given humanity a clue as to the nature of the purpose. A profound religious sense marked his thought from the start. In all mankind's long history, rationalism and atheism have been aberrations.

'Mankind's earliest cave paintings show him making religion to assist the hunt. They also show him using weapons. That was the start of science. A profound scientific sense also marks mankind's thought – although it has often been at war with the religious promptings. Those two characteristics had to be at odds, or there would have been no deep questioning. Mankind was going through its difficult childhood phase. You understand?'

'Oh yes.'

'By the time of mankind's first limited flights into space, it was generally understood that hydrogen was the basic building block of the universe. Then the idea was disseminated that consciousness might be even more basic to the universe than hydrogen. It seemed a mystical idea at first, and we don't know who were its first advocates – the astronauts themselves, possibly. They had been given the chance to see further than other men.'

'I'm tired, Nupor,' Tom yawned.

'Very well, Tom, let's talk more tomorrow evening.'

The lad's concentration was short, but Nupor persevered. He talked again about the age of early space flight. He explained that, just as scientific and religious thought represented two different strands of approach to a spiritual life, so there were also two major approaches to politico-economic life, the capitalist and communist ideologies whose rivalries pushed space flight into reality.

The capitalist system was old and easygoing. In the end it was overcome by the more stringent communist system in a series of wars, some openly, some almost secretly waged.

These wars were really attempts to establish the role of the individual in relation to the state. At the same time, research was continued into the nature of the human brain. Brilliant minds, both communist and capitalist, came to perceive that the brain has a dual function. 'The dual nature of man' was an old cliché. The dual nature of the brain was a striking new fact. It was a receiver of information, and hence a scientific instrument; it was also a religious instrument. The brain acts as an extremely complex amplifier of the sub-atomic, for only at subatomic levels can the mechanisms of intelligence and consciousness take place. Above the sub-atomic lies the great deterministic universe, with no place for consciousness. Below the subatomic lies the all-embracing cosmic consciousness we perceive as God. Throughout the universe, only the human brain – and to a much lesser extent animal brains – serves as a transmitter-receiver between the deterministic macrocosm and the all-pervasive world of God.

Such concepts were totally beyond Tom's comprehension. Although he knew very little, having lived all his eighteen years in the settlement on Bormidoor, he was far from unintelligent. But there was a sort of stubbornness in his character – in his very mind it seemed – which prevented him from moving from premise to premise. Nupor swallowed his anger and continued the lessons, night after night.

This grandiose concept of the nature of the human brain, and hence of humanity and its role in the cosmos, was at first regarded with alarm. Many labelled it anthropocentric. But something happened which lent credence to the idea.

As space flight developed, and mankind reached towards planets beyond his own stellar system, no other intelligent beings were found. Man was the unique interpreter of God to the universe.

At this period, 'Man' meant 'Soviet mankind'. The communist system had triumphed, taking over the older capitalist system as that system crumbled under its own defects. The Earth entered a long, bleak period of history.

Yet the act of digesting the more liberal system inevitably liberalised communism. The hidden mysticism of it burst forth. This new flowering was assisted by a perception of mankind's special purpose. The less doctrinaire of the world's new rulers began to understand that there was no solution to that vexed question of the role of the individual versus the state; but each individual contained God, and god-individuals could not be in conflict with a holy state.

'You understand all that, Tom? Science and religion became one, and politics became irrelevant for the first time in ages. The human brain was seen as the interface between the physical world and the subatomic world of eternal consciousness, i.e. God. So the new universal religion, to which Ovits and I belong, Theomanity, was born.'

Tom nodded sleepily. 'Religion beat science in the end, right?'

'No, no. It was only through science that a true religion was achieved. Theomanity is both religion and science.' Nupor looked pained. Not all human brains were capable of sustaining consciousness. Or even conversation.

Despite continuous physical work, Nupor began to suffer from sleeplessness. Despair would drive him out of his bunk in the middle of the night. He would go to stare at the remorseless ocean, staring as unintelligible lights flashed far out in the deeps – phosphorescence or something trying to be born.

'Always, always I yearn for something I know not. Where are you, God, if you are within me? Why don't I feel you?'

He looked across the breakers at the great universe. He was blind, unable to sense God.

He felt a rage at Aprav, and at Aprav's absence. The fellow had been away far too long. If he had died in the New Union settlement, then damn him. If he had not died, then double-damn him, for he was neglecting his duties. He might be with the leader. Every day, Aprav's undeserving eyes might rest upon that woman with the lips of the red of the bird's wing. Why, he might even speak with her, perchance touch her sleeve. If she was still alive ...

Ovits was no company. A dull, empty clone, thought Nupor, self-punitively. Ovits did not work hard enough, Ovits appeared so thoroughly content with his lot. He accepted whatever befell without protest. The worst of it was, Tom obviously enjoyed Ovits' company, and shunned Nupor's.

Huh. Ovits. Ovits? Ovits. Ovits, one more flavourless computer-bestowed name. Ovits ...

One morning after prayers, after a worse bout of insomnia than ever, Nupor took Ovits aside. He spoke to him above the roar of the machines.

'Soon we shall start drilling the shaft and the chamber for the centre. I do not think this is a suitable place for our shaft.'

'What do you mean?' Ovits asked the question without inflection.

Nupor indicated the muddle of their site, the factroid, the goats, the straggling crop of wheat, the machines which shaped metal. 'All this. I don't think that this is a suitable place at which to drill. We must establish the centre elsewhere.'

'It's where we chose.'

'It's where Aprav chose. Aprav made a mistake. It's more important to find a stable site than to be near water.'

'He isn't here to ask.'

'I know that. We must make our own decisions. Look, as winter descends on this planet, there are going to be storms such as you've never seen before. The whole climate of Bormidoor is going to change. It's going to get dark for ever, and this place here on the coast is going to flood. If the centre was built here, it could be washed away in fifty years. Don't you find that just a bit depressing, Ovits?'

Ovits shrugged.

'It's nature, isn't it?'

'You mean, you're indifferent.'

Ovits shrugged again, turning to stare blankly across the area. 'We'll be gone by then.'

'Yes, and the Theomane centre will be gone too – washed away, all that we came here to achieve, washed away. Nothing will stand in this sandy soil.'

'What should we do?'

He trembled inwardly before he dared to bring out the words. 'We change the site. We move to higher ground and start again.'

It took a week of days before Ovits could agree to the plan. He said he would fly to the settlement and see what had happened to Aprav, but their programme did not allow for such excursions; nor did they know precisely where New Union was. In the end, he yielded to Nupor's will, submitting neither willingly nor grudgingly to the prospect of months of extra work ahead.

Before they could lift the church, they had to dismantle the barn. They began one morning after prayers. Ovits was working on the roof of the building when he slipped. He clutched at the eaves and missed. Next moment he was falling. He landed almost at Nupor's feet. Nupor seized him, lifted up the broken body, crying Ovits' name.

Ovits opened his eyes. He looked dreamily at Nupor and smiled, a pure smile free of anger or reproach, a smile of simple friendship for his clone-brother. Then he died.

The new camp was established above the mine, on an eminence which gave fine views of the river and the surrounding territory. This site would remain intact even when the entire landscape was blotted out by darkness and its attendant ice. The church lifted its spire to heaven. Nupor promised Tom everything he wanted, even an eventual passage back to Earth, even a cessation of lectures, if he would help work with the machines. Tom agreed with sulky grace, saying he had no alternative.

Their labours went slowly ahead once more. Nupor planted anew, set a simple machine to work at the job of protecting crops. He had a powerbike built in the factroid, on which he could run easily back and forth to the old site by the dunes. He brought the goats inland to a field which he surrounded by a metal fence. After a while, he started machines drilling down to the mantle, preparing the way for the centre.

The day came when he called Plovol into the church. The great animal bounded to his side. It had a thick white coat. There was something of the bear in it, something of the dog. It was intelligent and affectionate. On friendless Bormidoor, Plovol had been a good friend. With sorrow, Nupor slipped the hypodermic into its muscle. Plovol fell at his feet, unconscious. Its living body would be used to nurture the DNA from human brain cells in the freeze bank. It would remain on Bormidoor after the Erlauries had gone, after Dooriz had shrunk to a mere fistful of light.

'Why?' asked Tom.

'We leave a gigantic human brain here,' Nupor said. 'A new interface between the physical universe and God. The time will come when every planet will be linked with God.'

'Are there that many berunds in the world?' asked Tom in astonishment.

The drilling was dangerous and took weeks. They worked slowly down to the desired temperature. If the brain was to remain in action over thousands of years – and that objective was the sole point of their labours on Bormidoor – then a permanent source of heat was needed. It was not the Devil but God who enjoyed fire.

The wet weeks and the months passed.

When not tending the machines, Nupor and the lad established their food cycle. The goat meat was good; so were the first crops of potatoes and beans, and their first loaf of bread.

'There's no end to the work,' said Tom, munching at a crusty loaf.

'There's never been an end to man's work. Never. Never will be. This work is no worse than man has always endured. Only the cause has changed for the better.'

With pride, he thought that he had spoken almost like one of the theologians in the Religious Academy at Korovsk. He said reflectively to Tom, 'Even before spaceflight, there were men and women who dreamed that we would go out and fill the galaxy. But they could not imagine why we would do it. They thought of the great expansion in terms of conquest or trade, because that was what they understood in those days. Neither conquest nor trade is possible among the stars. But religion, Theomanity – among the stars is its true home. Only religion begets spaceflight.'

'Religion seems to beget work.'

Despite the death of Ovits, the new site was a success. Yet Nupor missed the ocean. When the shafts were drilled and lined, when the chamber above the shafts was drilled, when the room that was to house the brain was almost fabricated, Nupor decided that he would give himself the day off. The whim came on him; he fought with it but it won.

Ordering Tom to stay on guard, he made an excuse, mounted the powerbike, and headed for the coast. The sun shone. He reached the shore and ran along the sand.

An extraordinary feeling of freedom possessed him. The sensation that he longed for something he had never known remained with him, but today it was transformed into something positive; he perceived that the condition of wanting something was positive. He pulled off his stained clothes and – for the first time – flung himself into the waves that broke upon the beach. The salty water came dancing up and embraced him.

He splashed and swam and laughed. Given the right company here, how happy he could be. If God was inside him, God would also be happier.

Poor old God, imprisoned inside a neuclone.

The breakers finally exhausted him. Gasping, he ran up

the beach to his clothes. Aprav stood there, fists on hips, watching.

Every day that the planet tunnelled its way towards its apogee, the slow-burning antagonism between Aprav and Nupor grew. Tom was no buffer. Rather, in his dim way, he delighted at setting the two neuclones against each other.

Nupor assumed that Aprav hated him because he had changed the site; his surmise was reinforced by the way in which Aprav never referred to this deviation from the original plan. Aprav offered no explanation of why he had remained in New Union so long, beyond saying that he had tended the sick and converted some of them to the Theomane Church.

They worked side by side in an all-enveloping silence. The brain, nourished on what remained of Plovol, was installed in its special chamber.

'That's done,' said Tom, with evident relief. 'Do we all go home now?'

'Now comes the difficult bit. We teach it to think,' Aprav said.

As they worked with the computer to bring the brain to consciousness, severe storms began. The coast was inundated to a distance of several kilometres inland, but the new site was safe. Nupor said nothing.

Most of the work on the brain was performed by the computer. Thought-instruction was too delicate a matter to be left to mere neuclone missionaries. The men stood by as, day by day, machines taught the brain to prattle. God's voice was as weak as an infant's. But this infant learned rapidly.

As Nupor trudged over to the church to fetch the next programme spool of material from the freeze, he happened to see Aprav climbing into the air vehicle. Shouting, he ran to the other man and clutched his arm.

'Where are you off to?'

'Another fifteen days and the programming of the brain is complete. Then we have only to put it through its catechism and see that all is well. Soon we shall be off this world for good. I'm going to say goodbye to my friends in New Union.'

'What friends? What friends? How dare you have friends there? Don't go!'

Aprav waved his arm at the site. His voice was cold. 'This is all yours, not mine. You've made it yours. Get on with it.'

'I want to come with you, Aprav. We can leave the machines to work on their own. Please, Aprav.' He could not remember when he had said 'please' to Aprav before. He despised the note of pleading in his voice.

So evidently did Aprav. He gave Nupor a push in the chest; the unexpectedness of it as much as the force sent Nupor tumbling over backwards.

Aprav jumped into the pilot's seat. 'I'll remember you to the leader's lady when I see her.'

His system flooding with anger, Nupor shook his fist and yelled, 'Be back on time, Aprav, or I'm leaving the planet without you.'

'Oh no you're not! I've got the ignition key!' Aprav's voice carried above the quiet throb of the engine. He waved cordially as the plane lifted. It circled above the site and flew inland.

After a while, Nupor picked himself up and brushed his clothes. He stood for a long time staring after the dwindling shape of the plane.

Tom came up behind him. 'Don't worry, Nupor. It's horrid in New Union. They're always starving in that dump.'

So unexpected was the word of comfort that Nupor turned and said bitterly, 'Yes, but at least they starve together, they live and breathe and speak and sleep together and touch each other.'

'Go there on your powerbike if you think that's so great. You've only got to follow the river. God'll help you, won't he? What's stopping you?'

Like the heat flowing from the ground, Nupor's anger erupted at last. Seizing up a wooden post from the ground, he swung it hard. It caught Tom across the ribs. Tom fell, staggered up, ran away howling.

Next morning, the powerbike was gone. Tom had taken it and his own advice.

The brain was immense and perfect. It spoke to Nupor. 'You have reason to feel pleased. You have fulfilled your task. Meritorious Nupor! Soon you will return to Earth and pass the rest of your days in comfort.'

'I don't honestly know how that will suit me. I don't want to seem ungrateful, but I may feel like a tool that has been laid aside.' He felt a bit of a fool, standing talking into a line of instruments and looking at the brain through a glass panel.

'We are all the tools of consciousness.'

At this Nupor remained silent. He considered it a fatuous answer, while marvelling that he, Nupor, should hold such outrageous views.

'You wish to ask me something?'

'No. Yes.' He wanted to ask about the leader's lady in New Union, or, indeed, about ladies in general, but he did not know how to frame the question. Besides, what could a mere brain tell him? After a pause, he thought to camouflage his feelings and asked, 'I suppose you feel yourself in close contact with God, so perhaps you can tell me if he has existed eternally or only since the beginning of the universe. It was a question that used to bother us in early religious training.'

The brain said, 'The correct answer is neither that God has existed eternally, nor that he came into existence with the universe. God came into existence only when the human brain first began to interpret God into the physical world. He is still coming into being.'

'I see.' But it was surprising and needed some thinking over. 'What happens when he comes fully into being?'

'I can't see into the future.'

Indifference

Leaving the brain, going back to sit by himself in the church, Nupor thought over what the brain had said. Not so much its meaning as the cool, indifferent way it had confessed its limitations. The thing was so big, it should be ashamed of not seeing into the future. He trembled.

A period of wet weather followed. Nupor wondered what it would feel like to have friends and to know non-cloned women. He also wondered why God should remain so detestably mysterious if a part of him was in every human being. Eventually he was driven to ask the brain more questions.

'You say that God has not come fully into being yet, although the universe has existed for so many millions of millions of years. How could the universe come into existence without God? It makes no sense to talk about God unless we are speaking of the force that created our universe.'

The brain was silent. Presumably not thinking but simply existing. Then it spoke.

'You imagine you are in control of yourself. Yet the central "I" of your self has not yet formed properly. It needs time. Perhaps it will never form; then your life will be a failure. Why should the universe be a success? Did you ever think of that?'

Nupor swore. He was astonished to find he knew the words.

'You bloody brain, I've sweated my guts to make you. Answer my question.'

'I did answer your question, Nupor, meritorious Nupor, but I will give you a second answer. Like your "I", God – the "I" of the universe – needs time. God is not properly formed yet or you would not have to labour on his behalf. Nor is the universe properly formed, contrary to what you believe. Both God and universe are process. When God and universe are finished, process is complete. Everything vanishes in a puff of smoke. Metaphorically speaking. I could cite the math.'

Nupor found himself swearing again. 'Stuff your math. What a rotten swindle it all sounds.'

His religious training kept him from doing anything about his anger.

He marched outside and let the rain beat over his head.

As he fed the goats, he thought that he would have to release them before he left the planet. They would live for many happy goat-generations before the cold killed them off. Perhaps they would multiply and provide food for the unfortunate heathens of New Union.

He wondered if those heathens would attempt to destroy the brain. But they were peaceful people after all, and too preoccupied with their own problems to bother with such a harmless – if irritating – object.

The goats nibbled timidly at his hand. They knew Nupor well, would come to nobody else. He wondered if they loved him. Nobody else did.

Except God.

'I love you,' he said to the goats, as they skipped about him in delight. It did not sound quite right. It was the first time in his life he had attempted the sentence aloud.

In the afternoon, he looked up and saw the air vehicle approaching. It progressed in swoops.

Nupor waved to it, and then felt ridiculous. He was meant to hate Aprav. If he hated him, how could he be glad to see him? Or was he glad to see him because Aprav brought the vital ignition key?

It began to rain as the flier made a bad landing on the side of the hill. The raindrops were cold and hard against Nupor's cheek. He found himself running. Something was wrong.

But Aprav was smiling as he pushed up the transparent canopy.

'I've brought you back the ignition key,' he said. His voice was husky. 'I've had a bit of trouble. They'll be coming – I should leave – '

'Aprav, let me help you! What's wrong?' He reached out a hand.

Aprav smiled a ghastly smile. 'Trouble over that lady –
Nupor – '

He rose up and then fell forward. He slumped against the
cockpit and did not move.

And Nupor thought, It's that disease again! He forced
himself to touch Aprav because the man had died – if he
had died – with his name on his lips.

He hauled Aprav out of the vehicle. There was blood about
Aprav's waist. He had received a stab-wound in the stomach.
The way back must have been agony, but he had returned
simply for Nupor's sake. The ignition key was in his jacket
pocket. Now Nupor could go home.

He went to let the goats loose.

There the story should end. Indeed, the important part of the
story has ended. But I take the chance of finishing too the
slender personal tale of Nupor Erlaurie.

I can no longer write of myself impersonally. I was never
a real, fulfilled person, but at least I still retain an 'I' before
I go to join the universal consciousness, and I will end as
I. I am Nupor. Meritorious Nupor ...

I have my reward. I fulfilled my objectives. Now I live out
my remaining days in a Mission of Rest. There are heated
corridors here. I sleep in a bunk in a dormitory with fifty
other neuclones whose work is also done. I exercise in a courtyard protected by a dome from the black sky outside. I eat
three meals of synthetic food a day, elbowed at table by my
fellows.

We pray morning and evening, as we have done all our
lives.

Outside is Mars. I was not lucky enough to finish up on
Earth, but Mars gravity is easier on an ailing heart. Days
must be lighter on Bormidoor still than they are outside on
Mars. A dull little planet, Mars, indifferent to life. Yet God
is there, and still spreading throughout the universe, through
mankind's dedication.

'He led a lonely life, mitigated by good behaviour and

dedicated hard work ... ' That is what it says on the Church's citation which hangs by my bunk. I also have a picture there of a bird in flight. A terrestrial bird, of course – Mars supports no birds, nor even winged insects. A bird with a bright red dash under its wing.

No, inwardly the life of Nupor Erlaurie has not been the success it may appear from outside. I never managed to accept God in my heart. I see too clearly a three-fold Principle of Indifference operating on a personal level, on the level of the Church, and also on the universal cosmic level. Where the indifference started, I cannot say; I only know how it has spread. Perhaps it has spread from God.

If it has spread from God, then I have only one thought for those who come after me, and let them heed it. In recent centuries, mankind has become very close to God, or its concept of God. That's not enough. God is indifferent.

Remember this. If there is a God, then we must become morally better than He.

The Impossible Puppet Show

A Life-Cycle of Thirteen Plays for Anti-Theatre

Author's note   Before presenting the scripts of these thirteen plays, or 'mini-mirages', as one critic unkindly and trendily called them, perhaps a word of explanation is needed. Late in 1969, after the First (and, as it transpired, Only) Symposium for Inner and Outer Pollution, in Luxembourg, I was asked to prepare a propagandist Event which could be enacted all round the world, particularly the Third World. Alas, the resultant plays never even reached the First World. The Macedonian crisis intervened.

My brief was simply that I should be entertaining while delivering the perfectly serious – indeed doom-laden – message of the S.I.O.P. Apart from that, I was given absolute latitude by the board. Since the board consisted of a mixture of ecologists, biologists, psychologists, biochemists, engineers, politicians, historians, pundits, and on-the-make theatrical impresarios, not to speak of representatives of four faiths and fifteen countries, it could hardly have been otherwise.

But I was paid for the work, and well-paid, since S.I.O.P. is funded by UNESCO. And it is true that two of the scripts were used almost as originally planned. My gratitude goes to Télévision Luxembourgeois, the National Television Company of Luxembourg, for their showing of *The Shipyard in the Clouds*, and to Radio Armenia for their broadcast of *The Day the Textbooks Closed*. For the rest, the plays appear here for the first time beyond the pages of the UNESCO *Culture Yearbook for 1971*.

1978   B.W.A.

I Eutrophication Begins At Home

A chemist's shop, loaded with drugs and patent remedies and vitamins and influenza cures in tins, packets, bottles, and jars. Time: late 1956, towards evening. Soft music: Mike Barenboim and his Brazilian Serenaders giving out with 'The Last Throes of Summer'.

Enter R. B. POLLARD *and* JIM, *both masked, dragging* ALDOUS HUXLEY *behind them.*

R. B. POLLARD: Right, Jim, stuff all them throat-lozenges into your sack, and look smart about it. The night-watchmen will be round in twenty-five minutes.

JIM: Time and tide wait for no man. No matter how bright the rose, noon will bring football and fighting. A minute saved, a shark denied.

R. B. POLLARD: Better get some Tampax for Florrie while you're about it. I'll take care of the till. (*Hits cash till with old piano leg, opens drawer, removes an assortment of crawling things, pockets them. Jim takes gun from pocket, fires. Hits jar.*)

HUXLEY (*weakly*): Help, help!

R. B. POLLARD: What was that shot in aid of?

JIM: I thought I heard someone outside. Or maybe it was an anteater inside. Big ears do little pitchers grow. The darling ass is just before the door. As my old mother used to say.

R. B. POLLARD (*bending over Huxley*): Now, you bastard, which one of these drugs is going to save the world?

HUXLEY: I don't know, I tell you! The world situation is nothing to *do* with me. I didn't invent it, I've been dead for years, No, NO, not my arm, please – (*Screams.*)

JIM (*pointing and laughing*): At least I hit something. No firing without smoke (*He has pierced a jar high on a shelf.*

White powder pours from it, covering the floor and mounting higher.)

R. B. POLLARD (*kicking Huxley*): Better hurry up and tell me! You got us in this rotten mess. Which drug will save us?

HUXLEY: No, no, please, please! No! I know nothing! I didn't do it! Ask Aristotle – it's probably his fault as much as anybody's. Oh, oh, my crutch ... (*Groans.*)

JIM (*laughing*): You'll kill him, R.B., you *reely* don't care, do you?!

(*The powder still pours down. Now it rises round their ankles.*)

R. B. POLLARD: You're going to suffer until you tell us, matey, you and all the other stinking intellectuals I can get my mitts on! How's *that*, eh?

HUXLEY (*screaming, face half-buried in the rising powder*): All right, I'll tell, I'll tell. This is the drug, this stuff coming up round us. It could save us all, stop evolution, make us all better people, anything you say!

R. B. POLLARD (*throwing Huxley down*): Right, Jim, that's what we wanted to know! Fill up the other bag – hey watch it! Oh! Jim, you've – !

(*The white powder rises and covers him. The chemist's shop is filled to the roof.*)

Curtain

II Overtones of an Undercurrent

VOLTAIRE *is in the kitchen, sleeves rolled up, stirring holly into a Christmas pudding. Enter* MRS VOLTAIRE.

MRS VOLTAIRE (*suspiciously*): What's that noise in here? You're not writing *Candide* again, are you?

VOLTAIRE (*hastily*): No, no, of course not. As you can see, I'm reading this anteater – I mean, letter.

MRS VOLTAIRE: The amount you must spend on postage

every year! Well, who's it from? An anteater, I suppose?

VOLTAIRE: It's from that nice man who called last month and told us those funny tales about weavers' concubines in Manchester.

MRS VOLTAIRE: Manchester, England?

VOLTAIRE: Naturally. There are no weavers to my knowledge in Manchester, France.

(*Enter* ALDOUS HUXLEY, *holding his crutch. Nods to Voltaire. Exits.*)

MRS VOLTAIRE (*smiling and wriggling*): Oh, you mean that nice Mr Boswell! How is he? Such a nice man, spoke funny Cantonese.

VOLTAIRE: That was a Scottish accent, you silly woman. Not a very acute remark!

MRS VOLTAIRE: But an acute accent. I'll pour you some Graves while you tell me what he says. Does he send his love to me and confess that the tears which spring naturally to the bosom of affection are closely related to that tenderness which man must naturally feel, though all unwittingly, in the presence of someone under whose skirts there beats a heart renowned for its lodes of gold?

VOLTAIRE: Sorry to disappoint you, but there's nothing like that. Just a receipt for jugged hare that he had from Rousseau.

MRS VOLTAIRE: Trust Rousseau to get in on the act! (*Takes a swig from the bottle.*)

VOLTAIRE: Two can play at that game. (*Drops his trousers.* BOSWELL *emerges.*)

BOSWELL: You're not writing *Candide* again, are you?

VOLTAIRE (*with the wit that made him the toast of Europe*): As you can see, I'm burning the toast with my trousers down.

MRS VOLTAIRE (*drinking again*): So here's a bumper to His Majesty.

(*They all embrace. A dog barks significantly.*)

Curtain

III A War Memorial Smiles and Wriggles

Enter two loss-adjusters disguised as chartered accountants. They are carrying a filing cabinet, which they set down by the war memorial.

JIM (*wiping his brow*): They'll never believe this story.

ALDOUS HUXLEY: How else are we going to get across the Pacific? Oh brave new world that hath such filing cabinets in it!

JIM: Quite right. As we have begun, so we must go on. A skilled workman replaces his own slates as they blow off. Mrs Parkinson was born on a Monday, but where's Jack-O'-Nine-Tales?

ALDOUS HUXLEY: Apart from the proverbial wisdom, why isn't there a clock on this bloody war memorial? Besides, it needs repainting.

JIM (*wiping his brow*): Of course, we could still go via microscope instead.

ALDOUS HUXLEY: It is a problem. I still prefer the filing cabinet. After all, it has been in our family since the Bronze Age. The Bronze Anteater Age.

(*Enter* ANDRÉ BEAVERBROOK FIRKOFFSKI, *a Russian poet*)

FIRKOFFSKI: Besides, it needs repainting. (*He produces a 15-inch solid state colour television receiver and commences to film them with it. Enter* SIR ANTHONY HOPE HAWKINS *with* DOLLY.)

SIR ANTHONY HOPE HAWKINS: Good, good, there's the war memorial! Now, Dolly, since my name's longer than any of yours, I'm going to suggest that there's something a bit incongruous about this legend saying DIED IN THE GREAT WAR, 1914–1918. What do you think to that, eh?

DOLLY (*wiping her brow*): What's so incongruous about that? It refers to the men named underneath, not to the memorial. Memorials don't die.

SIR ANTHONY HOPE HAWKINS (*removes his cravat, scarf, tie, haversack, cap and silk hat*): I'll tell you all what's incongruous. The war hasn't even started yet! This year is only 1895!

DOLLY: By the seven-starred feet of the Lord Absalom Apollo-Smith, I believe you're right! (*Looks in filing cabinet, pulls out a bottle of Graves.*) Yes, this letter is dated July, 1750 — that's just six minutes ago!

SIR ANTHONY HOPE HAWKINS (*wiping his brow*): Which proves my point. There was no July in 1750!

DOLLY (*removing her brow*): Then you must be — !
(*Supreme moment of revelation. Hidden orchestra plays 'The Smut Report Polka'.*)

SIR ANTHONY HOPE HAWKINS (*Opens cloak wide to reveal a brace of partridges, a full-scale map of Belgium, assorted bicycle-chains, a bust of Aldous Huxley, and a Do-It-Yourself Volkswagen kit.*): Yes, darling!

DOLLY (*rushing to him, arms waving*): Mother! At last! Mother! Oh, what a homecoming! (*They embrace. The war memorial wriggles and smiles.*)

Curtain

IV The Pasteurised Milk Skyscraper

A skyscraper is revealed. Milk runs down the front of it.

ALBERT EINSTEIN: It's no good saying you're sorry. It's too late to be sorry.

R. B. POLLARD: Don't be like that!

EINSTEIN: I'm *not* being like that. It's not my doing. (*Hint of whine in voice.*) It's nothing to do with me. *I* didn't invent the universe!

R. B. POLLARD: Nobody said you did. But you were the bloke as brought it to my attention, weren't you? (*Twists Einstein's arm.*)

EINSTEIN (*yelling*): You'll break my bloody arm, man! Leggo!

R. B. POLLARD: I'll break more than your bloody arm if you don't put the world back to rights, and be quick about it!

EINSTEIN: It wasn't me, I tell you! You want to get on to Malthus or John Stuart Mill or Pasteur or Fleming or that Russian chap, Firkoffski —

R. B. POLLARD: Don't give me that! Them names mean nothing to me. Nor to Florrie either, do they, Florrie?

FLORRIE POLLARD: The name John Stuart Mill is tolerably familiar. If memory serves, he's the chap who invented chastity belts, the sod!
(*Einstein laughs.*)

R. B. POLLARD: I'll teach you to laugh! You'll clear up all this mess for that!

EINSTEIN: You lot, really, you're so ignorant! It's not *my* fault, it's yours, it's all your fault! (*Starts to shout.*) Are you listening, world? It's me, Albert Einstein that was, enduring the torments of the damned! I didn't do it! It was R. B. Pollard and his wife, Florrie the Flue. They mistake ignorance for innocence, the lousy rotten — Owwwww! Oh, oh, my balls ...

FLORRIE (*savagely*): That's it, Bob — now one in the throat! (*Einstein sobs.*)

R. B. POLLARD (*panting*): That'll keep the swine quiet for a bit. Makes you feel good, a good beating up (*Pause.*) But it don't stop the ruddy milk boiling over, do it?
(*The stage grows dark. R. B. Pollard drags Einstein off, left. Florrie is left alone in front of the skyscraper. The milk is a torrent now.*)

FLORRIE: Oh, I'll give him 'equations' ... Him and John Stuart Bloody Mill ...

Curtain

V The Phantom Ladies of Salonica

Soup has been poured over the stage to represent passing time. Five people sit on a bench with their feet in the soup. One is a man dressed as a woman, one is a man dressed as an ape, one is an ape dressed as a man, one is a woman dressed as an ape, one is an elephant dressed as a small boy (in cheap productions, the elephant's role is sometimes played by an actor).

Enter a PIANIST.

PIANIST (*laughing in the key of G*): I'm sorry, for a moment I thought this was my dressing room.

ELEPHANT (*laughing in the key of X*): No, as you can see, this is Salonica. Hence the ladies.

PIANIST (*jumping astride his piano*): I don't see any ladies!

FIVE PEOPLE (*sitting on bench*): That's why they're the Phantom Ladies of Salonica!

PIANIST (*falling off piano in rage*): You damnable dirty-livered stable-state majestic sons of racehorses! How is it that whenever I happen to meet five people sitting on a bench, one dressed as a woman, one dressed as an ape, one dressed as a man, one dressed as another ape, and one dressed as a small boy, they immediately – (*Pauses.*)

FIVE PEOPLE: What?

PIANIST (*leaping back on to the piano*): I've forgotten what I was going to say. (*Scampers along the keys to the tune of a ragtime 'Auld Lang Syne'.*) Yes, that's it – something about coughing. No, no, wait! Something really significant. Something about an octopus stuck in an apple tree …

FIVE PEOPLE (*standing in the soup*): An octopus stuck in an apple tree!

PIANIST (*guiltily*): No, not an apple tree. My apologies. A war memorial.

APE (*sneering and producing a sausage roll made of old letters from Voltaire*): There are no war memorials in Salonica, you little fool! You're a born loser, you know that?

PIANIST (*running up to ape and shaking his chest*): Come out, come out, whoever you are! You think I don't know a war memorial when I see one? In any case, I have a certificate here (*fiddles in hip pocket and produces a much-thumbed roll of carpet with a pattern of red and white tongues on it*) to prove I'm not a born loser. (*Reads*): 'To Whom It May Concern, I'm sorry, for a moment I thought this was my dressing room.'

ELEPHANT (*laughing as it exits left on the piano*): No, as you can see, it is your script. Hence the ladies. (*Exeunt severally, pursued by bears, until pianist is alone.*)

PIANIST: I don't see any ladies. (*Kneels and laps soup*).

Curtain

VI The Shipyard in the Clouds, or how to Laugh Through Life with Voltaire

A jungle. Time: 1941, one afternoon towards sunrise. Two men are painting a tree. One uses red paint, one blue. A tiger crawls towards them on hands and knees. The band plays tiger music (or 'Teddy Bears' Picnic' or similar.)

Enter MILKMAN *with milk-cart and two mammals of the genus* Myrmecophaga tridactyla *clinging to either side of his head.*

MILKMAN (*smiling as if in memory of Voltaire*): I have anteaters for ears.

TIGER (*looking up, startled*): That's funny! I haven't eaten for years either!

(*Confused sounds of pursuit.*)

PIANIST (*dashing on*): I don't see any ladies!

EARTHWORM (*or Elephant*): ...

(*A cloud passes. It might conceal a helium-filled coal-mine or a shipyard.*)

Curtain

VII Where the Lion Laughs Last

A village that looks like a jungle. Vines grow on every door-step, towering above the few puny inhabitants, who are dead. Time: 1941, one afternoon soon after sunrise. A tree stands downstage. One side of it has been painted red, one blue. Two pots of paint lie by the tree. Two men lie by the pots of paint. One tiger lies by the two men. One milkman lies by the tiger. Two anteaters lie by the milkman. One earthworm lies by the anteaters. Music: something suggestive. A Can-Can or Fred Christian Sorenson Bach's Missa Solemnis.

Enter R. B. POLLARD, *carrying a copy of* The UNESCO Culture Yearbook *for* 1967.

R. B. POLLARD: Sorry, I thought someone called. (*Exit.*)

Enter FLORRIE POLLARD: Where's my bastarding chastity sodding belt fucking pissed off to? (*Exit.*)

(*Enter* JOE POLLARD, *hurriedly filling in a dot-to-dot picture of Voltaire mixing a Christmas pudding.*)

JOE POLLARD (*finishing filling in a dot-to-dot picture of Voltaire mixing a Christmas pudding*): Where have they all gone? (*Looks round.*) I'm sorry I look round – it's all this Christmas pudding. (*Exit.*)

(*Enter* ADAM.)

ADAM (*looking round*): How quiet it is ... I can't recall when it was last as quiet as this ... Oh, yes, I can ... My God ... (*Looks up.*) Crikey, it must be ... (*Looks frightened.*) Yes, it's the end of the world. Everyone's dead, except for the Pollard family and their lodger, Firkoffski, the Soviet Unionist. (*Re-enter* FLORRIE POLLARD.) And you – you, you beautiful creature! – you ... must be my new Eve!

FLORRIE POLLARD: Where's my bastarding chastity sodding belt fucking pissed off to? (*Exit, running.*)

ADAM: Moral, once is enough. (*Goes to lie with earthworm.*) (*Enter* R. B. POLLARD.)

R. B. POLLARD: Sorry, I can't take morality plays. (*Vomits, has diarrhoea, dandruff, and galloping gout, and collapses from epilepsy. Dies.*)

JOE POLLARD (*off*): Did someone call? (*Silence.*)

Curtain

VIII The Mince Pies of Lower Upper Windcheater

Two ANTEATERS *sit feasting at a table. Scene: a lonely ant-hill below a hypotenuse factory in Lower Upper Windcheater, Hollybank. Music: The Polovtsian Anteaters from Borodin's 'Prince Anteater'.*

1st ANTEATER (*munching*): … and then again, human beings are always worrying about relationships in a totally unnecessary way.

2nd ANTEATER: I entirely agree. We've a lot to be thankful for, being anteaters. I mean, I couldn't care less whether you're my father, brother, husband, or uncle.

1st ANTEATER: Precisely, and I don't mind a bit whether you're my wife, sister, aunt, or mother – or grandmother, come to that, as long as you make me a good spouse. You certainly make me a good mince pie.

2nd ANTEATER (*wiping her lips*): Absolutely. There is one discordant note, however …

1st ANTEATER (*protesting gesture*): Please, no discord after these delicious ant mince pies, darling!

2nd ANTEATER: That's what I wanted to talk to you about. We have now eaten the last of the ants.

1st ANTEATER: No problem – go down to the automat and get more.

2nd ANTEATER (*wiping her brow*): Darling, there *are* no more ants. We anteaters have eaten all the ants in the world.

1st ANTEATER (*suspiciously*): Are you sure? I saw one crawling up my leg yesterday ... My God, I ate it instead of letting it breed! What are we going to do?

(*Exit 2nd* ANTEATER. *1st* ANTEATER *performs balancing tricks on a war memorial to fill in time until she returns. Enter 2nd* ANTEATER *with dish.*)

2nd ANTEATER (*placing dish before mate*): Now, try this. It's human being mince pie. We have to change our diet.

1st ANTEATER (*groaning*): To think it's come to this, and me who had a father or son or whatever he was who served as – I forget – either the first anteater in the Eighth Army or the eighth anteater in the First Army ...

(*They eat.*)

2nd ANTEATER: Not too bad ...

1st ANTEATER: It's going to be several generations before we adapt to this diet.

2nd ANTEATER: Eat it up. There's lots more human beings where this one came from.

(*Enter* JOE POLLARD.)

JOE POLLARD: Did someone call? (*They eat him, slowly and with revulsion.*)

Curtain

IX Afloat with Henry Wilson Henty

The scene is a stony desert. Nothing moves except an army consisting of three brigades of four battalions of five platoons of six sections of seven men each, making a total of eight hundred thousand, six hundred and seventy-four point oh four men in all. They are led by a surly-looking loss-adjuster.

The Impossible Puppet Show

LOSS-ADJUSTER (*shouting*): Eighth Army, Eighth Army —
HAAAAALT!
(*Eighth Army halts.*)

SERGEANT CANNISTER: Can we fall out, sir?

LOSS-ADJUSTER: Fall out of *what*, sergeant?

SERGEANT CANNISTER: This canister, sir.

LOSS-ADJUSTER (*taking him by the collar and going red in face*): No jokes at a moment like this, sergeant, and in any case, what's that book you're presuming to read in the middle of a ding-dong war?

SERGEANT CANNISTER: That's not a book, sir. It's just my pet anteater, and it's called 'Afloat with Henry Wilson Henty'.

LOSS-ADJUSTER (*angrily*): Funny name for a pet anteater!

EIGHTH ARMY (*in unison*): It's a funny pet anteater!
(*Laughter.*)

LOSS-ADJUSTER (*drawing himself up to someone else's full height*): That's enough fun, men! Attention! Now I'm going to tell you all just why I have brought you here to this particular spot in this stony anteater. As you know, our objective is to wipe out Lance-Corporal Rommel and his forces before they get promotion. Now it's not going to be easy. I don't pretend it's going to be easy. We are confronted by an army twice our size — in fact, I've heard it said that some of them are as much as fifteen feet high. That may be an exaggeration, but one never knows. We must take precautions, and that's why you are all wearing high heels instead of Army Regulation Boots. Now, Lance-Corporal Rommel is a cunning adversary, make no mistake about that. Make no mistake! I'm not saying that he may not be even cleverer than I am. But that's no reason to be — no reason to be — no reason — (*Pause.*) What was I going to say?

EIGHTH ARMY (*in unison*): You were going to tell us why you brought us here to this particular spot.

LOSS-ADJUSTER (*laughing gaily and tossing his hair over his shoulder*): Yes, of course! Silence in the anteaters! I brought you to this particular spot because I have lost the confounded map and have absolutely no idea where we are. Absolutely no idea! But that is no reason why – no reason – sergeant, wake up, man! Tell them what I was going to say!

SERGEANT CANNISTER: It's just my pet anteater, and it's called 'Afloat with Henry Wilson Henty'.

LOSS-ADJUSTER: Thank you, sergeant, and if you have any other requests, please send them to me – on a postcard please – care of Radio Andorra, Irish Guest House, Manchester, Saskatchewan, Sasketoon, Wisconsin, U.S.A., Alberta, Europe, marking your letters PARCEL POST in the lower top bottom corner of the envelope. Remember to post early in the day, the month, and the anteater. And remember that we have only one record, for reasons of economy, 'Come Back to Sorrento, Ohio', so please make sure that whatever record you want, you ask for that one, and then we'll be happy to play it for you.

(*Enter* PIANIST.)

PIANIST: Sorry , I thought this was my dressing room!

SERGEANT CANNISTER: Just a moment, my lad – not so fast! I can see you're a pianist, perhaps you'd be good enough to tell us how to get out of this stony desert.

PIANIST (*laughing*): Wait a minute, don't I know you? Isn't your name Wilfred Blackleg Petersen, and didn't we used to call you Queen of Scots?

SERGEANT CANNISTER (*blankly*): No.

PIANIST: Are you sure?

SERGEANT CANNISTER: No, I tell you – I've never seen you in my life before! – It was my anteater you're thinking of, perhaps.

PIANIST: Don't be ruddy daft, man, who ever heard of an anteater called Wilfred Blackleg Petersen? (*Turns away, throws off silk hat, puts on black wig and beard.*) Now do you recognise me?

EIGHTH ARMY (*in unison*): It's Lance-Corporal Rommel!

SERGEANT CANNISTER (*reprovingly*): No, it's not, it's my long lost Uncle Ken. Uncle! Uncle!

PIANIST (*irritably*): Don't be silly, I'm a parrot-catcher called Tony Einstein. You may have seen my show.

LOSS-ADJUSTER (*aside*): Why does every flipping parrot-catcher in the world have to be called Tony Einstein? Is there no justice?

PIANIST: I have a parrot called Leontine who once wrote a hit-song called 'Come Back to Sorrento, Ohio'.

EIGHTH ARMY (*in unison*): That lousy song was never a hit!

SERGEANT CANNISTER: It was in Sorrento, Ohio (*His anteater takes hold of the pianist and the two of them walk off arm-in-arm. Night falls slowly.*)

Curtain

X If Winter Comes, Can a War Memorial?

The stage is dark except for fifteen searchlights and the band of Walt Disney's Grenadier Coldstream Guards bearing banners displaying the features of Aldous Huxley.

Enter an EARTHWORM.

EARTHWORM (*unheard above the din*): ...

THE BAND: 'Here's fifteen thousand corned beef cakes shall know the reason why!'

EARTHWORM (*unheard below the din*): ...

THE BAND: 'A war memorial, it's more pictorial Than the Escorial ... '

(*Enter* JIM, *wiping his brow.*)

JIM: They'll never believe this story.

TONY (*entering late, wiping his brow*): Apart from the proverbial wisdom, why is this band playing and singing about a war memorial?

JIM: Because it's a War Memorial Band! (*They fall about laughing. Enter a filing cabinet. Cannot get out.*)

TONY (*inside the cabinet*): How right you were. As we have begun, so must we go on. How soon the summer snows turn to reindeer-moss. The wind that blows at night means gulls along the Great Barrier Reef. We bow the head and do not understand.

WAR MEMORIAL: I'd just like to qualify that (*Falls silent, strikes twelve.*)

EARTHWORM: ...

(*Exit band, playing 'French Bank Rate Street Rag'.*)

JIM (*inside cabinet*): It's fun being in a musical for a change.

TONY (*inside cabinet*): Let's keep very quiet and see if we can think of a pair of red-haired loss-adjusters.

JIM (*inside cabinet*): Are they wearing green shirts?

TONY (*inside cabinet*): Only just.

(*They keep very quiet and think of a pair of red-haired loss-adjusters just wearing green shirts. Winter falls.*)

Curtain

XI Out of the Suits of Babes and Sucklings

A luxurious gentleman's study with books bound in blue vellum on two walls. Nudes by Etty, Boucher, Titian, and Bertrand Russell Flint on the third. Time: stationary, but not less than six. A family string quartet heard, off. Enter two figures in space suits. One lands on desk, one on side table piled with whisky, soda syphons, glasses.

TONY (*wiping his brow*): I wonder what they call this planet?

JIM: It obviously isn't inhabited. There's nobody here, is there?

(*Walks across ceiling.*)

WOODWORM: ... (*Exits left.*)

TONY: They've killed off all the animals, insects and ant-eaters. That broke the chain of life, the humans also died. Sir Walter Scott – dead as mutton! Nothing left but this desert. Not a trace of their culture.

JIM (*staring at nudes*): No, not a trace. Serve them right, probably. Always out to exploit their environment. A bird in the hand means two less in the bush. Never clout a cassowary before May is out.

(*Enter* JAMES WATT, *dressed in red-haired loss-adjusters with green shirt and obviously well-wined and dined. They grab him.*)

WATT (*staggering*): Och, ye two devils again! What is it the noo?

TONY (*punching him in the guts*): You invented the steam engine, you little Scots swine! You started the whole damned lousy rotten Industrial Revolution! But for you, we'd not be stuck in these damned space suits — you realise we have to wear diapers inside here, like a couple of babies?

JIM (*getting in a quick punch to Watt's mouth*): Yes, and my diaper's full already, and we're not going to be home for a week. Many a muckle makes light work!

WATT (*falling with bleeding mouth again his desk*): I've told ye before, my invention was for the common guid. I can't help it if everyone got wiped out instead.

TONY: Common good! Common good! And us togged up in this square gear! You must be joking! Why, Jim and me make nothing but sweet music in the wild state.

WATT (*rising*): Is that so? Well, I was an ape in the wild state! (*Removes his James Watt suit to reveal smiling gorilla.*)

TONY and JIM (*in unison*): Ha! Ha! Ha! (*They remove their space suits.*)

Curtain as the ape and the two pianos confront each other.

XII Up in Kafka's Room

Franz Kafka's apartment, luxuriously appointed with a chandelier at one end and a swimming pool at the other. Kafka, in eyeshade and purple velvet pyjamas, reclines against a red Moygashel war memorial, sipping a tankard full of onions and playing-card holders. Music plays: The Warts from Tsiolkovsky's 'Sleeping Beauty'.

New Arrivals, Old Encounters

There is a knock at the door. Enter KAFKA'S FATHER, *disguised as the Russian poet, Aldous Huxleysky.*

MUJIB ONANISM: Franz, my dear boy! So I've found you at last!

KAFKA: Who are you? I've never seen you before in my life.

MUJIB ONANISM: Franz, my darling boy, you must remember me! You are — you *are* the Franz Kafka who wrote *The Trial*, aren't you?

KAFKA (*defensively, hopping on to a passing war memorial*): Well, that was a bit of a mistake. A typographical mistake. It's actually *The Trail*. It's a cowboy yarn. Under my pen name, I'm the best-sellingest Western author since Zane Gray.

MUJIB ONANISM: My darling boy, you don't mean you're —

KAFKA (*clasping the swimming pool to his breast*): Yes, yes, it's true! I'm R. B. 'Sidewhisker' Pollard, none other, author of 'Finnegan's Wake in the Saddle', 'Shoot-Out at the Northanger Abbey Ranch', 'Stampede on the Bounty', 'Billy the Kidnapped', 'Moby Dick Rides Again', 'Riders of the Purple Pickwick', 'Tarzan at the Earth's Corral', 'Round-Up of Things Past', 'Wuthering Gulch', 'Dr Jekyll and Mr Rawhide', 'The Tale of Sioux Cities', 'The Two-Gun New Testament', and many other well-known best-sellers.

MUJIB ONANISM: Not so fast! How could you have written those well-known best-sellers? I have evidence which proves that you were in Manhattan all last week.

KAFKA (*wiping his brow*): Little you know of the pressures of literary life! Besides, come to that, I don't think you've met my wife. (*Shouts.*) Mistinguette!

MISTINGUETTE (*entering nude, right*): Right! (*Singing.*) 'They call me Mistinguette. It was misty when we met. But don't forget, In a mist you get All you missed of Mistinguette ... ' You called, Franz?

KAFKA: No, I called 'Mistinguette'. Tell this personage that you're my wife.

MISTINGUETTE (*drawing back*): But I'm not, I'm not your wife. I've never seen you before in my life, you odious little imposter! You were sent round here to clean my war memorials by the Berlin and Stalingrad Itinerant War Memorial Renovating Company.

MUJIB ONANISM (*taking Mistinguette's hand*): I endorse that, every word of it.

MISTINGUETTE (*loftily*): Give me back my hand. (*He passes it to her.*) Now tell me who *you* are.

MUJIB ONANISM: Surely that's obvious. I'm the real R. B. 'Sidewhisker' Pollard. You'll find my name on your war memorial. (*Shoots himself.*)

MISTINGUETTE: Men! (*Jumps into swimming pool.*)

Curtain

XIII The Day the Textbooks Closed

A clearing in the jungle. André Beaverbrook Firkoffski, Russian poet extraordinary, is seated at a table writing a letter. The time: Doomsday.

FIRKOFFSKI (*muttering as he writes, so indistinctly that audience cannot hear*): ' ... into seven or eight feet of stilbestrol, and was never seen again. And so perhaps now, my dear little Father, you comprehend the terrible thing that has happened in the great world of which, together, we were so proud. I am the last man alive, with only my faithful old upright piano for company ... mmm ... mmm ... her petting to climax, she whispered. But perhaps I should not be telling you these things. However, this surely is the night of nights for truth, the last little gleam of truth in the world, in this great Siberian jungle ... '

(*The light fades. Night is indicated by the roar of a tiger, the cough of a coffin, and the sound of 'When the Moon Comes Over Canoga Park' played on a solitary bagpipe. Light returns.*)

FIRKOFFSKI (*still writing*): ' ... keep thinking I am Kafka or R. B. Pollard, but when I strip my furs and my clothes off, I observe I am still myself, so there is hope yet – hope, yes, but not time ... mmm ... mmm ... of course it has all been fun, and my deepest regret is that you should have had to spend the last twenty years in labour camps ... mmm ...

(*It begins to rain.*)

EARTHWORM (*wriggling*): ...

FIRKOFFSKI (*still writing*): ' ... mmm ... mmm ... last year in Marienbad ... mmm ... mmm ... blame ourselves for trying to live rationally within the crazy irrationality of the firmament, but then I suppose you have tried these positions yourself in your young days, when you first married dear little Mother ... ' (*Drops pen, picks up mother, who is in old gin bottle standing on table.*)

MOTHER: Give him my love, dear.

FIRKOFFSKI: It's too late, little Mother. They've all gone. Everyone. Only just you and me, sitting here in this jungle clearing in someone's head.

MOTHER: You don't mean that the actors –

FIRKOFFSKI: As I foretold, they're all spirits, even you're in an old spirit bottle, and the great globe itself –

MOTHER: You're having me on!

FIRKOFFSKI: Well, I'm certainly not having it off, am I? That's all over ...

MOTHER (*bitterly, and peering over shoulder through glass*): But only because *he* says it's over. It's inhuman ...

FIRKOFFSKI (*resignedly*): I'm resigned to it. Someone has to pronounce. The great ecosphere itself, all which it doth inherit – even Moscow ... Sh, what was that?

MOTHER: I heard it before. My darling boy, they're chopping down the cherry trees. (*They listen.*)

(*Sound of cherry trees being chopped down. Buzzing, crashing, confusion. The rain stops. The light dies. Enter anteaters.*)

Curtain